DIVER'S PARADISE

DIVER'S PARADISE

A ROSCOE CONKLIN MYSTERY

DAVIN GOODWIN

OCEANVIEW PUBLISHING
SARASOTA, FLORIDA

ISBN 978-1-60809-383-0

Published in the United States of America by Oceanview Publishing

Sarasota, Florida

www.oceanviewpub.com

10 9 8 7 6 5 4 3 2 1

PRINTED IN THE UNITED STATES OF AMERICA

For the most inspirational, influential person in my life, my father, Mr. Roscoe C. Goodwin. Thank you, Boss, for always being there. I miss you and will love you forever. Hope you enjoy Paradise.

ACKNOWLEDGEMENTS

To my lovely wife, Leslie (Double L). Her countless proofreads, tenacity to detail, and steadfast dedication to story continuity were paramount. None of this would've been possible without your love and support.

To Bob and Pat Gussin and the wonderful people at Oceanview Publishing. Your flawless guidance and feedback have made my writing the best it can be. Thanks for taking a chance on an unknown, debut author.

To my daughter, Elizabeth, for suggesting a breakthrough idea that propelled me past a major plot hurdle. Way to think outside the box, girl!

To Ruth van Tilburg-Obre, the undisputed Queen of Bonaire. Few could've provided the insights and knowledge regarding Bonaire that you did. As always, thanks for the love.

To all my beta readers—Geoff Goodwin, Tim Goodwin, Jerry Goodwin, Tom Weber, Thad Jakusz, John Belknap, Josephine Boeckman, John Anderson, and Roy Wickham. Your time, feedback, and effort were greatly appreciated.

CHAPTER 1

EARLY MORNING, MID-JANUARY,
ROCKFORD, ILLINOIS

HE'D NEVER FIRED this gun before—or any gun, for that matter—and the blast from the Colt was louder than he had thought possible. Ears ringing, hands trembling, he laid the revolver on the dinette table.

Marybeth had always called him the "best neighbor in the world." He lived across the street and visited the Rybergs, Bill and Marybeth, every few days, lending a helping hand, saying encouraging things about their shitty landscaping, and even pretending to enjoy Bill's old stories.

An early morning visit wasn't uncommon, and The Neighbor's appearance hadn't surprised Marybeth. She'd looked up from the L-shaped counter as he came through the sliding glass door, a bright smile on her face, ready to offer him a pleasant greeting, a split second before the back half of her skull splattered across the kitchen.

Wonder what she'd say about him now.

The Neighbor took a moment and examined the room. His dad always said a .357 Magnum made one hell of a mess. Growing up, his dad had told him lots of things. Some of it was even true. Most of it, though, was total bullshit. But the old man was right about the .357 Magnum.

It does *make one hell of a mess.*

Especially up close, and *especially* pointed at the face.

Blood on the opposite wall, bone fragments on the stovetop, a dead body on the floor. But what did The Neighbor care? He wouldn't be cleaning it up. Besides, he had completed the job, or at least half of it, for today.

The stench of burnt gunpowder couldn't overpower the aroma of fresh-brewed coffee. Near the sink, with two mugs sitting alongside, a coffeemaker dripped black nectar into a small glass pot. He took a cup—not just any cup, but the one imprinted with *World's Best Husband*—and partially filled it.

He got on his tiptoes and retrieved a bottle of Baileys Irish Cream from the cabinet above the microwave. He had watched Ryberg stash it there a few nights ago. The level hadn't changed, and The Neighbor shook his head while unscrewing the cap.

Damn teetotalers.

The Neighbor poured a shot into his coffee. Not too much, though, just enough to steady his hands. Needed to keep his wits about him for Ryberg's return.

Eyes closed; he savored the numbing effects of the alcohol as it traveled down his throat. This had been his dad's favorite drink, and The Neighbor found it fitting to drink it now. He opened his eyes, held the cup up in a mock toast. "Here's to you, Dad."

The morning newspaper lay open on the table. He sat and used a section of the paper to cover the gun, then took the opportunity to flip through the other pages. After a few moments, he realized he had no interest in the news, sports, weather, or anything else. Besides, other than one spot in the classifieds, he wasn't here to read.

The wall clock read 5:40 and, soon, *Mister* Ryberg, the man of the house, would return from his morning walk. He'd stroll through the same sliding door The Neighbor himself had passed through just a few moments ago.

The Neighbor grew anxious considering Ryberg's return. What if he returned with someone in tow? Maybe the guy next door, or that idiot down the street, the one with the fake windmill in his yard, who sometimes joined Ryberg on his morning walks. No problem. There'd be three dead bodies instead of two. The Neighbor smiled and pointed his finger at the sliding door, making a pretend shooting motion, twice. Four rounds left in the gun, and at this range, even *he* couldn't miss. Too bad for the others. For them, it'd be the wrong place, wrong time.

The Neighbor chuckled. What'd the military call it? Collateral damage?

Ryberg might come back talking on his cellphone. It'd be unlikely this early in the morning, but it *could* happen. Have to wait and see on that one.

Worse yet, someone nearby may have heard the noise. The gun-generated concussion wave and recoil were jarring, and the ear-splitting crack could easily have penetrated the walls of the house. The Neighbor knew the house wasn't a fortress, and he guessed the walls were flimsy and paper thin. Not many people fired guns indoors, so no point in wasting money on extra soundproofing.

He decided not to worry about the things he couldn't change. If someone came investigating, he'd shoot them. Walk right up and pull the trigger. Just as he'd done with Marybeth.

It'd be a different story, though, if the cops happened by. The Neighbor knew he'd lose that encounter. Never stand a chance.

Don't worry about the things you can't change.

Dawn had just broken when The Neighbor caught his weak reflection in the sliding glass door. First thing every morning, even in January, when darkness prevailed till well after six, Marybeth opened every blind in the house.

The Neighbor turned his head left and right, examining his full profiles for several long moments. An article he had read—or was it a TV show he had seen?—came to mind that claimed a successful killer couldn't look like a monster. People believed a killer looked a certain way. He raised his chin and turned his head in both directions, again studying his reflection.

"Nope," he said to himself, "no monster here."

As he swallowed the last drop of his Baileys and coffee, the door slid open. A stout, heavy-breathing man in his early sixties stepped into the house and stood by the table. No one else, no cops, and no cellphone.

"Hello, Bill," The Neighbor said.

Bill Ryberg stomped his feet on the entry mat, knocking a dusting of snow from his boots. He wore a baseball-style cap with *Rockford Police Department* embroidered on the front.

"Hey," Ryberg said as he slid the door shut. "You have breakfast yet?"

The Neighbor moved the newspaper aside, exposing the gun.

"What the fuck's with that?" Ryberg asked, jerking his head at the pistol.

Not saying a word, The Neighbor picked up the gun and pointed it at Ryberg.

"What the *fuck*?" Ryberg said. He stepped toward The Neighbor, reaching for the gun, but caught a glimpse of the lifeless, bloody body of his wife.

"Marybeth!" Ignoring the gun pointed at him, Ryberg hurried around the counter and knelt beside her. His face flushed, and his breathing quickened.

"It's retribution time, Bill." The Neighbor stood and walked to where Ryberg knelt on the blood-covered tile floor. He raised the gun and pointed it at Ryberg's forehead.

"You go to hell," Ryberg said. He raised himself off the floor, maintaining eye contact with The Neighbor. Ryberg's knuckles turned white as his hands clenched into tight fists.

The Neighbor had waited a long time for this and wanted to see Ryberg sweat and, hopefully, beg for his life. But to The Neighbor's surprise, Ryberg lunged forward and grabbed the gun. The full weight of the older man crashed into The Neighbor, slamming him into a doorframe. The pistol discharged, and the bullet streaked wide of Ryberg's ear. Using his free hand, Ryberg delivered a glancing jab to The Neighbor's nose. Although weak, the strike dazed The Neighbor, snapping his head back and blurring his vision.

Ryberg clinched The Neighbor's arm with one hand and his neck with the other. Nearly overpowered, The Neighbor managed to twist sideways in a quick, practiced maneuver and delivered a kick—his sensei at the dojo called it a fumakomi geri—to the older man's leg, an inch below the knee. Ryberg's face contorted and he screamed, crumbling to the floor, bone protruding through his sweatpants from a compound tibia fracture, blood pumping onto the tile. His complexion growing pale, he wrapped both hands around his leg and dry-heaved onto the floor.

Panting, eyes half-closed, Ryberg crawled across the floor to the body of his dead wife and scowled at The Neighbor. "Go to hell," he said through pursed lips. His narrowed eyes met The Neighbor's and didn't waver.

The Neighbor used the back of his sleeve to wipe a single drop of blood from his nose. Well worth it, he thought. Standing on the blood-covered tile, he looked down at Ryberg and pointed the gun at the retired detective's head.

"You said that already."

The Neighbor took a breath, squeezed the trigger, and relished the sound of the blast.

CHAPTER 2

WITH THE WINDOWS down and the top off, the warm Bonaire-island breeze flowed through the cabin of my four-door Jeep Wrangler. I glanced right, across the sea, savoring the salt-filled air. A brilliant shade of blue—one found only in the Caribbean—filled the cloudless sky.

Living on Bonaire, I never worried about traffic lights or big-city hustle and bustle. With fewer crowds and more locals, I considered this tiny island my undiscovered paradise, not yet spoiled by restaurant chains, high-rises, or all-inclusive resorts. Scooters and bicycles were primary transportation for many, while others walked, greeting each other with smiles and waves. The culture, best described as laid-back with an unhurried pace, continued to have that slow, relaxed feel of the *old* Caribbean.

Unhurried, unspoiled, unforgettable.

My phone rang as I turned left, heading north on the road called Kaya International, toward Kralendijk. Even island life has its flaws.

Damn cellphones.

"Hello, Erika," I said.

"Hello, R. You are on your way back?"

My full name is Roscoe Conklin. However, most folks refer to me as R. "Yes. Do you need anything?"

"It is Friday," she said. A Bonaire native, and having lived on the island her entire life, Erika spoke English as a third, maybe fourth, language. As with most of the local population, her speech contained a hint of Dutch accent and reminded me of someone who wanted to sound formal and correct, but sometimes placed words in the wrong order.

"Yes, it *is* Friday . . . all day," I said.

"I must leave early today."

She had reminded me three times since noon. I smiled, downshifting around a curve.

"I know, I know. You must have a wonderful boss."

"I did have a wonderful boss. Now I work for you."

"Yes, you do." I sighed. "Need anything?"

"I need a raise."

I shook my head. "Anything else?"

"I do not think so."

"See you soon."

A few turns later, I stopped for a road-crossing iguana, or tree chicken as they're called on Bonaire. It stood in the middle of the lane and swiveled an eye in my direction, which I considered a gesture of gratitude for saving its life. Even so, this guy had better quicken the pace. Many locals considered iguanas a food source, and one this size— maybe three feet long from head to tail—would be a prized catch.

We studied each other a moment or two, then I beeped the horn, ending our one-sided standoff. The iguana scurried away and found refuge in the roadside underbrush.

I pulled into the parking lot of the YellowRock Resort, which I owned, courtesy of my life savings and a large chunk of my pension. The *Resort* part, however, was a bit of a misnomer. It was a ten-unit ma-and-pa-type hotel with a front reception area and a small apartment upstairs where I lived.

Guilt shot through me knowing the roof leaked in several units, and, scattered along the path, yellow flakes of paint reminded me of some much-needed upkeep. Bonaire is an island for water lovers and, most days, I wished for more time in the sea. Retired, and in no hurry to overwork myself, I struggled to stay ahead of the repairs. Erika seemed her happiest when keeping me busy.

I'd be lost, though, without her.

Before going into the office, I walked around the side of the building. Mounds of dirt, a cement mixing tool, and several wooden forms laid haphazardly around a partially repaired section of the foundation. The mess had cluttered the small side yard between the YellowRock and the building next door for several weeks. Neither the contractor responsible for the work nor any of his crew had bothered to show for work in several days. He wanted more money to finish; I wanted the job completed before paying him another cent. A stalemate like this on Bonaire—on *island time*—could last for months. Shaking my head, I walked into the guest reception area, which also doubled as the office, on the first floor.

Erika sat behind an old gray desk that reminded me of something from a 1960s secretarial office. I did my work on an identical one against the back wall, and a third, stacked high with papers and other junk, gathered dust in the corner. The place needed an upgrade, but the retro decor of our cozy office served our function and suited us well.

Erika punched away at a computer keyboard, acting as if she hadn't seen me enter. Her yellow polo, embroidered with *YellowRock Resort* on the upper left shoulder, deepened the tint of her dark skin. She refused to tell me her age, but insisted she was older than me "*by several years.*" I loved her like a big sister, and most of the time, she treated me like a little brother.

With black-rimmed glasses perched halfway down her nose, she rolled her eyes as I walked by her desk. "There are *still* some papers on your desk that *still* need your signature," she said, turning back to her work.

"Hello to you, too."

I laid a plastic bag on my desk and retrieved a bottle of water—or *awa* as it's called in the native language of Papiamento—from the small fridge in the corner. I sat and put my feet on Erika's desk, playing a game with myself by blocking out most of her face with my size eleven sandals. Her modest afro formed a dark halo around the tops of my toes.

"You *still* have not fixed the problem with that bathroom light." She continued to gaze at the computer, not giving me the satisfaction of showing the least bit of aggravation.

I didn't say anything and hoped she'd notice the soles of my sandals.

"The light?" she said.

I decided I'd better answer. "Which unit?" I glanced at the bags I'd placed on my desk. They contained several packages of light bulbs.

"You know which unit."

"It's just a light bulb."

"Then it will be easy to fix, yes?"

"I'll get it tomorrow."

She moved her head to see around my sandals. "That is what you said last month about the paint." She grabbed a small stack of papers, slapped my feet with them, and turned back to her work, muttering "*hende fresku.*"

My Papiamento wasn't good, but I got the gist of what she said. "What would I do without you?" I lowered my feet to the floor.

Knowing how far to push was most of the fun.

"Don't forget you have some friends arriving on tomorrow afternoon's flight," Erika said. "You'll need to meet them at the airport."

"Yup, I remember. Tiffany and her boyfriend."

She removed her glasses, laid them on the desk, and leaned forward resting on her elbows. "And how does that make you feel?"

I knew what she trolled for but didn't bite. Tiffany and I had met during a case many years ago and were friends long before I moved to the island. She had visited me on Bonaire in the past and decided to bring her new boyfriend along on this trip.

"I feel fine about it."

"You know what I mean." She leaned back in her chair. "When do you plan to introduce her to Arabella?"

"Tiffany is a *friend*. That's all she's ever been. Nothing more, nothing less." I took a swig of water and wiped my mouth with the back of my arm. Letting out an exaggerated "Ahh," I concentrated on screwing the cap on the bottle before continuing. "Erika, you think you know more than you actually do."

"Uh-huh." She put her glasses back on, grabbed the stack of papers, and walked to the filing cabinet.

Wanting the conversation to end, I stood and headed up the stairs leading from the office to my apartment. "I'm going to take a shower. Have a nice weekend and don't forget to lock up when you leave."

Entering my apartment, I went straight to the fridge for a cold beer, my favorite being an Amstel Bright. The advertisements described it as a "Euro Pale Lager," whatever that meant. Most of the bars and restaurants served it with a slice of lime wedged atop the bottle's neck. At home, I didn't waste time slicing limes.

Unlike Jeff "The Big" Lebowski, I liked the Eagles *and* Creedence, so I popped *The Eagles Greatest Hits, Volume 1* into the CD player and sat in front of my computer to check email. Twelve new messages. Eleven went straight to my junk folder, but one had a recognizable address—Marko Martijn, the contractor responsible for the unfinished foundation work. Before I clicked it open, my cellphone rang.

"What's up, Bella?" I said.

"Hey, Conklin, happy birthday."

I laughed. "Thanks, but you're a little early."

"I know, but since it will be the big five-oh, I thought your memory might slip and needed a reminder."

"Yeah, that's funny." Arabella De Groot was from the Netherlands, and I'd found sarcasm doesn't always work on the Dutch.

"I thought so. I called to see how you are doing."

"Well . . . I'm about to take a shower. Want to join me?"

"I wish I could, but I am on my way to work. They called me in to work the desk tonight."

"That's too bad."

"Yes, for both of us. It is that new inspector, Schleper. He thinks we are at his beck and call."

I walked out on the balcony and sat on a lounger facing the sea. "Yup, sounds familiar."

"*Ach.* You think he would give me more respect." She exhaled a short, hard breath. "I have been a cop for ten years on this island. Longer than him!"

Changing the conversation, I asked, "We still running tomorrow morning?"

"You bet. Eight kilometers?"

"If you mean four point nine miles, then yes."

She laughed. "No, I mean eight *kilometers.*"

"Ah, forgive me. My measurements are still strictly American."

"I will forgive you. You are drinking a beer right now?"

"Yup. Need to drink away my sorrows before I shower. Alone."

"Do not drink too much. I do not want to hear excuses for tomorrow's run."

"Maybe one more, then I have some paperwork to do. Or maybe change a light bulb."

"Yeah, right. You are drinking, so you will not do more work tonight."

"Hey . . ."

"I will see you tomorrow. Usual time?"

"Yup. Good night."

She chuckled. "I will send you a text reminder."

I seldom read text messages and never answered them, but the phone pinged as soon as I set it down. She'd included the words "old man" as part of the reminder about our run.

The sun had moved closer to the distant horizon, creating an orange aura behind the few low clouds. Palm trees and sunsets. Tough to find a more relaxing setting. I nursed my beer and watched the sparse traffic crawl along the one-lane road that ran between the YellowRock Resort and the sea.

I imagined Erika's delight in arriving at work in the morning and finding the light fixed. It'd be easy—just a bulb. As I headed toward the stairs to retrieve the bags sitting on my office desk, the landline phone rang; the one used most often for off-island communications. It might've been a future guest wanting to make a reservation at the YellowRock or maybe an old friend from the States calling to chat me up about retirement in paradise.

Darkness was settling over the vast, smooth sea, and I took a swig of beer, not interested in answering the phone, content with letting voicemail do its job. Besides, the Eagles were telling me to take it easy, and, regardless of the light bulb, that sounded like a good idea. Arabella was right. I was drinking; my work finished for the night.

Second ring.

Nearby, my banjo sat on its stand. Erika had kept me busy enough lately that practice had eluded me. Picking some tunes sounded good.

Third ring.

Turning around, I noticed my old 7-iron propped in the corner. I hadn't played golf since moving to Bonaire five years ago but still fed the urge to practice my swing. Make sure my elbow stayed tucked, and the clubface didn't open.

Fourth ring.

Or I could swap the Eagles CD for Creedence, sit on the balcony, and drink another beer or two or three, watching the sun settle below the horizon. Maybe skip the shower, doze off early, and catch a few Zs to the rhythm of the waves.

Fifth ring.

I could've done any of those things but didn't.

Instead, I went to my desk and answered the phone.

CHAPTER 3

THE CALLER WAS Mike Traverso. We had worked together for a short time in the Violent Crimes Division of the Rockford Police Department and hadn't spoken since my retirement.

"Mike . . . What's up?"

Mike wasn't much of a talker and got straight to the point. "It's Bill Ryberg . . . he's dead."

I slumped into a chair. Traverso stayed quiet for a moment, allowing me to absorb the news. I used my hand to prop up my head and stared at the darkness beneath the desk, trying to make sense of what he had said.

Too many late nights, crappy food on the go, and high levels of stress had taken a toll on Bill. Large doses of coffee and beer hadn't helped either. For years, his doctor had insisted he take better care of himself, but like most tough-guy cops, Bill ignored the advice. After his retirement and the clearing of a blood clot, he finally wised up and began to listen. In addition to eating healthy, he quit drinking—cold turkey—and started walking every morning. Last time we talked, he said he felt better than he had in a long time.

Too little, too late.

"R," Traverso said, "he was murdered."

The word *murdered* jolted me like a punch to the chest, a punch so hard it nearly stopped my heart or, at least, made it skip several beats. The room spun a bit, and I closed my eyes to keep from being sick.

Traverso took a breath. "Yesterday morning. He and Marybeth were both shot. At home."

"Shot? Both of them?" I leaned forward in the chair, neck hairs bristling.

"I thought you should know," he said.

"Marybeth?"

Mike paused a beat or two before answering. "Yeah."

Nose tingling, eyes welling with tears, my mind swirled, and I wasn't sure what to do except fight the urge to break down. If anyone other than Traverso had told me this, I wouldn't have believed it. Maybe even laughed it off as a joke.

But I wasn't laughing.

The anger—closer to rage—surged. I'd seen it many times.

The detective in me wanted to drill Traverso for information, and, as impossible as it sounded, take the investigative lead myself. To track down the monster who killed my buddy and his wife.

"I need to put you on hold," Traverso said. He didn't wait for a response, and the phone went quiet.

My career as a detective with the Rockford Police Department had exposed me to a lifetime's worth of crime and tragedy. Murder is a common offense in Rockford, ranked fifth worst in violent crime statistics for the entire United States. Even worse than nearby Chicago.

Sometimes, the atrocities had happened to acquaintances. After a while, a sense of numbness set in, and I treated all cases with a sense of distant professionalism, removing myself emotionally from the situation to remain sane. Do the job while investing as little feeling as possible. Not easy, and maybe, since my retirement, some of the walls I'd built around me had collapsed. After all, this wasn't just anyone.

Nor was it just an acquaintance.

Traverso kept me on hold for several minutes, long enough for me to formulate a page full of questions.

"I'm back," Traverso said.

My voice cracked. "Tell me what happened."

"Not much to tell. The coroner puts death between five and seven a.m. No witnesses, of course. We're canvassing the neighborhood. We know there was a struggle because Bill's leg was shattered."

"Robbery?"

"Don't think so. It doesn't look like anything is missing, and no signs of B and E or forced entry."

"Someone they knew."

"Yeah or knew them."

"Who found them?"

"Anonymous call. We couldn't trace it so probably a burner phone."

One of those cheap, limited-use cellphones sold at drug stores, convenience shops, and gas stations. They're impossible to trace because the numbers associated with the phones aren't assigned or registered to specific individuals. Make a few calls, then dump it in the trash. The answer to every criminal's prayers.

"That doesn't sound random," I said. "Not many people walking around with untraceable phones at the ready."

Mike was quiet.

I asked about a link analysis—a process of combing through all aspects of Bill's cases, both former and active at the time of his retirement. People, vehicles, addresses, and a host of other information would be loaded into a computer program and cross-referenced against current leads on other cases.

"Started, but nothing yet. We're digging," Traverso said.

"Dig deep, Mike."

"You know how this works, R. It's my highest priority. I've got everything and anything I need. We're on top of this and will take care of it."

Mike let out a long, exaggerated sigh. We both wanted the same thing. He'd bypassed protocol and given me useful information, knowing I would've done the same for him.

"I'm sorry. It's a big shock," I said.

"I understand."

We were both quiet for a moment.

"I have to go," he said. "If we get more, I'll try calling you back."

"Thanks. I know it's delicate but keep me in the loop. Please."

"No promises, but I'll do my best."

Traverso hung up. I went to the fridge and counted four Brights. Not even close to what I needed.

I opened one and took a swig. All of a sudden, my world seemed a lot emptier.

And lonelier.

CHAPTER 4

ARABELLA AND I usually meet for our runs at seven in the morning, but I liked to arrive a few minutes early to enjoy the quiet sunrise. Most tourists anticipated the sunsets on Bonaire, a time to recover from the day's dives, have a cocktail or two, and plan the evening's events. But the calm and serenity of the dawn, the tranquility of the island coming to life and preparing for a new day, was meditative.

After a mostly sleepless, turbulent night, images and memories of my old partner dominating my consciousness, I savored the peaceful morning. Alone with my thoughts, I sat on a concrete bench at a location known as Windsock, a small stretch of beach a few minutes south of Kralendijk, and listened to the gentle rhythm of the sea.

My elbows rested on my knees, hands cradling my chin. A distant oil tanker, its massive hull riding high in the water, headed west, on course for the neighboring island of Curacao. Not far offshore, a pair of kayakers paddled across the smooth, glass-like water. My restlessness worked against enjoying the morning and the freshness of a new day.

There had to be a motive. Bill always said, "Start at the end and work forward. Find the motive."

And how did Marybeth figure into the motive?

Too many questions had haunted me the night before. I watched the ceiling fan go round and round and woke in the morning with no answers. Not even guesses.

I stood, raised my arms over my head, and arched my back, trying to stretch away the sluggishness. It didn't work, and I yawned. My muscles resisted movement, the lack of sleep taking hold of me. Not to mention last night's beers. Like a dog shaking its fur to dry, my body quivered as if trying to toss away reality.

Off to my right, down the shoreline, two pelicans were perched on a trunk-sized boulder, their heads moving back and forth, scanning the water. They sat motionless and waited for the sun to penetrate the shallows and illuminate unsuspecting fish to snag for breakfast.

Hard to believe it'd been five years since I'd last seen Bill. When I first moved to the island, we'd make contact every couple of weeks. Over time, the frequency grew longer and longer and became every couple of months. Not surprising. Once the work's gone, partners have less in common. He often talked about visiting the island, wanting to experience life for the "other half," but he—we—never planned an actual trip. Even though life found us on different paths, we were still good friends.

Bill was smart, but, more importantly, he possessed the three characteristics that made him the most effective investigator I'd ever known: objectivity, logic, and common sense.

He'd been the better detective and maybe the best in the department. No one else could hold a notepad and pencil to his abilities. I wasn't a slapstick Keystone Cop, nor had I considered myself a bumbling fool as portrayed in TV cop sitcoms, but too often I became sold on a suspect early in an investigation. Bill stayed objective and countered my tendency to shape or interpret evidence to support my theories. He remained open-minded and willing to consider all suspects and alternatives.

A car horn beeped, interrupting my trance and sending the pelicans flying down the shoreline. My running partner, Arabella, slowed to a stop and parked her secondhand Toyota on the gravel shoulder. She gave a quick wave, gulped from a water bottle, and got out.

Her Nike running shoes were in desperate need of replacement, showing generous wear and tear from many miles of road work. The blue in her sports bra, along with the red and white of her nylon shorts, completed a colorful ensemble of Old Glory. I considered mentioning something about her misplaced patriotism when I remembered the flag of her native Netherlands contained the same colors.

She carried a fluorescent pink tank top, which she slipped into as she walked, her thighs flexing with each step. The shirt had a black swoosh across the front, large letters on top, which read *I Run Like a Girl*, and below, *Try to Keep Up!*

Large doses of exercise and an insanely high metabolism kept her body weight proportional and well distributed. With curved sport-glasses and blond hair pulled back in a tight ponytail, she could've easily walked onto the cover of *Runner's World* magazine. A short, fleshy nose, shallow cheekbones, and modest overbite might prevent most men from considering her attractive, but I found her striking. The edges of her mouth were always curved upward, just slightly, as if ready to break out in a smile or spontaneous laughter. Taking in the sight, I remembered why I enjoyed running with her.

My pulse quickened.

She put her arms around my neck and kissed me. "Are you ready?" she asked, the twinkle in her blue eyes reminding me of sunrays reflecting off the sea. At a tad under six feet, she stood almost as tall as me and was the first woman I'd ever seen eye to eye with, literally and figuratively.

"Well, that depends," I said. "Are you referring to the run?"

"Yes. But I want to apologize for the shower last night."

"The one I took by myself?"

She smiled. "Yes, that one."

"I never realized Dutch women were such a tease." I gave her a peck on the lips.

"Going to be hot today." Bending at the waist, she placed her palms on the ground several times.

I didn't attempt any stretching and looked down the road, south, in the direction we'd be going. My preferred method of exercise was swimming; however, Arabella enjoyed running so I indulged her and went along several times a week.

"Should we not start?" she said, beginning a slow jog and pressing the start button on her watch.

My knees creaked a few times as I slipped in alongside her, my mouth already dry. If it weren't for the salty air and the lingering strawberry scent of Arabella's shampoo, I might've smelled the beer pouring out of my skin disguised as sweat.

Yesterday, this sounded like a good idea. This morning, not so much.

Flat and straight, the road before us seemed to stretch forever. A light breeze did little to offset the heat radiating off the pavement, already sizzling from the intense rays of the morning sun. On our right side, calm and pristine, the sea, like a seductive siren, beckoned me to end this madness and plunge myself into her refreshing waters.

We reached the turnaround point, a blue X painted on the edge of the pavement. Arabella runs specific distances. It's never *about eight kilometers* or *a little over five miles* or any such nonsense. Years ago, she had used a GPS to locate and mark the exact halfway point. Precisely eight kilometers, round trip. No more. No less.

We crossed the road and headed back north. Arabella glanced at her watch and grimaced. My face throbbed as sweat streamed down my neck and chest. She would never point it out, but we both knew I was slowing her down. The sun and heat didn't affect her, and at ten years my junior, she could outrun me on any given day.

Especially after last night.

"Bella, you go on. I'm going to slow down a bit."

She nodded and surged ahead a few yards. My pace slacked off just enough to put her a few yards in front of me. I didn't mind. Running behind her was the most enjoyable exercise imaginable, watching the sweat roll down her back and soak her nylon shorts. Her hamstrings and butt muscles worked in perfect harmony as they propelled her forward.

By the time I returned to Windsock, my feet were like anvils and throbbed with every step. Arabella had removed her tank top and was sipping from a bottle of water, her damp hair and flat belly gleaming with moisture. She strode toward me.

"Need some water, old man?"

Bent at the waist, my breathing deep and rapid, I couldn't respond. By the time I managed to raise my head, the bottle was in midair. I caught it, downed a long hard swallow, and leaned against the hood of my Wrangler.

Windsock derived its name from its proximity to the island's airport. On the other side of the road, a few yards beyond a security fence, a large orange windsock swayed in the breeze alongside the approach end of the runway. From here, using my 7-iron, I could put a golf ball on the tarmac. Arabella talked shop, something about last night's shift, but my mind wandered, and I only caught every third word or so.

A small, twin-engine commuter taxied into position for takeoff, destined, no doubt, for one of the neighboring islands. After sitting at the end of the runway for a moment, the engines revved, and prop wash blew across Windsock Beach as the plane began its takeoff roll.

It sped down the runway, raised its nose into the air, and clawed for altitude into the clear sky, leaving all of us and our troubles behind.

Arabella stepped into my field of vision. "Hellooo, Conklin. Are you with me?"

The plane made a left turn and continued its climb, becoming a small dot, engulfed by endless blue. Arabella snapped her fingers in my face, and after a moment, I looked down.

"What?" she asked.

I moved bits of gravel with my foot, then raised my head and let out a deep sigh. "Bill Ryberg is dead."

Her shoulders slumped, and she put a hand on my arm. "Oh no. That is terrible."

"He and Marybeth were both shot. In their home."

Eyes wide, her jaw dropped. "What happened?"

"Not sure, but it wasn't a robbery." A shrug and a shake of my head. "Probably someone they knew. Revenge, maybe?"

She leaned beside me against the Wrangler and stared at the gravel. "What are you going to do?"

Across the street, the windsock held at a forty-five-degree angle. I wished the breeze could blow all this away.

"Not sure," I said.

"You are going back to the States?"

"Why would I do that?"

She bounced the palm of her hand off her forehead. "Do you not want to go to the funeral?"

"Won't be one. They both wanted cremation."

"But there will be a ceremony or something? You would want to attend?"

Funerals—or ceremonies or memorials or whatever—were for the living. The dead didn't care. I shook my head. "No one there I need to see or talk to."

We were both quiet for a bit. Arabella watched me dig more gravel with my foot.

"There is another reason to go back," she finally said. When I didn't respond, she added, "To help find who did this."

"No one wants my help." I paused a moment. "I'm retired, remember? I don't do that anymore."

"But—"

"I'm not going back," I said, shaking my head with every word.

Arabella pushed away from the Wrangler and stood in front of me, hands on her hips. "You have to do something."

"I'm two thousand miles away." I began counting on my fingers. "I don't know how the scene was secured; no photographs; don't know who the witnesses are, let alone any chance to interview them; no access to physical evidence; no ballistics; no coroner's report—"

She held up her hands. "Okay, okay." She resumed her lean against the Wrangler.

"Not to mention access to possible suspects and interrogation notes."

Neither of us spoke.

After a moment, she said in a low voice, "Maybe I can help. I have some experience."

I held back a smile. "I know you do." I took her arms and pulled her close. "I'll make some calls and see what I can find out. To be honest, I want to know more, but I don't want to get my hopes up. I'm not sure what I can do from here."

Arabella wrapped her arms around my neck and moved even closer. "I will help. You must tell me what to do." She kissed me.

After the kiss, we rested against each other's forehead. "Let me make those calls. Then I'll let you know what I think."

She looked me in the eyes. "I am sorry for your friends."

We hugged. After a moment, a passing motorist honked, and we pulled apart, laughing.

"Are you coming over tonight?" I asked.

"I want to, but I have that new exercise class."

I shook my head. "You exercise too much."

"See this?" She squeezed a portion of her belly skin between two fingers. "Too much fat. I must get rid of this and stay in shape."

"You know, we could create an exercise class of our own."

She smiled and shook her head.

"Call me later?" I asked.

"Of course. Do I always?"

A truck pulled off the road onto the gravel shoulder and skidded to a stop in front of Arabella's car. Stenciled on the tailgate was "M + M Concrete." The driver's door flung open, and a towering figure stepped out and walked in our direction. Concrete dust covered the lower half of his worn jeans and boots. Dried sweat, and perhaps yesterday's dirt—or last week's dirt for that matter—stained his white T-shirt. No sunglasses or hat.

Marko Martijn, the contractor I was at odds with regarding the foundation work at the YellowRock.

Sauntering toward me, his shoulder-length dreadlocks swung back and forth in cadence with his strides. He stood several inches over six feet, large by Bonaire standards, and possessed the build expected of someone who worked with concrete blocks and cement all day. He leaned in, poked a dust-covered finger at my chest.

"I want my money, Conklin."

Hairs on the back of my neck stood and adrenaline pulsed through my veins. I counted to ten.

"As soon as you finish the job." I spoke in a low voice and maintained eye contact with him.

He moved closer, pumping his finger at my chest several more times. "Not good enough."

Arabella stepped partway behind his left side, out of his direct line of sight.

"Best I can do," I said.

His lower jaw quivered. "You think you are pretty funny, right?"

I smiled. "I have my moments."

"You do not have many friends on this island."

"Well, at least we have each other."

"Pay me."

I leaned against the hood of the Wrangler and placed a foot on the fender. Hands in my lap, I sighed, and studied him.

"You will see what happens to people who cheat me," he said.

"Is that a threat?" Arabella said.

I put up a hand, palm facing her, and mouthed the word "no."

Martijn cranked his neck, looked at her for an instant, then back at me. "Ha. Your woman cop. I do not give a shit about any of that." He spat on the ground near my feet. "Remember. Pay me or else." He leaned into me, his nose a scant few inches from mine.

"I'm really easy to get along with," I said, "once you learn to see things my way."

"You haven't seen the last of me." His warm breath had a hint of stale tobacco mixed with coffee.

"Hope not. Wouldn't want to lose another friend."

After glaring at me for a few seconds, he turned and walked to his truck. He opened the door, turned back pointing a finger at me, then drove away.

"We have had problems with him before," Arabella said. "Want me to do something?"

"No, don't bother." Marko Martijn didn't make my short list of concerns and problems. "I need to get a couple of things done today, so I'll see you later."

Arabella narrowed her brow. "Like what?"

I drew in some air, long and slow. "I'll make a few phone calls to Rockford. But I have to be at the airport this afternoon to—"

"That is right. Your old girlfriend is coming for a visit. I cannot wait to meet her."

"What is it with you and Erika? Tiffany is an old *friend*, not an old *girlfriend*."

"Okay. If you say so." Her smile was persistent. "When are we all getting together?"

"I'm not sure we will."

She laughed. "Oh, I know we will. Call you later."

I got in my Wrangler, started the motor, and, in a fit of adolescent showmanship, spun my tires in the gravel leaving the road shoulder. I caught Arabella in the rearview mirror. She smiled and got in her car.

A few moments later, my cellphone pinged. Arabella had sent a selfie.

Below the picture, it read *Just 4 U.*

CHAPTER 5

SHOWERED AND WITH a beer and ham sandwich in hand, I plopped into my office desk chair. I wore a clean pair of khaki cargo shorts and a dark blue Longtail T-shirt from Duluth Trading Company. Sandals and no socks. My daily attire since moving to the island.

Erika sat at her desk, punching away on her keyboard, doing whatever it is she does. The main door was latched open, and a gentle breeze pushed fresh Caribbean air through our work area, forcing Erika to employ her stapler as a part-time paperweight. The blinds on the front window were positioned for sunlight to burst through, causing a glare on my seldom-used computer screen. The hum of midday traffic and bits of conversations filtered into the office.

I chewed a bite of sandwich and leaned back. Finding something better to do—anything—would be easy. But my promise to Arabella hung over me. I needed to make some calls that, hopefully, would appease her while satisfying bits of my own curiosity as well. Tourists wandered past the open door, their laughter and overly-exposed-to-the-sun skin forcing me to concentrate hard on the task at hand.

No need to search for the number to the Rockford Police Department headquarters. It was as fresh in my mind as it had been the day of my retirement. The switchboard operator answered, and I asked for Larry Penn, who worked in the Violent Crimes Division. We had always gotten along well, and I was sure he owed me a favor.

Larry claimed to be from Arkansas and wanted people to call him by both his first and middle names, implying a multi-generational, Southern tradition of some sort. In a thick, overly emphasized Southern drawl, he had told many a waitress, "Darlin', a Southern gentleman is always known by his first *and* middle names."

I needed his help, so best to indulge him.

He answered on the second ring. "Penn."

"Larry David, its R. Conklin." He didn't say anything. After a moment, I said, "Larry, I have a favor to ask."

"Figured as much. I know Traverso talked to you." His voice cracked, and he paused. Larry possessed an engineering degree and had modified his office chair to recline further than usual. I pictured him leaned back as we talked, tossing a 2016 World Series Chicago Cubs autographed baseball in the air and catching it in his hand. It's how he handled stress.

He started to say something, but hesitated, his voice cracking again. After another moment, he continued. "What can I do for you?"

I was sure he already knew. "Can you send me the pictures? Paperwork? I'll take anything you got."

"The whole file? Man, Traverso will have my ass."

"Traverso doesn't have to know."

"Yeah. But . . ." His voice trailed off. "Anything else instead?"

"I want to see them."

He paused a moment and moaned a few times. He threw in a "Jeez" and "Shit" for good measure. "Alright, I'll try." He sighed heavily into the phone. "Email?"

"That'd be great." I gave him my email address. "Are you sending them now?"

"Christ, R, I'm not a fricking magician. I'll have to send them from my personal computer, so it'll probably be later this evening."

"Okay. Thanks, Larry. I appreciate it."

"If I do this, and I'm not saying I'll be able to, you owe me. Big-time!"

"Sure, anything." I decided to push further. "Can you include the coroner's report, too?"

"While we're at it, want to know who killed Kennedy? Or maybe where Hoffa's buried?"

"Larry David—"

"I need to go. Talk to you later."

He didn't hang up right away, nor did I. We both felt the pain, neither of us knowing what to say. After a few quiet moments, he disconnected.

CHAPTER 6

I leaned on my Wrangler, drinking a beer in the parking lot of Bonaire's Flamingo International Airport. A light gray overcast failed to block the scorching rays of the afternoon sun. Three miles out, over the sea, the outline of a 737 on final approach cut through the afternoon haze, accented by the glare of the jet's landing lights.

Tiffany's previous trip to Bonaire clouded my thoughts. Like a sappy flick on the Lifetime Movie Network, frame by frame, it rolled through my mind. My heart raced with anticipation, butterflies bouncing off the inside of my stomach.

Not to mention the new boyfriend, whom I hadn't met. No clue what to expect from him.

As the jet taxied to the ramp, I finished my beer and meandered my way across the small parking lot to the open-air main terminal. No need to hurry—it'd take several minutes for them to clear immigration, customs, and retrieve their luggage. I bought a beer at the bar and waited.

Bill and Marybeth's murders happened yesterday morning, so it was possible Tiffany didn't know. With last-minute packing and travel preparations, she might not have watched the news. She'd never been one for news-watching, anyway, content with not knowing, for the most part, what happened in the world. Something to be said for that.

Her demeanor would let me know whether or not she knew, so I'd play it by ear about whether to say anything right away. She deserved to know, but I didn't want to ruin her vacation immediately. Details were scant, and hopefully, in a day or so, there'd be more information from Traverso or Penn—maybe a motive or a lead on a suspect—something to help put this in perspective.

I shook my head. Retirement should've meant I didn't have to deliver news like that anymore, especially not to a friend.

I reached into my pocket and fished out a piece of paper Erika had given me on my way out the door. She had scribbled the name of another guest arriving on this flight. This person had made plans of their own to get to the YellowRock, so I didn't need to meet or transport them. Not sure why Erika gave me the name, but sometimes Erika's ways were confusing to me.

The guest's name was Mandy W. Driver.

The name "Mandy" brought back memories. A long time ago, I dated a girl named Mandy. I liked her, but we were together for only a short time, and I couldn't remember her last name. One afternoon she wised up, grabbing her coat, and slamming the door on her way out as she described in full detail what she thought of me and where I could stick my opinions.

Maybe this Mandy was her, and she had seen the error of her ways. Had she tracked me down to tell me what a mistake she'd made all those years ago? Maybe beg my forgiveness? Tell me that my opinions *did* matter?

I put the paper back in my pocket. Not likely.

Tiffany walked through the doors separating the luggage area from the main lobby. I chugged the last of my Bright and left the bar, walking in her direction. She strolled across the terminal, her head swiveling back and forth until our eyes locked. She waved. I waved back.

"Roscoe!" she yelled.

A colorful, yet worn, *Rockford College* T-shirt half covered her spandex shorts. Swept by the wind, her delicate, dark hair lay loose on her shoulders, and the tone of her skin disclosed a distant Hispanic heritage. She had midnight dark eyes and a petite nose, and if my math was correct, she was thirty-three years old. Whereas Erika sometimes felt and acted like my big sister, Tiffany played the role of my little sister. Biologically, I'd never had either.

She dropped her luggage and jumped into my arms. I didn't resist. She kissed me on the cheek, and we hugged again. Finally, after what felt like a full minute, I sat her down.

"It's great to see you," she said. "I've been looking forward to this for a long time."

No mention of Bill and Marybeth—so she didn't know. Good, and bad.

"I'm glad you're here." I looked her over. "How was your flight?"

"It was good." She smiled, and her cheeks flushed a little. "I slept most of the way."

Being fixated on Tiffany, I hadn't noticed a guy next to her until she put her arm around him. Must be the mysterious boyfriend. He stood a couple of inches taller than me; his polo shirt stretched tight across his shoulders, chest, and biceps. He had short brown hair and brown eyes. I guessed him to be Tiffany's age or a few years older.

Tiffany gestured toward him. "Roscoe, this is Lester Jeffrey. The guy I emailed you about." She leaned in close to me and lowered her voice. "Isn't he gorgeous?"

I stuck out my hand. "Good to meet you, Lester. I'm Roscoe Conklin. You can call me R."

He smiled and shook my hand, squeezing it harder than necessary. First impressions are lasting impressions. If he wanted to start a macho-guy competition, he'd barked up the wrong tree.

"Wow, that's some handshake," I said, rubbing my hand to help the circulation return. "First time to Bonaire, Lester?"

"Yes."

"He learned to scuba last summer," Tiffany said. "He's only made a few dives and never in the ocean." She leaned into me again and, again, lowered her voice. "I may ask you to join us on some dives, just to be on the safe side."

"Well," I said with a brief glance at Lester, "I have a trip set up for us tomorrow. My buddy Jan will be taking us out on his boat."

"Sounds great," Tiffany said.

I studied Lester's face. "What happened to your nose?"

Lester shrugged.

"Winter in northern Illinois," Tiffany said. "He slipped on the ice getting out of his car yesterday morning and cracked his nose on the door. The doctor said it's not broken, but badly bruised." She touched Lester's arm, and he flinched. "The day before we leave on vacation. Such bad luck." She eased up on her toes and kissed him on his neck, but he turned his head away from her. She sighed and looked at me, then snapped her fingers. "I have something for you, Roscoe." She knelt, unzipped her checked luggage, and began rummaging through it.

"Jeez," Lester said to Tiffany, shaking his head. Then to me, "Where do I pick up our rental truck?"

I stared at him a moment. If they had a rental truck reserved, they didn't need a ride from the airport. Again, Erika's ways sometimes confused me.

"Over there," I said, pointing at a one-story, white building on the other side of the parking lot. Lester began walking toward the building. "I'll load your luggage into my Wrangler while you get your truck."

"Here it is," Tiffany said, as she removed a square, flat cardboard box from her duffel bag. She stood and handed it to me. "Apple donuts. Marybeth gave them to me a couple of days ago to bring to you."

Marybeth knew my weakness for the apple donuts made by a specific apple orchard outside of Rockford. She had sent some with Tiffany on her last trip as well. I took the box and stared at it. My nose tingled.

"Thanks," I said, opening the box.

"I froze them yesterday, then packed the box. I hope they'll be alright."

The donuts were firm, but no longer frozen. "They'll be fine." The tingling in my nose was receding, and I turned my head into the wind to help dry my eyes. After a short moment, I turned back to Tiffany. "I'll keep them in the fridge and when I want one, zap it a few seconds in the microwave. They'll be perfect. Thanks."

She put her hand on my shoulder. "You're welcome. Oh, and Bill and Marybeth said they send you their love."

Before my eyes could water again, I ushered Tiffany toward the bar for a beer.

Lester arrived with the rental as Tiffany and I returned, both of us sipping on Brights. Small pickup trucks were popular with dive tourists visiting Bonaire because the open bed made for easy loading and transporting of gear. Lester and Tiffany rented one from a place called Abby's Seaside Truck Rental. Abby's vehicles had ocean creatures painted on the tailgate.

Tiffany's shoulders slumped when she saw the truck. "Crap. We got a seahorse. I asked for a turtle."

Patting her on the shoulder, I said, "Yeah, but what a pretty seahorse it is." She laughed and leaned against me for a moment.

Lester hadn't gotten out and honked the horn. "Let's go," he yelled out the window.

Breaking it off with Tiffany, I walked to the Wrangler and got in behind the wheel. Tiffany got in on the passenger side.

"Shouldn't you be riding with Lester, your *boyfriend*?"

"I guess not. He's the one who said I should ride with you."

I looked at her a moment, eventually shrugged, and pulled out of the parking lot.

Along the way, Tiffany talked about her two-year-old son, Ozzie. She said he was doing well and that her folks were watching him so that she could make the trip to Bonaire. I'd never asked Tiffany who Ozzie's father was, figuring if she wanted me to know, she'd tell me. Unlike Bill and Marybeth, I had never met Ozzie.

We entered the office at the YellowRock, and Tiffany scurried over to Erika's desk and they hugged. As Tiffany introduced Erika to Lester, I took a beer from the fridge and sat with my feet propped on my desk. Erika went through the mechanics of registering Tiffany and Lester and getting them squared away with keys and such. Lester had a litany of questions, and Erika showed great tolerance in answering them. I might not have been so patient.

After a few moments, and a short hug with Tiffany, I bolted up the stairs to my apartment, anticipating a freshly microwaved apple donut.

CHAPTER 7

I CHECKED EMAIL on the computer in my apartment, and one of them was from Penn. Larry David had come through much earlier than expected. Not sure how he did it and I didn't care.

I moved the cursor over Penn's email but didn't click it open. Not right away. I hesitated, knowing what the photos would show. What I might see. This email was likely most, if not all, of the information Traverso's team had on the case and could tell me a lot. My hand shook as I clicked the mouse.

The first of six attachments was labeled REPORT. The Rockford Police Department used a standard reporting form to record the facts, listed in chronological order, regarding the investigation of the case. The structure changed as deemed necessary by supervisors and management, who came and went every few years or so. This form was similar to the one I had used before my retirement and contained the same facts, albeit in a different layout.

Sections for a date, time, and incident-type told me nothing new; it matched the information from Traverso. Penn included an audio attachment of the 9-1-1 call made to the station.

"Anonymous call. We couldn't trace it so probably a burner phone," Traverso had said.

I played the recording, all four seconds of it. *Two dead bodies at Bill Ryberg's house. You figure out the address.* It sounded like a man's voice, thick with no discernable accent. Not that of a harried friend or neighbor who happened to discover the bodies. The caller had a steady, almost clocklike cadence, every word pronounced and delivered with precision. I played it several times and couldn't detect the caller making any attempt to disguise or mask his voice.

"*No witnesses, of course,*" Traverso had said, so the report didn't include any witness statements.

As far as anyone knew, nothing was missing and no sign of forced entry. Nothing new—Traverso had mentioned all of this.

The report concluded with a disposition of *Active, Open,* which told me the department was actively working the case. The next step, currently in progress, was to canvass the neighborhood for statements or additional information and wait for completion of the link analysis process.

Penn included an attachment containing the crime scene sketch, a rough drawing made by an on-scene detective, as opposed to a detailed description—or *scale* sketch—created later by a draftsman. Well done, a sketch could be more descriptive than hundreds of words and was a crucial investigative aid. It showed the location of doors, windows, furniture, plants, room sizes, distances, and everything else in the vicinity of the crime scene.

In this situation, though, even a spectacular sketch would be of limited use to me. Not from lack of information or any flaw in the drawing, but because of how well I knew the crime scene and vicinity.

I'd been to the Ryberg home countless times and knew the room sizes and locations of all the doors and windows. The walls were yellow, the trim white, and the kitchen wallpaper above the cabinets faded and peeling. Pictures of distant family and friends lined the hallway. A bathroom light switch was installed upside down—toggle down for on; toggle up for off. Because the fridge door stuck shut, an extra nudge was needed to open it and grab a beer. Bill often joked about his right arm being stronger than his left based on the sheer number of times he had opened the refrigerator.

The only information I'd be able to glean from this sketch was the location and position of the victims—the spot where Bill and Marybeth fell.

I opened the attachment.

On the floor in the kitchen, in front of the fridge with the sticky door, were the outlines of two bodies. An M labeled one shape, and the other had an F. There was an X on the head portion of both, indicating headshots. The M structure overlaid the upper part of the F one. Bill was lying on top of Marybeth's torso. In death, as in life, they were together.

I closed the attachment. It couldn't tell me anything more.

For now, I skipped the attachment labeled BODIES and opened the one labeled SCENE. These were long-range shots of the Rybergs' road, street signs, the exterior of the house from all sides, the neighbors' houses, along with their front and back yards. The attachment included a series of 3D color-enhanced interior photos that echoed the crime scene sketch, showing the doors, windows, picture-laden hallway, kitchen area, and dinette table. A coffee mug and an open newspaper lay on the table.

A series of overlapping photos was used to establish the scale and dimension of the crime scene, creating a panoramic effect with a focus on the dinette and kitchen area where the bodies were found.

None of the photos revealed any useful information. The images were all too familiar—Bill and Marybeth's home. On any given day, I could've taken the shots.

Except for one.

One photo caught my attention. It was a close-up shot of the newspaper on the table, opened to the used truck classifieds section. One of the ads was circled in dark red and read "Four-wheel drive. Call Bill." The words "Four-wheel drive" were double underlined in red, but not the same red as the circle. Whereas the ring was thicker and less defined, the double underline was precise, like a fine-point pen. The intent was clear, though, to highlight the ad.

The ad didn't give a phone number, nor was there a make and model of vehicle. No description of the condition or the miles, year, or anything else that might entice a person to call.

Bill had a small pickup, but I couldn't remember whether it was a four-wheel drive. Could be the newspaper messed up. Maybe Bill had checked the ad, caught the errors, and circled it as a reminder to call and have it corrected.

After studying the photo and considering the ad for a while longer, I moved on to the coroner's report.

More precisely, Penn had sent the *preliminary* coroner's report. The coroner would issue the final statement after completion of the autopsies. This initial report, written early in the investigation, contained mostly routine data such as the estimated time of death, cause, victims' names, and their locations.

The cause of death, listed as a gunshot wound, or GSW, surprised me. Listed beside the GSW was the notation .357 MAG. Ballistics could never be so precise. The only way to determine it had been a .357 was to have the weapon.

I looked at the crime scene sketch again. The table was sketched out, surrounded by four chairs. Sketched on the table was a rectangle with the letters NP, and near the NP were the letters CM. The NP and CM corresponded to the newspaper and coffee mug shown sitting on the table in the photos I had seen earlier. On the sketch of the table, near the CM, was the letter G. I couldn't remember anything from the images that a G might represent.

I reopened the attachment labeled SCENE and paged through the photos looking for the one of the dinette table. It showed the newspaper and a coffee mug, but no other section of the table. Nothing showing its entirety, just the one showing part of it.

G could have stood for gun and would have made sense. They'd need the gun to list the GSW as a .357 Magnum. I made a note to ask Penn about that and the ad.

I dreaded the last attachment the most, the one labeled BODIES. Stalling for time, I went to the microwave and zapped another apple donut. My hand trembled. Before sitting back at the desk, I stood over the laptop, staring at the screen.

The attachment had two dozen photos of Bill and Marybeth lying on the kitchen floor in their own blood. The pictures showed multiple angles and various distances. All the photos contained the same subject matter—the dead bodies of my friends.

I clicked through at a steady pace—slow enough to get a sense of what was in the frame, but quick enough not to dwell on them. Bill and I hadn't seen one another since my retirement, and neither of us were Facebook types, nor did we send a lot of photos back and forth, so I was surprised at how much grayer and thinner his hair had become. Marybeth had emailed me a picture of her and Bill from a few years ago, an anniversary or birthday party or something. Comparing that photo and the one taken at the crime scene, it appeared Bill might've put on a few pounds since then, even with his healthier lifestyle.

Criticizing a friend's appearance based on photos of his dead body was cold, but I chalked it up to a weird, internal defense mechanism on my part, something deep inside my psyche trying desperately to convince me none of this was real. Create as much distance as possible.

I rapidly clicked through the pictures of Marybeth's face and head. She had taken pride in her appearance and always looked her best for Bill. Crime scene photos weren't a fair way to remember her.

None of these photographs should've caught me off guard. I was a cop and had seen this stuff before. But the last one was the kicker, the one that jolted me. I'd seen the sketch of the crime scene and knew it to be a representation of Bill and Marybeth's bodies.

But a sketch and a photograph are two different things.

I froze and gasped at the same time. I stood and paced the floor a few moments, using my sleeve to wipe a tear before continuing.

The photo was from the front at a forty-five-degree angle with the intent to show the upper portions of their bodies. It showed Bill and Marybeth the way they had fallen. He was on top of her from the waist up, his legs twisted, sticking out at a strange angle. Their faces—what remained of them—were in the center of the frame.

The focus and detail were good. Too good.

I put my elbows on the table and rested my chin in the palms of my hands with my fingers over my cheeks and stared at the picture. Not sure how long I held that position, but long enough for my donut to begin to go stale.

How had things come to this? Two friends lost to murder. Two friends I'd never see or talk to again.

I touched the screen, moving my fingers along the edges of their faces several times. Finally, with a deep sigh and feeling as if I were saying goodbye, I closed the attachment.

CHAPTER 8

TIFFANY AND I had agreed that she and Lester would rendezvous with me midmorning the next day, load our gear into my Wrangler, and head to the dock to do their first scuba dive. They arrived later than we had planned, but "midmorning" on Bonaire is very ambiguous. Setting the clock to Island Time is almost automatic.

Strange, and maybe out of place, diving less than forty-eight hours after learning of Bill and Marybeth, but I hoped the dive would be a diversion from all the questions bouncing through my head. Still wasn't sure how—or when—to tell Tiffany. Telling her needed to be done, but right now didn't seem right, although I didn't know what "right" would feel like. Or when it would come.

Packed in a mesh bag, most of my gear sat in the same area of the Wrangler as Tiffany and Lester's. My swim fins were too large to fit in the bag, so I had laid them alongside. They were oversized, purchased several years ago in a drunken state of testosterone-fueled machoism. If needed, the larger size provided additional power, thus speed, underwater.

Tiffany placed a hand on one of my fins. "Nice fins," she said.

"I can chase down a dolphin with those monsters," I said.

"Yeah, right." Her eyes widened. "But it'd be cool to try."

"What about oxygen tanks?" Lester asked.

Tiffany elbowed Lester in the ribs. "They're not *oxygen* tanks," she said.

Lester rolled his eyes. "What fucking ever," he said.

Tiffany was correct, and Lester's question—not to mention his attitude—gave me pause. An experienced diver wouldn't refer to them as oxygen tanks. The tanks contained *air*, not oxygen. Two different gases.

"Jan has those on the boat. All included with the price," I said.

We piled into the Wrangler and headed for the pier.

"How's the nose?" I asked Lester.

"Fine," he said with a shrug. "No different than yesterday."

"Remember, the nose plays an important part in scuba. As we descend in the water, the pressure on your ears will increase. To help clear the pressure—"

"Yeah, yeah, I know. Scuba 101," Lester said.

I sighed and tried again. "When you pinch your nose and try to breathe through it to clear the pressure, signal me if you have any problems. We don't want any trouble, especially on your first dive."

Tiffany placed a hand on Lester's shoulder. "I'll be there, too. If you need help, let me know."

Lester brushed her hand away. "I'll be fine, for God's sake." He tried to pinch his nose, his hand jerking away like he had touched a hot plate. Under his breath, I heard, "Shit."

We parked in the gravel alongside the road near one of the northern piers. Jan stood on the shore-end of the dock waving, a massive smile on his sun-wrinkled face. Over the years, Jan's skin had developed an all-over honey-brown color, which brought out the blue of his eyes.

He wore an untucked white button-down shirt with the sleeves cut off and a pair of red, knee-length swim shorts. His white beachcomber hat was wrinkled, stained with salt, and pulled low on his head to keep from being blown off. No shoes, sandals, or flip-flops. Ever.

I heaved the mesh bag over my shoulder and grabbed my fins. Tiffany and Lester grabbed their gear, and we marched toward the dock and Jan's outstretched hand.

"Good to see you, my friend," he said, slapping me on the shoulder.

After I introduced Tiffany to Jan, he proceeded to give her the customary Dutch three-kiss greeting on the cheek. I smiled. Tiffany, like most Americans, became uncomfortable having her personal space violated with a series of kisses—not to mention from someone she had met just a few moments ago. Her cheeks flushed and she tried to hide a sheepish grin. I puckered my lips at her.

"Your name is *Jan*?" Lester asked. "What kind of name is that?"

Tiffany jabbed Lester in the side with her elbow. "Lester," she said with clenched teeth.

Jan stiffened, narrowed his eyes at Lester. "Yes. Jan. It is Dutch."

I wedged myself partway between Lester and Jan. "It's pronounced like *John*," I said to Lester, "except with a *Y* instead of a *J*. It's the Dutch version of John."

Lester shook his head. "Whatever."

Jan stared at Lester a moment, then turned and led us to his boat, *The Dutchman's Pleasure*. "Let's get your gear loaded and get out on the water."

The boat rocked in the light waves as Tiffany, Lester, and I handed our gear over the boat rail to Jan. We couldn't board until Jan stowed the gear and gave us his standard safety speech.

After a ten-minute briefing on emergency procedures, basic radio operation, where to stand, where not to stand, first aid equipment, and a host of other items, Jan helped Tiffany and Lester step aboard. He started the engines, and I untied the mooring lines, tossed them onto the boat's deck, and jumped aboard as we eased away from the dock. Tiffany and Lester sat near the stern in the blazing heat, each with a water bottle in hand. I stood next to Jan on the helmsman's deck, protected from the sun by the overhead canopy.

Jan used *The Dutchman's Pleasure* for hired fishing excursions, but, on occasion, worked scuba trips. The boat was an older vessel, known as a Topaz, circa 1988. At thirty-six feet in length, it easily navigated the Bonaire coastal waters. Aside from his wife, *The Dutchman's Pleasure* was Jan's pride and joy, and he kept it in pristine condition. When not tending bar downtown, he was on the *Pleasure* fixing small maintenance items or cleaning its hull of barnacles.

"Hey, Roscoe," Tiffany said, "where we diving?"

Making a fake slap to my forehead, I said, "Oh yeah. I forgot to mention that." I pointed south. "How about a site called Tori's Reef? We'll stay shallow and spend the entire dive in depths of twenty-five to forty feet. There'll be plenty of coral and fish. It's also a good place to see spotted eagle rays."

At that moment, as if on cue, Jan pulled back the throttles, and the big engines changed pitch. The buoy indicating the Tori's Reef dive site floated just beyond the boat's bow. We'd be there in a few seconds.

"R, get the bow," Jan said.

"Aye-aye, Skipper."

Using the railing to steady myself, I made my way to the front of the boat and unstrapped a long pole with a hook on one end. Jan altered the power settings of the engines, holding the *Pleasure* in position so I could snare a rope floating on the surface connected to the buoy and secure it to the bowline. The line went taught as *The Dutchman's Pleasure* settled into a downwind position, small waves lapping against the hull, rocking us from side to side.

Tiffany sprang to her feet. "Let's do this."

CHAPTER 9

WHILE I SLIPPED into my wetsuit, tank, and fins, Jan helped Tiffany and Lester assemble and test their gear. Earlier, Jan and I had agreed that I should be in the water first, ready to help when Lester and Tiffany entered.

I sat on the side of the boat and watched Lester attach the air regulator to his tank backward. Jan knelt beside him and helped correct the situation, explaining to Lester what he should've already known. Lester exhibited the classic signs of a nervous beginner—shaky hands; rapid breathing; repetitive stares over the rail at the water.

"Nothing to worry about, Lester," I said. "You'll be fine. This is a good dive site."

I caught Jan's attention and pointed a finger at my chest then over the side. He nodded. With one hand over my mask and the other holding the regulator in my mouth, I took a breath and rolled backward off the boat. Drops of seawater worked their way between the regulator and my lips, giving me a quick taste of salt. I gave Jan a signal to indicate that everything was okay and swam to the stern.

Tiffany waddled to the platform at the rear of the boat, stopping every step or two to steady her balance. Her scuba ensemble made quite a statement. Her mask and fins were bright pink. Her wetsuit, which was all-over black, had pink accents along the arm, waist, and legs. Even her weight belt was pink. I wouldn't have been surprised to see the price tags still attached.

She held her mask and regulator in place with her hands and looked straight out at the horizon. She extended one leg forward, the other trailing behind, as she "stepped" into the water, executing what's known as a *giant stride* entry. I motioned for her to hold onto the drift line, a rope floating on the surface behind the boat.

She shook her head, removed the regulator from her mouth. "I'm okay," she said. "There isn't much current." She placed the regulator back in her mouth.

I raised my arm out of the water, my hand holding the line. She moaned into her regulator and grabbed the rope, smacking her hand on the water as she did so.

Safety is never an accident.

The wake from a passing vessel sent several large waves pounding against the hull of *The Dutchman's Pleasure*. The boat rocked while Lester was trying to walk to the stern in full scuba gear. He lost his balance and Jan grabbed his arm, but Lester fell on his keister, his tank scratching the side wall of the *Pleasure*. Jan's face turned red, and he let out a stream of Dutch profanity—then helped Lester to his feet. Out of the corner of my eye, I saw Jan rubbing the mark with his foot, shaking his head.

As Tiffany and I rode the shallow waves behind the boat, holding the drift line, Jan succeeded in helping Lester into the water. His entry wasn't graceful, and he floundered on the surface, splashing water with his hands and lunging for the drift line. His eyes were the size of golf balls, and his regulator whined from his rapid, deep breathing. He should've been relaxed and floating, but, instead, he kicked hard, trying to keep his upper body high above the surface.

I considered canceling the dive and getting everyone back on the boat. However, many new divers experience anxiety on the surface, but, once below the water—and the waves—they relax and have an enjoyable dive. I hoped this would be the case with Lester.

Forming a circle with my index finger and thumb—the international scuba "okay" sign—I flashed it at my dive partners. They nodded and reciprocated. Next, I extended an arm, thumb pointing down. We released the air from our buoyancy compensators and sank below the surface. As we descended, noise from the surface vanished, the only sound our exhaled air as it vented through the regulators and bubbled its way to the surface. I kept a watchful eye on Tiffany and Lester.

We halted our descent a few feet above the reef at a depth of twenty feet. The current was minimal, with visibility at seventy-five feet. My dive computer showed the water temperature at eighty-one degrees. Near perfect conditions.

Tiffany swam to me, pointing at her mask. During our descent, it had leaked around the edges, filling halfway with water. Using a tried-and-true scuba method for removing the water, she tilted her head back and exhaled through her nose, forcing the water out around the edges of the mask. With it cleared, she gave me the okay sign.

The three of us glided along the reef at depths ranging between twenty-five and forty feet. Eels, a large barracuda, and numerous small reef creatures scurried about the coral. Several tarpons, three to four feet in length, swam gracefully behind us. Tarpons posed no threat to humans, but over time, had learned to use divers as cover to ambush small reef fish. They cruised behind and off to the side of a diver, then swooshed past and toward the coral to snag unsuspecting fish. If a diver was unaware of this behavior, it could be a startling experience.

I regularly checked on Lester. Breathing normal now, he seemed relaxed. He swam along the reef calmly, proving himself capable, and didn't exhibit any signs of the surface-fueled anxiety. Tiffany swam an arm's length from his side, her gaze alternating between him and the coral below.

After twenty minutes on the reef, and at a depth of forty feet, I signaled to Tiffany and Lester to turn around. Time to head back to the boat.

As Lester turned, a tarpon darted between him and Tiffany, headed for the coral below. In doing so, it swam closer to Lester than to Tiffany, nearly brushing his mask.

The sudden movement startled Lester and he panicked, looking from side to side, then at the surface. Sometimes, the first course of action by a diver struck with panic or fear is an uncontrolled desire to get out of the water, resulting in a beeline to the surface. It's a fight-or-flight response, and since there's nothing to fight, the diver instantly opts for the flight option. Rapid ascents increase the chance of severe injury and make divers much more susceptible to air embolisms and decompression sickness—better known as the bends—which are sometimes fatal. Student divers are taught to make slow ascents, breathing slowly and regularly. But panic sometimes negates training, especially for beginners.

Tiffany acted immediately. When Lester started his move to the surface, she grabbed his weight belt and used her body weight as drag to slow his ascent. Lester looked up, feet kicking, arms flailing, clawing for the surface. Lester wanted out of the water and Tiffany was doing everything she could to slow his ascent.

Thanks to my oversized fins, I swam to Lester's side in four kicks. His mask was full of blood and mucus, which, I guessed, had something to do with his injured nose. There weren't any bubbles coming from his regulator, which became my immediate problem; Lester was holding his breath.

Divers should never hold their breath, especially on an ascent. Air in the lungs expands and, like rapid ascents, can cause pulmonary barotrauma and possibly death. Lester needed to start breathing again—and soon. No way I could communicate the importance of that to him underwater, so I placed one hand on his regulator and with my other hand, punched him in the gut. Not hard, but forceful enough to get him to exhale. He exhaled so hard that if I hadn't been holding his regulator to his mouth, he'd have involuntarily spit it out. I didn't want to hit him but saw no other way. Wide-eyed, he inhaled, then continued regular breathing, albeit at a rapid pace.

His struggling and thrashing increased. A swing of his arm knocked Tiffany's mask off her face. Dread shot through me. I watched her for a few seconds, worried she might panic.

But unconcerned with her own discomfort or safety, Tiffany closed her eyes and maintained a firm grasp on Lester. I watched her mask sink to the bottom—slowly descending, a pink circle in a field of blue, coming to rest sixty feet below the surface on top of a round green sponge coral.

A glance at my dive computer showed our ascent rate within acceptable parameters. Our best option was to maintain this pace to the surface.

Our ascent took close to a minute, my heart pounding the entire way. As soon as his head popped above the surface, Lester tore off his mask and regulator, gasping for air but, instead, getting a mouth full of water. He coughed and gagged, his face turning a blotchy red. To increase his buoyancy, I reached over and removed the weight belt from around his waist. His thrashing slowed, and he seemed to calm somewhat. I grabbed the bright orange lifesaver attached to the end of the rope Jan had thrown in our direction and tucked it under Lester's arms. I told him to hold on. He nodded and breathed heavy, eyes fixated on the boat, gasping and coughing.

Tiffany kicked over to Lester. She removed the regulator from her mouth. "You'll be okay, hon. Just breathe normally."

Lester pushed her away and continued to stare at the boat. "Pull me in," he tried to yell but caught another mouth full of seawater.

I took the regulator out of my mouth and said to Tiffany, "You okay?" She said she was and placed the regulator back in her mouth. I handed her my mask and told her to put it on. "Stay here, above your mask. I'll take Lester to the boat, grab a mask from Jan, and come back to get yours."

"I can get it," she said.

"No, not solo." I looked at the boat, then at Lester. He couldn't be left alone on the surface, so I needed to stay with him the entire way back. "I'll be back here in three minutes."

"Roscoe—"

"Wait for me to get back."

She put the regulator back in her mouth.

"Promise?" I said.

After a moment, her face muscles tightened, and she flashed the okay sign.

I swam alongside Lester as Jan pulled him toward the boat. Lester clutched the lifesaver and grunted each time a wave washed over him. Breathing rapidly and white-knuckled, he gripped the lifesaver so fiercely, I feared his fingers might leave permanent impressions. Something else to upset Jan.

I glanced at Tiffany every few seconds as she floated on the surface. Occasionally, she'd put her head in the water and adjust her position slightly in order to stay above the green coral, but mostly, she watched Lester and me make our way to the boat. Each time she caught me watching her, she'd flash me the okay sign.

"Why is she not coming with you?" Jan yelled as we neared.

"She dropped her mask. I'm going to return and get it for her as soon as I help Lester aboard. Keep an eye on her, okay?"

Jan nodded and turned back to watch Tiffany.

Lester and I made our way to the ladder at the stern of the boat. I helped Lester remove his fins, and, on the second attempt, he hauled himself onto the first rung.

"There she goes," Jan said. He pointed to where Tiffany should've been floating on the surface. Much to my horror and dismay, she was gone.

"Right when Lester got on the ladder, she went under," Jan said.

I smacked a fist on the water's surface, then reached up and yanked Lester's mask out of his hand. I rinsed out most of the blood and snot, pulled it over my face, and swam to the spot where Tiffany's bubbles breached the surface. Before I descended, Tiffany surfaced, holding her mask up in a one-handed victory wave, unable to supress a smile sneeking across her face.

Then she signaled okay, turned, and swam toward the boat. I followed and counted to ten.

As we neared the boat, I heard Jan ask Lester, "What happened to your nose?"

Lester shook his head, eyebrows pursed. "A simple bloody nose and those two get all panicked." He glared at me working my way up the ladder. "And that fucker punched me in the gut."

Jan smiled at me. I waved the matter off.

Lester threw his fins down and unbuckled his gear, dropping it to the deck.

Jan straightened and took a step toward me, shooting a finger at Lester. "He doesn't come back."

I unzipped my wetsuit and sat on a wooden seat that ran along the side of the boat. "I understand." I looked at Tiffany and shrugged.

With the mooring line released, Jan cranked the engines and headed north, back to the pier. As *The Dutchman's Pleasure* bounced through the surf, I sat near the back of the boat, nursing a Bright I'd borrowed from Jan's cooler.

Tiffany walked over and sat next to me, putting her arm around my shoulders. "Thanks for your help, Roscoe," she said. "I'm glad you were there. I wasn't sure exactly what to do."

"What happened?" I asked.

"It happened so fast, I'm not sure." She reached over and took my beer, keeping it for herself after downing a sip. "Everything seemed to be going along fine. Lester was doing well."

I walked over to the cooler, grabbed a beer of my own. Soaking up some sun, Lester lay motionless on the deck near the bow. Relaxed and under control, he held an ice pack on his nose.

Tiffany continued, "Then, that tarpon went by. I saw blood pouring out—covering the inside of his mask. It freaked me out and then all hell broke loose."

"That's when he started to go up?"

"Yeah, that's right. He bolted for the surface. I knew that was bad, so I grabbed him, hoping he would settle down." She took a sip of beer. "As I said, I'm glad you came along. Not sure how much longer I could've held him."

"You did good, but we'll need to talk about your broken promise back there."

"Roscoe—"

"Not now, but you shouldn't be solo diving." I took a swig, pointed a finger at her. "You know that."

She let out a sigh, leaned back on the rail, and curled her toes. "What a way to start a vacation."

Jan slowed the engines as we approached the pier. Like a well-trained dolphin, I stood and started toward the bow, knowing all too well my role in getting us secured to the dock. I took a step and turned back to Tiffany. "You know . . . you probably saved him from serious injury."

"Oh, c'mon," she said.

I swallowed the last of my beer and tossed the empty bottle into the cooler. "I'm not kidding. Maybe even saved his life. Sure hope he appreciates it."

CHAPTER 10

No one spoke during the drive back to the YellowRock—all seven minutes of it. Lester sat in the back seat; head tilted back with an ice pack on his nose. The bleeding had stopped, but the swelling caused a whistling sound every time he breathed. At my suggestion of a doctor, he held out an open hand, palm facing me. I shrugged. Okay, have it your way.

Tiffany sat in the front seat with a Bright in her hand, the smell of her spearmint chewing gum doing little to mask that of the alcohol. Staring out the open window, she released a deep sigh every third or fourth exhale. She turned my way once, shook her head, and returned to the window.

I parked in front of their unit. We unloaded the gear and hung it to dry in the shed out back. Lester didn't say anything and disappeared into their room as soon as we finished. Tiffany kissed me on the cheek and said she'd stop by later. I watched as she entered and closed the door behind her, the one with a number five nailed to it.

I walked back to the office, unlocked the door, and went inside. Since it was Sunday, Erika had the day off, so the office was unattended. I pressed the delete button upon hearing the threatening message Marko Martijn—the contractor responsible for the unfinished foundation work—had left on my answering machine and then hit the stairs to my apartment anticipating a cold beer. I went to the desk in my living room and fired up the internet. The dive having done nothing to quiet—or answer—the dozens of questions still banging around in my head.

The *Rockford Register Star* was the leading newspaper in Rockford. The edition open on Bill's table and visible in the crime scene photos correlated to the NP—or "newspaper"—on the crime scene sketch.

I dialed the number listed on the *Rockford Register Star* website and got an automated answering system. The pleasant female voice told me to listen carefully because their menu options may have changed.

Are people calling the newspaper often enough to memorize their menu options?

Orny Adams, one of my favorite comedians, came to mind. *"If people are calling often enough to memorize your menu options,"* he says during his stand-up routine, *"then fix your damn product!"*

Smiling, I pressed the button for the classified department. The same pleasant voice told me the regular hours for the classified department were eight to five, Monday through Friday—currently closed. I went back to the menu and selected the button for the circulation department. A gravelly voiced guy answered.

"I'm hoping you can help me," I said.

"Whatcha need, bub?" Loud, repetitive machine sounds echoed in the background. He yelled as he spoke, and I pulled the receiver away from my ear.

"Can you tell me about an ad in your classifieds?" I half-yelled back at him.

"This is circulation."

"I know, but can you help me?"

"You gotta talk to the ad department."

"They're closed. I just have a few questions—"

"Can't help ya. Call tomorrow and ask for *ads*." He hung up. So much for customer service. I considered my next phone call.

The website for Jay's Automotive, the single-owner repair shop in Rockford where Bill took his vehicles, showed closed on Sundays. Bill and Jay were old high school chums, and Bill was a loyal customer. He told me once he'd never go anywhere but Jay's. If anyone knew Bill's truck, it'd be Jay. He might even know if Bill had mentioned anything about selling it.

I dialed the number. No answer and no option to leave a message—just endless ringing. After ten minutes, I tried again. Same result.

Next, I dialed the Rockford Police Department and asked for Penn. Usually, he wouldn't be working on a Sunday, but considering Bill's murder, I guessed he'd be in the office.

Larry David answered on the second ring, and I asked, "You got the weapon?"

"What?" he said.

"You got the weapon?"

He hesitated a moment. "R?" I was silent. "What are you talking about?"

"The sketch shows a weapon on the table."

"You're seeing things."

"Why does the coroner's report list a .357 Magnum? You'd need the weapon to know that."

Penn didn't say anything.

"Sketch and coroner's report," I said. "You have the weapon, don't you?"

He sighed into the phone. "Look, R, I can't comment on that. I messed up. You were only supposed to get the pictures, not the sketch or reports."

"Speaking of the pictures, what's with that ad? The one circled in red?"

"No comment there, either," he said.

"Anything you *can* tell me?"

"After the lashing Traverso gave me? Nope, nothing. No more than you already know, that is."

"But I don't know anything," I said.

He was quiet for a moment, then said, "Exactly."

CHAPTER 11

HAVING GOTTEN NOWHERE with three phone calls, I went out to the veranda. Sitting on the lounger with a Bright, I reached over and took my banjo off its stand. I'd been playing the 5-string since the age of sixteen, but still wasn't very good. Probably never would be. Besides putting me in a relaxed, almost Zen state of mind, playing the banjo did one of two things: it either took my mind off everything that was bothering me, or it made me think more intensely about the things that *were* bothering me. But until the playing started, I never knew which one it'd be.

Most locals had grown accustomed to the tinny sound of my banjo, not giving it a second thought. The tourists, expecting steel drum melodies and every incarnation of "Margaritaville" possible, paused and looked around for the source of the odd, unexpected music. Sitting against the back wall of my veranda, observing through the railing balusters, I watched them as they swiveled their heads in bewilderment. And it never failed. There was always one clown in each crowd who would break out in a poor rendition of a square dancer, forcing laughter from the rest of the group.

And today was no exception.

Gawking at the fun-loving tourists that day didn't bring the usual smile to my face, the banjo playing having taken me to the think-more-intensely-about-what-is-bothering-me state of mind. My brain swam with thoughts of Bill, Marybeth, and their murders. The weapon. The classified ad: *Four-wheel drive. Call Bill.*

No answers.

"Hey there, Mr. Clampett."

Tiffany stood on the veranda, smiling and mimicking my playing by doing her version of an air banjo. My music having taken me someplace I didn't want to go, I hadn't noticed her walk up the outside stairs.

A white, see-through sarong, tied loosely around her waist, covered the lower portion of a dark blue swimsuit, and a white, short-sleeved button-down shirt hid the top. Her hair lay loose on her shoulders, and a canvas bag hung over her shoulder.

I stopped playing, leaned back on the lounger, and grabbed my beer. "Jed Clampett didn't play the banjo."

"Whatever." She set the bag on the floor. "You have another one of those?"

I bit my lower lip and held back a smile. "Nope." I shrugged and held my banjo out in front of me. "As far as I know, this is the only banjo on the island."

She glared at me and leaned forward, hands on her hips. "Do. You. Have. A. Nother. Beer. Smartass?"

"Oooohhhh. Why didn't you say so? I always have another beer." I motioned my head toward the kitchen. "In the fridge and ignore the mess."

Tiffany headed for the kitchen. "Are you saving these chips?"

"Help yourself and bring me another beer, please." Since my playing time was over for the moment, I set the banjo back on its stand.

"How's Lester?" I asked as Tiffany handed me the beer, her mouth full of potato chips.

"He'll be fine, I guess." She leaned against the railing and licked salt off her fingers. "He won't go to the doctor, but that's just the way he is." She caught me with the corner of her eye. "I know someone else like that."

"Go on."

She chased the chips with a sip of beer. "He says he doesn't want to go anywhere or do anything the rest of the day. Maybe not even tomorrow." She shook her head.

Tiffany had kept her composure and handled herself well at Tori's Reef. If she hadn't, the dive might've turned into a disaster. Her confidence and dive skills impressed me, especially for a vacation diver.

"You did good this afternoon," I said. "Well, mostly anyway."

"Thanks, Roscoe. That means a lot coming from you. But to tell the truth, I was a bit scared. I know I shouldn't have gone for the mask alone." She stared at her toes. "It won't happen again."

"Promise?"

She hesitated a moment, then snapped to attention, placed a hand over her heart, and said, "Promise."

"Okay, okay. I hope it doesn't ruin your vacation."

"Well, it won't ruin mine. Lester can do whatever he wants. He can pout in his room, or he can get on with it and enjoy the island. It's his call."

"Sounds reasonable . . . What are you doing the rest of the day?"

"I think I'll go lay in the sun for a while." She jerked a thumb at the beach across the street.

"Good place to do it."

"Beyond that, I'm not sure. Hopefully, Lester will want to go out or something." She raised her eyebrows. "Hey, when am I going to meet Arabella?"

"Never."

"Don't be like that. What's the problem?"

"Kind of like when Mr. Scott would warn Captain Kirk about mixing matter and antimatter."

She stared at me. How could she know Jed Clampett and the *Beverley Hillbillies*, but not Captain Kirk, Mr. Scott, or *Star Trek*? I shook my head. "Never mind. Maybe we'll get together tomorrow."

Tiffany concentrated on the floor, head bopping, toe tapping as if keeping time to an internal beat only she heard. Eyes fixed on a precise spot a few inches beyond her feet, she seemed to have something to say but was holding back. I leaned over to my banjo, sitting on its stand, and ran my finger across the strings. The open G chord brought her around.

"So . . . when do you think you're going back to the States?" she asked.

My heart skipped a beat as sweat pooled and ran along my spine, the temperature feeling as though it had risen twenty degrees in the last second. She must've known about Bill and Marybeth and thought I'd be going back for the ceremonies. Maybe she had known all along and was waiting for me to say something. I wasn't sure how that conversation was supposed to start, or how it'd go, but this wasn't the way I'd pictured it.

I blurted out the first thing that came to mind.

"What?"

Her mouth opened, but she closed it before saying anything. She stared at me a moment, then looked at the floor again. I got out of the lounger and stood next to her against the railing. I took a sip of beer and scanned the beach area across the street. Kids were jumping off the pier, sandpipers were scurrying near the trash cans scavenging for food scraps, and someone was practicing a martial arts routine—a *kata*—in the sand. Several local fishermen, motoring along in their handmade wooden boats, were returning to the docks after a long day on the sea, ready to sell their *Catch of the Day* to the seaside restaurants.

I waited.

After a few long moments, she looked at me. A solitary tear ran down her cheek.

"I'm going to the beach," she said, pushing off the railing and picking up her bag.

She crossed the street, spread her blanket on the sand, and lay down, apparently not giving me a second thought.

Not even a glance.

CHAPTER 12

TIFFANY AND ARABELLA were determined to meet, so I gave in and planned to have everyone over for food and beer. My apartment was the quintessential bachelor pad, and as such, in desperate need of cleaning.

With a trash bag in each arm, I walked around the corner of the building and heaved open the dumpster lid. My nostrils flared, and my eyes watered as the stench reached out and swallowed me. Before I threw the bags on the smelly heap, I heard a footstep and turned around.

Someone hit me in my right eye.

I dropped the bags, and before I could straighten, was struck on the other side of the face. My head spun and jerked as my legs began to buckle. A third hit caught me square in the jaw and knocked me to the ground.

I slumped to my knees, and before looking up, got kicked in the lower rib cage. My diaphragm collapsed, forcing the air from my lungs, and I hit the ground hard, unable to breathe.

Lying on the gravel, the salty taste of blood tickling my tongue, oozing from my upper lip into my mouth, time meant nothing—it could've been a few seconds, or it could've been a few hours. I didn't know. My right eye was already difficult to open, and I swallowed hard to choke back bile. Consciousness began to slip, and I fought to remain lucid.

A faint voice yelled "Hey." I heard footsteps, maybe running, and in the next few seconds, someone helped me stand and lean against the Wrangler.

"Are you alright, mister?" someone said. "I think you blacked out for a second."

With the world spiraling out of control, I spit blood on the ground, mumbled something even I didn't understand, and sought to find the source of the voices. My eyes were slow to focus, but two blurred figures, males, stood in front of me.

"Which way?" I asked.

"That way," one of the guys said, pointing down the street toward the business district.

It hurt, but I sucked in several breaths, then squinted and peered down the street. A figure, walking casually, turned the corner two blocks away and disappeared.

"Thanks," I said and patted one of them on the shoulder.

After the first stride, pain shot through my midsection. I straightened and, with a hand, applied pressure to my upper abdomen. Teeth clenched, I squeezed my eyes shut. The throbbing pain in my lower rib cage was no stranger, and I knew it'd prevent me from running.

A bruised rib.

"Maybe I should call the cops or an ambulance or something," one of the guys said.

I shook my head and waved him off. Stopping the pursuit and losing my attacker wasn't an option. Every step was a struggle as I hobbled down the street, trying to keep myself upright. I dragged my feet more than walked and braced myself against every car, wall, or bench.

The pain worked its way up my side and into my shoulder. I wanted to stop and lie down but limped along the street to the downtown area of Kralendijk. Vehicles, moving no faster than snails, clawed their way through town, lining the one-lane road that spanned the length of the business district. Dinner guests crowded the open-air restaurants along the street, and the oceanfront bar, Vinny's, teamed with patrons. Smells of fresh lobster, wahoo, and swordfish filled the air, and the sound of people conversing in multiple languages echoed across the street.

Not a picture-perfect Bourbon Street during Mardi Gras, but crowded and hectic enough to lose sight of a person.

And lose him I did.

With a mixture of Cabana and Latin-style music playing at Vinny's and the faint sound of a steel drum band somewhere down the street, I made my way past each successive restaurant. I peered at the tourists, eager for a familiar face or any hint of an abnormal situation. Nothing. No sign of him. I turned and scanned the crowd at Vinny's.

Nothing.

Turning to start the long, painful journey home, I noticed Jan behind the bar at Vinny's, waving his hands at me, trying to get my attention. After raising my hand in acknowledgment, Jan pointed to a person sitting head-down at the bar.

Built on a wooden and concrete pier, Vinny's jutted out over the sea. I stepped onto the planks and nursed my body over to the bar and sat next to the guy Jan had pointed out.

At least the guy was conscious.

Chuck Studer, another American living on the island, had an apartment above one of the storefronts across the street making Vinny's his favorite—and closest—hangout. Out of synch with the music, he tapped his toe on the stool's footrest. His head rested on his left arm, which he had formed into a makeshift pillow. In his right hand, he held a half-empty bottle of beer. Thirty dollars in paper and coin lay scattered across the bar.

I placed a hand on his shoulder. "Chuck, you alright?"

Chuck stood five feet, nine inches tall with short-cropped graying hair and a clean-shaven face. He had served many years in the Air Force as an aviation mechanic and still maintained the build of a former military person, albeit, these days, a bit thicker around the waist, the result of beer, late nights, and too many late mornings. Beyond my comprehension, the island women—especially the younger ones—found him irresistible. Chuck was seldom alone.

He rolled his head, one eye open, peering at me over his arm. "What's up, R?" He fiddled with the money on the bar. "Want a beer?" He wore a surplus Air Force pilot suit, which he had claimed many times *"the chicks dig."*

I decided a beer couldn't hurt anything. My pursuit was finished . . . for the night, anyway. Besides, knowing Chuck, he wasn't going to leave until the last drop of beer disappeared from his bottle. Jan stood nearby and nodded when I held up two fingers. Bar service was on island time, and I had learned soon after moving to Bonaire to order two at a time.

The recent excitement faded, and my senses began to return, along with aches and pains in various parts of my body. Alcohol might be just what the doctor ordered.

"I meant to call you," Chuck said. He snapped his head up, one eye closed. "Hey, do you know why scuba divers roll backward off a boat into the water?"

He had told me this joke two days ago. "Yes, I do."

"Because if they rolled forward—" he began to chuckle—"they'd still be in the boat." Laughing, he placed his head back onto his arm-pillow.

"Chuck, you were going to call me?"

After a few moments, he spoke, head still down, into his folded arms. "Oh yeah, what are you doing tomorrow afternoon?"

I had a good idea where this was going.

He rolled his head a couple of times in his arms. "Can you take a flight for me, around three?"

Chuck owned a Cessna, model 180, single-engine airplane that he used in a sightseeing business on Bonaire. He gave rides to tourists, contractors, and anyone else who wanted an aerial view of the island. Occasionally, when something came up, but more often, when he was hungover, I would take a flight for him.

"Three o'clock?" I said. "You still be hungover by then?"

Chuck looked at me and smiled. "I have a date later tonight."

"A date? Tonight?"

"Yeah, when she gets off work," he said and closed his eyes. "I'm hoping it'll last till tomorrow."

I turned toward the sea and watched a pelican paddle along, probably hoping to snag a stray piece of bread or French fry that happened to float pass. I didn't mind helping. Besides, it kept my pilot skills from getting rusty. After a moment, I smiled and turned back to Chuck.

"Sure, I'll do it."

Chuck raised his head, opened both eyes. "Thanks." His brows crinkled, and his eyes narrowed a bit. "What happened to you?"

"It's been a rough night."

"You and me both." He lowered his head and resumed his near passed-out position on the bar, toe still tapping.

I clanked my bottle against his sitting on the bar. My first beer went down in one, quick upturn.

It was a typical crowd for Vinny's—a solid mixture of tourists and locals. They laughed and drank, not having a care in the world. A big-screen TV mounted on one end of the bar televised a Dutch soccer match. In the corner, a group cheered as one of the teams scored a goal, or point, or whatever it's called.

Another night in paradise.

A flood of recognition overtook me as I did a double take on a figure at the far end of the bar. His bruised nose made him impossible to miss. Lester Jeffrey held a bottle of beer and chatted with a local girl, who didn't appear interested in him.

No doubt, a woman with good taste.

No sign of Tiffany. I watched for her, thinking she might return from the bathroom or enter Vinny's off the street. After a few minutes, and half a beer, she hadn't done either.

Lester was here without her.

He hadn't noticed me yet and continued to annoy the girl sitting alongside him. He leaned in close to her several times, and each time she twisted her body, so more of her back faced him. She appeared to be part of a group of people mulling along that side of Vinny's and showed no interest in Lester.

Go figure.

Eventually picking up on her vibes, Lester abandoned his attempted conquest of her, and scanned the bar, possibly seeking out other prey. He froze when our eyes met, then held up his bottle, furrowed his brow, and took a swig. Maintaining his glare, he set the bottle on the bar with a loud clunk, prompting a scowl from Jan.

Tolerating Lester without Tiffany around would be impossible. "Let's go, Chuck. Time to get ready for your date." In my condition, hauling Chuck to his apartment would hurt.

Chuck reached for his half-full beer. "Wait, I still have some beer left."

Before he got the bottle to his mouth, I yanked it from his hand and polished off the contents, setting the empty on the bar. "No, you don't."

Chuck glared at the empty and moaned as if a prize marlin had thrown the hook. His jaw dropped, and his eyes widened. He waved at Jan for another one, but Jan was busy with other customers. I pried Chuck's hands from the edge of the bar, and half dragged him the first few steps.

We stopped at the far end of the bar.

"Are we getting a beer?" Chuck asked. I ignored him and moved between him and Lester.

"Lester, why are you here?" Chuck tried to move closer to the bar, but I tightened my grip on him. "I mean . . . where's Tiffany?"

Lester shrugged. A woman walked past, and he made a point of staring at her butt. "Tiff said she didn't want to come out tonight."

"So, you came alone?"

"Well, not exactly. Mandy is meeting me here."

"Mandy?"

"Yeah, Mandy." He rolled his eyes, shaking his head. "Another person staying at your place." When I didn't immediately say anything, he continued. "Unit seven?"

He meant Mandy Driver, whom I hadn't run into yet, which wasn't unusual during the high-tourist season. When the YellowRock was at near-full capacity, as it currently was, I didn't always meet each guest. But Erika did, and that's what mattered.

"But . . ." I couldn't finish the sentence. Didn't know what to say or think, except that Lester should be with Tiffany, not Mandy. That's how it worked in my world—bring your girlfriend to the tropics and spend time with her.

I stood in his face a moment, then began dragging Chuck toward the exit. When we got out of Vinny's and onto the street, he quit struggling and accepted his fate. He relaxed, seeming content to lean against me while I walked him to his apartment.

With my attention focused on Chuck, I bumped shoulders with a guy walking past.

"Sorry," the guy said.

"Me, too." I was about to turn away when my eyes locked on his face. Something about him seemed familiar. For a moment, I assumed the Chicago Bears hat or the sweat-stained Northern Illinois University

T-shirt he wore had caught my attention. NIU, located in DeKalb, was a scant forty miles from Rockford, so numerous alumni lived in the Rockford area. I couldn't narrow it down, but there was something more profound to this feeling of familiarization. More than his face or clothes.

He stood five feet, seven inches tall and weighed roughly one hundred and seventy pounds. Nothing out of the ordinary about him. Long blond hair, a pointed nose, and a physically fit appearance, the way laborers or union guys looked. Solid shoulders and slightly oversized forearms. He had workingman hands, scraped and red.

His eyes caught my attention. They reminded me of well-polished, dark brown marbles swimming in a sea of pale white, with a speck of black pigmentation in the white of the left one. It reminded me of a random, misplaced freckle.

Unique and somewhat distracting, I tried not to stare.

"I said I was sorry," the guy said, his voice louder and a bit more forceful. He balled his right hand into a fist.

As hard as I had tried not to, I realized that I had been staring. With one arm around Chuck, I held up the other, palm out. "Yeah, me, too. Sorry."

The guy relaxed and walked into Vinny's. He sat on a stool next to Lester, the one previously occupied by the woman Lester had been annoying. She must've wised up and left.

"You should meet this chick, R," Chuck said as we crossed the street, his speech slurred. "She's a knockout."

"Yeah, I'm sure she is."

He smiled from ear to ear. "Her name is Jasmine."

I turned back to Vinny's and gave Jan a quick wave. Perched on his barstool, Lester scowled at me. Head shaking, he eventually swiveled his stool sideways, and struck up a conversation with Freckle Eye.

CHAPTER 13

A FAMILIAR SOUND woke me. I opened my eyes, and through the sliding screen door connecting the bedroom to the balcony, spied the source—a small green parakeet native to Bonaire known as a *prikichis*. Most mornings either he or one of his cousins perched on the railing of my balcony and serenaded me out of slumber.

I wished the little guy would fly off and allow me to sleep. But he continued to sing away and was soon joined by another prikichis, their elaborate duet trying to brighten what I knew would be a rough, slow morning. Exhausted and in pain, I stared at the ceiling and tried to muster the strength to rise.

On returning home the previous night, I had iced my bruised rib and wrapped it in a body bandage. Jabs of pain shot through me each time I rolled over in bed or took a deep breath. Halfway through the night, tired but far from slumber, I rose and sat for several hours on the balcony.

This morning I counted six empty beer cans.

Using my trusty 7-iron as a cane, I limped to the bathroom, looked in the mirror, and noticed a black-and-blue shiner around my right eye. Overnight, my left eye had swollen half shut. Every blink created a rough, scratching sensation as if gravel were under each eyelid.

Lazing on a beach somewhere and letting the sun cook me for a while sounded good. I opened the medicine cabinet and grabbed a bottle of Tylenol with codeine. The expiration date had long since passed, but I shook the last three capsules into my mouth anyway and chased them down with a swig of water. The empty container bounced off both walls as I tossed it into the corner wastebasket. No matter what else happened today, at least I had already scored two points.

I scrutinized my reflection in the mirror again, examining the damage. Not the first time I'd been beaten up. I had suffered worse in the past but couldn't remember when.

Although food was the furthest thing from my mind, I leaned on the 7-iron and hobbled to the kitchen. My stomach growled, but after last night's beers, the storm in my belly wasn't hunger related. A glass of ice, a diet soda, and a slow trek to the balcony was the start of this day. Using as few abdominal muscles as possible, I lowered myself into the lounger and put my head back. Eyes closed, I breathed out through pursed lips.

The laughter and mumbled chatter of folks one story below lofted upward as they walked along the street in front of the YellowRock. Several loud cars drove past, kids with souped-up Mitsubishis or some other compact, showing off to the girls. Teenage boys are the same everywhere. A construction truck went by, suspension springs clanking as it passed over one of the speed bumps, known as *drempels*.

After a few minutes, my phone rang.

"Hey, Conklin. What are you doing?" Arabella asked.

"Just sitting here waiting for you to call."

She laughed. "Could I buy you lunch?"

"That'd be great."

"James and I are on patrol today, but we will need to eat. I will meet you at one o'clock? Coral Reef Café?"

"I like James, but can you lose him for lunch?"

She laughed again. "No problem." Her laughter seemed to make my rib feel better.

"Good. See you there at one."

The phone went silent, and I placed it back in my shirt pocket. I watched the sea and boats, and sipped on the soda, which worked to calm my stomach. I sighed but kept it shallow, my injured rib preventing my lungs from expanding too far.

Around noon, I hobbled downstairs to the office. Erika was curious about my condition and shook her head when I told her about last night. She didn't acknowledge when I mentioned meeting Arabella for lunch.

"Do not hurt yourself again," she said, as I stepped out of the office.

The Coral Reef Café was only a few blocks north of the YellowRock, and I preferred to walk, my bruised rib notwithstanding. Parking spots downtown are scarce, and at this time of day, anything available would probably be several blocks from the restaurant anyway.

I limped up Kaya C.E.B. Hellmund, the street that ran in front of the YellowRock and through the middle of downtown. A brick-paved pathway lined the side of the road next to the sea, palm trees sprouting through concrete boxes, and wooden benches, used most often for watching the water and sunsets, spaced at precise intervals. Multinational sailboats were moored a few yards offshore, each flying a flag denoting their country of registry. On one of the boats, someone worked atop the main mast, shirtless, pounding with a hammer.

Several dive boats sped toward the smaller island of Klein Bonaire— which means *Little Bonaire* in Dutch—located a half mile out to sea. Their foamy wakes rocked the sailboats, causing the guy on the mast to quit hammering for a few minutes until the waves subsided.

The open-air Coral Reef Café was on the opposite side of the street from the sea and about midway along the downtown strip. It occupied the lower floor of a newer, upscale three-story condominium complex, one of several built over the last few years. Arabella had not yet arrived, so I grabbed a sidewalk table underneath an oval Amstel light and ordered water and a glass of iced tea. The table offered a good view of the sea interspersed with the local foot and motor traffic.

An older couple held hands as they walked past on the other side of the street. They wore brightly colored, newish T-shirts with dive flag emblems embroidered on the backsides. Drawstrings drooped from the brims of their floppy hats, and they each had a pair of dark sunglasses. Their arms, legs, and necks were crispy red. When they sat at one of the benches, the man put his arm around the woman. They looked at each other for a moment, then gazed across the water.

They reminded me of Bill and Marybeth.

The memory wasn't sparked by their age, what they wore, or their appearance. It had to do with their display of affection toward one another. Bill and Marybeth were committed to each other and often held hands while walking.

I'd never been able to make a serious commitment to a woman and had always been jealous of Bill and Marybeth's relationship. Often, Bill told me that my noncommittal nature wasn't a big deal and not to worry about it. Conversely, Marybeth said I had a problem and needed to deal with it soon. If not, she said I'd end up a lonely old man.

Arabella would agree with Marybeth.

Or maybe not. Arabella and I had never talked about it, so perhaps she felt the same as me. As far as I knew, Arabella had similar commitment problems.

The waitress came by and refilled my tea. She was slender and in her mid-twenties. Her hair was several shades of purple, and she sprouted not one, but two nose rings. Multi-colored tattoos layered her arms and neck.

Turning fifty didn't make me feel old. However, my inability to relate to today's youth sometimes did.

Shortly after one o'clock, Arabella arrived. "Hey," she said, dropping into the chair next to me.

"Ready for some lunch?"

"*Ja hoor.*"

Arabella wore her full police uniform—or *Polis* in Papiamentu. Around her waist, a thick leather belt supported pouches for a set of handcuffs and two full pistol magazines. A leather holster attached to the belt cradled a Walther P-5 nine-millimeter semiautomatic pistol. By policy, she carried her weapon fully loaded, with a cartridge chambered, and the trigger de-cock mechanism engaged. Previously, she had confided in me that, thus far, in her law enforcement career she'd never used her service weapon in the line of duty.

Few ever did.

She tossed a couple of folded papers on the table and smiled.

I knew what they were before unfolding them—three-foot-high targets used at a shooting range. One had a silhouette of a person while the other had a five-ring mark in each corner and one in the middle. The inner ring in each target had two holes, indicating multiple rounds fired in succession.

Double taps.

The one with the silhouette had numerous holes in the head and chest area. Scanning the shape further, I noticed three holes in the groin section.

Better than I could do.

"Nice shooting." I pointed at the holes in the groin area of the silhouette target. "I hope this isn't a message to me."

Her smile vanished; her eyebrows tightened. "Of course not."

I folded the targets and handed them back to her.

"You know," she said, "you can join me on the range anytime."

Not the first time she had invited me to the range. It'd been a long time since I'd fired a handgun. Glancing at her weapon, I gave my pat answer. "Someday."

She knew that was as good as a no. Her shoulders slumped. "Well . . . Okay, but you never know when it might come in handy."

"One never knows," I said.

Purple Hair came by to take our order. Arabella glanced at the chalkboard menu over the bar and ordered an iced tea, French fries, and the daily special—karko stoba, a concoction of conch, rice, and fried plantains. My stomach churned like a mild hurricane, keeping my appetite at bay, not yet settled from last night's bender. I opted for an order of funchi, the island's version of cornbread. The Coral Reef Café added a special touch to funchi by toasting both sides, giving it a mild, crunchy exterior. A beer would've tasted good, but with this afternoon's flight, I opted to abstain.

"Only funchi?" Arabella asked.

"Moving slow this morning."

Arabella understood. A slight smile crept across her face.

"French fries?" I asked. "How is that healthy?"

"You know I am weak." She shrugged. "So how was last evening? Did you finish your cleaning?"

I removed my sunglasses.

"What happened?"

I explained last night, including my attempts to find the guy.

"I bet it was that Martijn creep. You should file a report." She pulled out a pencil and a notepad.

"Why? Could never prove it was him."

"It was him."

"I don't think so. Not big enough." I took a sip of water. "Besides, Martijn would've wanted me to know it was him. He wouldn't have run off. He would've stayed and pounded on me a little more."

"I will fill it out, and you can sign it."

"Maybe it was some punk wanting to grab something out of my Wrangler."

"I am going to question Martijn."

I grunted. "Okay, it doesn't matter to me."

"Did you see a doctor about your rib?"

"No . . . but I will."

Arabella sighed, knowing I wouldn't. Thankfully, our lunch arrived, and we began to eat. Arabella laced her fries with a squeeze of mayonnaise our Dutch waitress had knowingly placed on the table.

She dipped a fry into the mayo, and slowly laid it on her outstretched tongue. She tilted her head back, closed her eyes, and moaned, smacking her lips in the process.

"So good," she said.

She opened her eyes, brows raised, and pointed her chin in my direction.

"No thanks." Mayonnaise on French fries was a sin the Dutch would have to bear on their own.

From the corner of my eye, I caught the movement of someone walking up to our table.

"Hi, R."

Lester had crept up behind me. I put a hand on Arabella's shoulder. "Lester, this is Arabella."

Smiling, he nodded at Arabella then turned his attention back to me. "Look what I bought." He removed a large scuba knife from a plastic bag and set it on the table.

I stared at the knife a few moments, then unbuckled the strap securing the handle and slid the knife out of the sheath. The blade was titanium, close to seven inches long and two inches wide. One side had a smooth cutting edge; the other serrated along the outer half. Near the handle on the serrated side was a deep groove intended for hooking and cutting stray fishing line. The end tapered to a sharp point. I looked at Arabella. She shrugged. I returned the knife to its sheath and laid it back on the table.

"Lester, you don't need this. Not for Bonaire diving," I said.

"Maybe not, but you never know. Besides, it might be nice to have some protection."

"From what?"

"Anything . . . or anyone."

"I would suggest against it," Arabella said.

I gave up. "Just be careful," I said.

He held the knife in front of him, studying it. "Don't have to now. Not with this baby." He put the knife back in the plastic bag. "Hey, can Mandy come to your place tonight for the party?"

"Mandy?" I said, feeling like last night's conversation might happen all over.

"Yeah, Mandy."

"Why?"

He shrugged. "The more, the merrier, I guess."

For the life of me, I couldn't understand why he wanted Mandy around so much. Or why Tiffany tolerated it.

"Sure, why not," I said. After all, Mandy was a guest at the YellowRock, and I had yet to meet her. Be a good time to do so.

"Okay, great." He looked down the street. "I need to go. Meeting Mandy for lunch."

Arabella and I watched Lester walk away, disappearing into the crowd.

"I thought Lester was here with Tiffany," she said. "Why does he care about this Mandy person?"

Good question. Same one I had last night at Vinny's. I didn't say anything and shook my head. As Tiffany's self-proclaimed older brother, I was annoyed with Lester's attitude toward her.

"By the way, I filed a request to test for inspector," Arabella said.

My head snapped around. "Wow, that's great."

In the past, she had explained the test had three parts; physical conditioning, academics, and experience. Of the three, Arabella excelled at the physical portion and, when stressed, would fall into her comfort zone. The test was the trigger for her recent over-obsession with exercise.

"Soon I'll have to call you 'Inspector De Groot.'"

She smiled. "Yes, you will." She shoveled a fork full of karko stoba into her mouth. "What time should I come over tonight? I cannot wait to meet Tiffany."

"Whenever you want. Maybe you should come over early, so we can work on my Dutch."

Arabella had started teaching me Dutch about a year ago, although lately, any phrase the least bit similar to "study Dutch" had developed into a moniker meaning "getting in the sack and fooling around." It sure beat the crap out of studying.

"I'll bring my swimsuit. We can study on the beach."

"Not too early. I'm doing a flight for Chuck around three."

"Hungover again?"

"Yup. He had a late date."

Arabella faked a slight gag on a sip of tea. "Poor girl."

We sat a few moments, watching folks meander along the sidewalk.

Between swallows of funchi, I said, "I called Rockford and spoke to Larry Penn."

"And?"

I told her about my conversations with Penn and the email attachments, including the pictures of Bill and Marybeth.

"What do you think it means?" she asked.

"Not sure." I finished the funchi and took a sip of tea. Arabella waited. "The ad is weird. I'm going to call the place Bill took his truck for repair. Maybe he talked to them about selling it."

"Can I see the advertisement?"

"Sure, but only on my computer. I don't want to forward the email."

"Okay, that will be fine."

I leaned back and laced my hands behind my head, elbows pointing straight out. I extended my legs below the table, but my rib prevented me from fully stretching.

"I think they have the weapon," I said.

"What?"

"The murder weapon. Penn wouldn't say so, but I think they have it."

"Why do you say that?"

"They know it was a .357 Magnum." I tapped my index finger on the table. "To know that, they must have the weapon."

Arabella didn't say anything. She leaned back in her chair, furrowed her brow, and crossed her arms. The wheels in her noggin were spinning, but I wasn't sure whether she was mad or confused. Finally, she said, "Ballistics?"

"Maybe—some—but not completely."

"I do not understand."

That's when I remembered not all cops had the same level of ballistics knowledge. Over the years, I had acquired a lot of information from the lab guys while working every violent crime imaginable. Standard police training didn't teach a lot of this stuff, but those tidbits of knowledge had become second nature to me. The forensic teams were good, so there was never any reason to educate everyone on the specifics. I used to ask a lot of questions, and the lab guys were always eager to explain, sometimes with excruciating detail.

"A .357 round is close to a .38 caliber," I said. "It'd be difficult to tell the difference after impact deformation. The best would be to call it a medium-caliber round. They could never say it was a .357. Or a .38 for that matter."

"Yes," Arabella said, deep in thought. "That makes sense." She leaned forward in her chair and rested her arms on the table.

"You know what the Magnum part stands for, right?" I asked.

"Yes, that would be the amount of powder."

"Right, the powder load in the cartridge. But when the bullet is fired, the powder is burned—"

She snapped her fingers. "So how would people know the powder amount *after* the shooting?"

"Exactly."

Elbow on the table, she rested her forehead in her hand. After a moment, she slowly raised her head. "They must have the gun."

"To play devil's advocate, they could've found a shell casing. That would've told them exactly what cartridge." I held up my index finger. "But since most .357 Magnums are revolvers, it's unlikely a casing was lying around."

"Yes," she said shaking her head as if convincing herself, "and revolvers do not eject the spent casing. They stay in the cylinder. You also said the sketch had a G on it."

"Yeah, it all falls into place."

Arabella's eyebrows creased. "This is strange. Did they find a weapon or did they not?"

"I think yes."

"Why would the shooter leave it behind? Is there a reason?"

I shook my head. "I have no idea."

CHAPTER 14

AFTER LUNCH, I went back to my apartment to call the newspaper and Jay's Automotive. Unlike yesterday, when the automated system at the *Rockford Register Star* picked up, I knew which menu option to select to reach the classified ad section. I smiled. Maybe my newfound comedian, Orny Adams, isn't as smart as he thinks he is.

"I'd like to get some information about a classified in your paper," I said.

"Sure, I can help with that," said the lady who answered. Her voice reminded me of the voice on the menu system. "When did it run?"

"I don't know the entire run, but it was in last Friday's edition." She asked me for my name, phone number, and other items used to identify the owner of the ad. "I'm not the person who ran the ad. I just need some information."

She paused a moment. "Okay, that's unusual, but what do you need?"

"The ad said, 'Four-wheel drive. Call Bill.' I'd like to call Bill, but there isn't a number to call. Can you help me?"

I heard keyboard clicks in the background. "I found the ad. Give me a minute to see if I can find the account." She put me on hold, and the line went silent. No music or advertisements, just a silent emptiness. After a few moments, she returned. "I found the account, but this is interesting."

"How so?"

"Well, usually we require a phone number for the account, especially if paid with check or credit card, which most are. But this one was paid with cash."

"Do you have any information? I'd like to call this Bill guy."

"No, I'm sorry. There isn't any contact information. Only a name. Bill Ryberg."

"Bill Ryberg?"

"Yes. That's all."

"Nothing else?"

"Nope."

"Okay, thanks."

Had Bill paid for the ad? His name was on the account, so possibly. Again, I considered that he had circled the advertisement because he had noticed its vagueness and wanted to have it corrected. *No information* is still *information*. Usually in an investigation, especially early, it felt like a continual dead end. Until more facts become known, it's difficult to quantify the value of the current evidence.

Next, I called Jay's Automotive, asked for Jay, and a sassy lady named Kim put me on hold. Cheap Trick, a '70s rock band from Rockford, was playing through the receiver, singing about how much they needed me to need them. After a few minutes, Jay picked up.

"I'm a friend of Bill Ryberg's," I said.

"Yeah, I heard about Bill. What a shame," Jay said.

"It is."

"What can I do for you?"

"Did he mention anything about selling his truck?"

"Mmm . . . You mean the Ranger?"

"Yeah, I guess."

Car mechanics remember vehicles easier than people. Ask about a car or truck, and they correlate it to the owner.

Jay paused and said, "What's it to you?"

"I'm one of his old police buddies."

"Look, pal, I feel bad about Bill. He was an old friend and a good customer. But I got a waiting room full of customers. I ain't got time for stories."

"Please, a few more minutes."

He yelled something to someone in the shop, the words sounding distant and muffled. When he returned his attention to me, his voice was edgy. "Hurry up, then. Mondays are a busy day for me."

"Do you know if he was selling his truck?"

"Mmm . . . I don't know. Don't recall him saying anything about it. Hold on a minute."

He put me on hold. Mondays must've been Cheap Trick Day at Jay's Automotive. Now they told me my mommy and daddy were both alright. They just seemed a little weird.

"I checked the computer," Jay said when he took me off hold. "Bill had the Ranger in for new tires a couple of weeks ago. I don't remember him saying he was selling."

"Nothing, huh?"

"Nope, and you know how he liked to talk."

We were both quiet. No Cheap Trick either.

"Why do you ask?" Jay said.

I needed to be careful with what I said. I doubted the ad was public knowledge and didn't want to be the source of a leak.

"There was an ad in the newspaper, someone selling a four-wheel drive. It said to call Bill."

Jay was silent for a moment. "Bill's Ranger wasn't a four by four."

"It wasn't?"

"No. Bill's Ranger was a two-wheel drive."

CHAPTER 15

A HUNDRED YARDS west of Flamingo International Airport's main terminal sat a hangar that housed the general aviation businesses—anything unrelated to the commercial airlines. Chuck was too cheap to pay for hangar space, so he kept the Cessna 180 tied on the open tarmac, in front and slightly askew of the large hanger doors.

Pulling to a stop in the parking lot, I had to press the Wrangler's brake pedal harder than usual. I didn't know much about vehicles but figured the brake pads were starting to wear out and get thin. I made a mental note to get them checked.

Someone stood near the security gate. I grabbed my flight bag from the back seat and limped in that direction, my pace slowing as I approached and recognized him.

Lester.

"What are you doing here?" I asked, fishing through my flight bag for the security access card.

"I was about to ask you the same thing. I mean, what are *you* doing here?"

"Taking some folks for an airplane ride."

"That's weird. I'm here to *take* an airplane ride."

"What?" I scanned the parking lot, my mind a swamp of confusion, then leaned into Lester. "Where's Tiffany?"

Lester raised his chin and puffed his chest. "She's not here." He relaxed and looked at the ground a moment, then back at me. "Mandy was supposed to come with me, but plans changed a bit."

"But why take a plane ride? And without Tiffany."

"It was Mandy's idea, but I figured what the heck?" He paused a moment, met my eyes, and smiled. "Beats the hell out of scuba."

"Does Tiffany know about this?" I hesitated, and even though it wasn't any of my business, added, "And about Mandy?"

"No, and she doesn't need to. Besides, Mandy isn't here."

My first instinct was to call off the ride. Something wasn't right. Lester being here without Tiffany bothered me, and the Lester-Mandy relationship was becoming suspicious. Deceptive, to say the least. A game I didn't want to play.

"Maybe we shouldn't go," I said.

Lester huffed and said, "But Mandy already paid for it."

Chuck wouldn't have any sympathy for me canceling the flight. He had the money—money he wouldn't be enthusiastic to return, especially based on my anxieties. I tried to convince myself that how Lester and Tiffany spent their vacation was none of my business. If they chose not to spend time together, or spend it with other people, that was their decision. I wasn't a couple's therapist.

I scanned the parking lot one last time and resigned myself to the fact that Tiffany indeed wasn't here. "Okay, let's go."

We walked through the security gate and across the concrete toward the plane. Although a short distance, things happened fast on airport tarmacs, and I kept Lester close by my side. A spinning propeller can ruin a vacation.

Safety is never an accident.

When not flying, Chuck's Cessna spent its life on the concrete pad in front of the hangar, the sun and heat wreaking havoc on its cosmetics. The bare aluminum skin was visible where spots of the vintage

'80s red paint had peeled away. The red vinyl interior had long ago dried and cracked, being held together in places with duct tape, most of it peeling along the edges from the constant heat inside the cabin. The once black plastic instrument panel had seen better days, now faded to a light gray and warped in several places. Ripped and thread-bare carpet curled along the floor.

Granted, the appearance of the plane, serial number N7757U, left a lot to be desired. But mechanically, Chuck kept it tip-top, its flight worthiness never in doubt. Back in the States, Chuck had parlayed his military training and experience into a civilian career as a top-rated and well-respected FAA-certified airplane mechanic.

I propped open the doors, allowing the breeze to ventilate the swel-tering cabin. The familiar smell of hot plastic and moldy carpet mixed with traces of aviation fuel—or avgas as it's called—greeted my nostrils.

"What's with the big tires?" Lester asked, pointing at one of the main landing gear tires.

I shook my head. Chuck and his projects.

"They're called Alaska Tundra Tires," I said. "Bush pilots use them to land in places where there aren't any airports or runways. Strips made of dirt, gravel, old roads. The tires are oversized and cushion the landing." I didn't mention Chuck only dreamed of being a bush pilot. This set of Tundras hadn't landed on anything but pavement since being installed.

"Do you do landings like that?"

"Never."

As part of my preflight inspection, I did a thorough walk-around of the airplane, making sure everything was in good order. Then, I guided Lester into the front, right-side "co-pilot" seat.

As Lester got comfortable and I helped him locate and fasten his seat belt, he touched the top of the instrument panel, which absorbed the direct sunlight under the front windshield.

"Ouch!" he said, shaking his hand. "That's hot."

"Don't touch that," I said, failing to hold back a smile. "It's probably hot."

"Fuck you."

Yeah, this'll be fun.

Although Cessna claimed the 180 was one of their midsized single-engine models, the cabin was as cramped as a coffin. Pulling myself into the pilot's seat with a bruised rib was no easy chore. Sweat beaded and streamed down my face. Several grunts and moans later, I heaved myself into the cabin, careful to ease onto the hot vinyl, and parked my butt into the front left seat. I moved around a little in the cushion, fidgeting like a twelve-year-old at church, trying to find a spot where my rib pain would be tolerable. With little success, I gave up and began working through the before flight checklist.

Doors shut and locked.

Master switch on.

Flight instruments and radios set.

Engine primed.

The starter whined as I turned the ignition switch, the prop jerking into motion. The engine fired to life with a slight shudder on the propeller's third revolution. I worked the throttle to set the engine idle at one thousand RPMs and dialed the tower frequency into the radio.

Chuck scheduled these tours to coincide with low levels of commercial traffic. At three o'clock in the afternoon, the only other planes in the air near Bonaire would be the small puddle jumpers working their hops between islands, landing and taking off every thirty minutes or so.

The tower provided me with a takeoff clearance as we taxied to the runway. I positioned the Cessna on the runway centerline and pushed the throttle forward, my body sagging into the seat as the plane lunged forward and the flight instruments sprang to life. We rolled down the runway, the plane's nose becoming light as the airspeed indicator moved past seventy knots. A slight pull on the yoke and we were airborne, climbing into the blue Bonaire sky.

I leveled our climb at a thousand feet, which allowed for easy identification of objects on the ground. Also, at this altitude, the controllers weren't concerned about our flight disrupting any of the scheduled commuter flights.

The air was smooth, with a few small bumps here and there as we flew near the salt flats along the southern shore. The flamingo sanctuaries defined two restricted areas to avoid on the end of the island. I reversed course before going too far south and headed back to the north. To give Lester a picturesque view of the shoreline, I positioned the plane a quarter-mile off the coast. Lester didn't say anything, apparently not impressed with the sight. After several miles, I dropped the right wing, banking east, and headed for the other side of the island.

Bonaire is only twenty-four miles long, and at its widest, seven miles. We flew along the middle section of the island, which was four miles across. Even from our low altitude, both the east and west coasts were visible.

The motor droned on, almost hypnotic in its consistency. Most passengers want to talk, ask questions about the island, the plane, or a host of other topics. Not Lester. No chatter, smiles, or pointing at objects on the ground. He just sat there, stoic, and stared out the front. Impossible to tell whether he was scared, bored, or mad. Not the typical sightseeing trip.

It dawned on me that I'd yet to see him happy, or even content. A continual scowl, clenched jaw, and raised chin. He always seemed on edge, as if needing to prove something to everyone. Maybe to the world.

Or maybe just to *me*.

With an elbow, I nudged Lester on his side. "Would you like to fly it?" I often let people handle the yoke, the "steering wheel" of the air-craft. When trimmed correctly and in smooth air, the plane is de-signed to fly in a straight and level altitude. Handling the yoke, even in benign conditions, gave passengers a sense of piloting.

"Sure, I'll try." Lester quickly grabbed the yoke left-handed. Most people, when offered a chance to fly a small airplane, hesitate a few seconds before taking the controls. Some need extra prodding, and some won't do it at all.

Lester fell into a select group—eager and seemingly waiting for the opportunity to take control. Unusual.

"The air is smooth," I said, "so just hold the yoke steady."

People usually take the yoke with both hands, treating it like a car steering wheel during their initial days of Drivers Education class. Over the years, I had noticed that when someone did it one-handed, it's most often with their dominant hand. Something about Lester's left-handed grab of the yoke made me think about the crime scene pictures.

One of those photos showed a coffee mug sitting on the table along-side the newspaper. The vantage point of the picture was from the chair as if the photographer had been sitting at the table in front of the paper. The mug was to the left, with the handle pointing in the same direction. A lefthander would've set the cup in that position.

Bill and Marybeth were both right-handed.

"I don't like this. You should fly," Lester said and let go of the yoke, hands raised in a surrender fashion.

"Okay," I said and took back control of the plane.

I worked the trim a notch to fine-tune our altitude as my mind drifted back to my first flight lesson. Bill had told me I was nuts want-ing to be a pilot and said I'd die in a fiery crash. He saw no possible use for it; considered it dangerous and a waste of money.

"You can't haul a lot of people, you can't go far, and you can't drink beer while doing it," he would chastise. "So, what's the point?"

But after I earned my license, and flew him and Marybeth to Sandusky, Ohio, for an extended weekend, Bill became one of my most frequent passengers. When other guys were spending their Saturday mornings fishing, mowing, or gardening, Bill and I would be cramped in a small airplane, slicing through the air, landing and exploring a different airport each weekend.

I'd never fly again without remembering him; sitting next to me, scanning the maps, ready to locate the next checkpoint. He was a good co-pilot.

A great friend.

"That's impressive," Lester finally said, snapping me back to reality.

The east coast of Bonaire, also known as *The Wild Side*, is the windward side of the island and the shoreline is more dramatic than the west. It consists of massive rock cliffs and drop-offs whereas the west side of the island—the leeward side—is much less rugged. Also, the wind sweeping in from the Atlantic on the east side creates large waves and surf, making boating and scuba difficult. By contrast, the sea off the west coast of Bonaire, protected from the wind by the island itself, has a nearly flat surface, perfect for water recreation. From the air, these distinctions left most passengers in awe.

"Is that a lighthouse?" Lester asked.

I dipped one side of the plane so that he could get a better look. "Yeah, it's Spelonk Lighthouse."

"With these special tires, could you land on that dirt road?" Lester asked.

He pointed at the road in front of the lighthouse, running parallel to the coast. Several times, Chuck had considered landing in that exact spot. From the air, it seemed as smooth as an airport runway, but I knew that to be an illusion. Having driven the road several times, I knew it'd be a harsh landing.

No bush-pilot auditions today.

I turned my head and looked over my shoulder at him. "Why?"

"Maybe for fun?"

"Nope, not my idea of fun."

"We should at least try."

"No, we shouldn't."

He squirmed in his seat and muttered something I didn't hear. I was about to ask what he had said when he folded his arms across his chest, his entire body seeming to tighten.

I didn't want a confrontation with him and counted to ten, focusing on the flight instruments for a few moments. Finally, not being able to stand it any longer, I asked him, "What's the problem?"

He looked at the ground through the side window. "How well do you know Tiffany?"

"I've known her a long time."

"Yeah, I guess you know her *very* well."

I didn't say anything.

"How long were you a cop?" he asked.

I assumed he knew the answer—that Tiffany had probably told him. But I indulged him anyway. Sort of. "Long enough."

"Tiffany told me twenty-five years or something like that," he said.

I didn't say anything.

"All of it in Rockford, right?"

Again, this felt as though he were baiting me for some reason. For a fleeting moment, I considered pushing him out of the plane and scanned the horizon for a place to dump him. Lucky for Lester, the thought passed.

"Have you ever used anyone?" he continued. "As a cop, it would be easy to do, wouldn't it?"

I bit the inside of my cheek, remaining silent. Red-faced and eyes narrowed, he turned from the window, straight at me, and leaned in my direction. In the small cockpit, our shoulders had been touching the entire ride. Now, he towered over me. Any closer and he'd be in my lap.

"How many times have you gotten away with that?" he asked. "How many people have you hurt? Lives you've ruined?"

No idea what he expected from me. I tried not to react but was sure my face painted a picture of confusion.

I didn't have to like him, but being Tiffany's boyfriend, I needed to tolerate him. "For Tiffany's sake, let's get along. Okay, Lester?"

"Yeah, right." He resumed his stare out the side window, arms folded across his chest.

I'd had enough of this ride and banked the plane to the southwest, straight for the airport. I inched the throttle forward a few hundred RPMs, increasing our airspeed. The tower clearance was the only conversation for the remainder of the ride.

The landing was uneventful. I taxied to the parking area and exited the plane more abruptly than I should have, wincing from the pain that shot through my rib. Small price to pay to get away from Lester. After a few steps and clearing the overhead wing, I stood upright and stretched my side.

Lester fumbled his way out of the cabin, and I motioned for him to follow me across the tarmac to the security gate. He pushed through and made a beeline for his truck.

Not so much as thanks, see you later, or get lost.

CHAPTER 16

I FLOATED ON my back, hands behind my head, gazing up at the sky. The massaging effect of the salt water deadened the pain of my bruised rib, and I could've drifted like that till the next day.

Stars were twinkling to life, darkness waiting to overtake the island. A couple of schooners, moored at the edge of the reef, gently rocked in the light breeze, their masts casting long shadows across the glass-smooth water. A sliver of sun was visible on the horizon.

Arabella relaxed on the beach in a lounger. She had come by for my Dutch lesson, but we decided to answer the call of the sea and take a dip.

Before she arrived, I had checked the crime photos. The coffee cup was as I remembered, off to the left with the handle pointing left. Someone must've been sitting there using their left hand, but that didn't mean the person was left handed. Maybe some right-handed people used their left to hold cups.

Four pelicans swung over the beach, flying in an orderly formation. A couple of divers exited the water, having finished a late afternoon dive. I hobbled out of the water, onto the beach, and made my way to the lounger next to Arabella.

"Can you rub some lotion on my back?" she asked.

"Why?" I pointed at the horizon. "The sun is almost gone."

"Just a little?"

She was in no danger of sunburn. Arabella loved having her back rubbed, and I loved rubbing it, so I grabbed the tube and squirted a blob of lotion in my hand.

I began making small circles on her lower back. Gently, but with occasional mild force, I moved up her back and pressed my thumbs on the soft spot under her shoulder blades. I let my fingers find their way behind the strap of her suit.

She responded with a low moan, her respiration becoming more profound and audible. My breathing had changed as well. She closed her eyes and tilted her head, back arched, pressing herself against me. I pulled her closer and kissed the back of her neck. She turned and pressed her lips hard against mine. Then we stood, gathered our lotion, towels, and water bottles, and walked toward my apartment.

As we crossed the street, Tiffany and Lester appeared from around the corner with a cooler.

"You two ready for some food?" Tiffany asked.

Arabella and I stole a glance at each other, both biting our lower lips.

"I guess so," I said.

Arabella looked at me. "I *am* starved."

Tiffany stepped up to Arabella and stuck out her hand. "I'm Tiffany. You must be Arabella. It's great to meet you."

"It is good to meet you, too."

Arabella took Tiffany's hand, but then stepped in close and did the customary Dutch three-kiss greeting, just like Jan had done. Afterward, Tiffany stepped back and half-smiled. She looked at me for reassurance, but all I did was pucker my lips at her.

Tiffany gestured toward Lester. "This is my boyfriend, Lester."

Arabella started in with the three kisses again, but Lester stepped back, his features tightening. Arabella hesitated for a moment, then Lester extended his hand and she shook it. He looked at me and gave a cordial nod. For lack of anything better, I nodded back.

Lester handed me a brown paper bag. "Mandy is going to stop by later but asked me to give this to you now."

I removed a bottle of Baileys Irish Crème from the bag and glanced at Tiffany.

She shrugged.

"You know Mandy?" I asked her.

"Oh . . . we've met," she said.

"You okay?" I asked her.

"Sure she is," Lester said. "Aren't you, Tiff?"

"Like I said, whatever." She rolled her eyes.

As a hint to move along, Arabella poked me in the rib, luckily, the not-bruised side. I led everyone upstairs, albeit slowly. Tiffany asked about the limp, and I gave her an abbreviated version of what had happened. Lester managed an enthusiastic chuckle during the part about me getting beat up. Otherwise, he stayed quiet.

"Don't worry about diving with me," Tiffany said.

"We'll figure something out," I said.

"Seriously, I'll be fine."

I held the door to the apartment open for everyone, then led Tiffany and Lester to the fridge for a beer, dropping my sunglasses on the kitchen counter. Arabella volunteered to go for the food and slipped into the bedroom to change clothes.

Hoping to give Tiffany and Lester a taste of the island, I called and placed a *takeaway* order, as it's called on Bonaire, of kabritu stoba—goat stew with vegetables—and keshi yena—a variation of a Dutch cheese and chicken potpie. Tiffany liked sampling unique foods and would jump at the opportunity to try something new, but I wasn't as sure about Lester.

I fired up bits of small talk about diving and whether Tiffany and Lester were enjoying Bonaire. Lester's attitude was reserved. He said nothing and wandered around the apartment. Maybe he was embarrassed about our encounter at Vinny's or during our flight—a ride I assumed Tiffany still didn't know happened.

Lester wound up standing alone on the balcony holding a beer. I didn't care if he drank it or not, or whether he had a good time or not. His attitude wouldn't destroy my evening.

Arabella came out of the bedroom wearing a T-shirt with "Girls Like Guns, Too" printed on the front. The pocket linings on her blue-jean cutoffs hung below the edge of the frayed cut line. She wore my black *RPD* hat with her ponytail pulled through the back. She grabbed me behind my head, pulled me close, and kissed me hard.

"You have money for the takeaway?" she asked. I handed her a crinkled fifty, and she winked at me. "I will be back with the food soon." A quick shake of her ponytail and she sauntered through the apartment to the veranda and down the stairs into the darkness.

None of us spoke.

After a few moments, Tiffany cleared her throat and said, "Arabella speaks English well."

"Yes, she went to college in Florida and speaks several languages."

"She seems nice."

"She is. Very."

Lester pointed down the hall.

"Down the hall and on your right," I said.

He walked to the bathroom and closed the door. Tiffany peered down the hall, turned to me, and spoke. Her voice was low, and I had to lean in close to hear her. "Roscoe, there's something I need to talk to you about," she said.

"Okay, shoot."

"No. Not here, not now." She looked down the hallway again. "We'll talk later. It's important."

Lester came around the corner from the hall. He resumed his quiet demeanor on the balcony, and Tiffany sat on the couch. They stared at each other for a moment, then he shrugged, and she looked away.

The old cliché about the tension being thick enough to cut with a knife came to mind. Hopefully, Arabella would arrive soon with our takeaway order. That should help.

Tiffany took a drink of beer and touched the frame of a picture sitting on the end table. "Which lighthouse is this?" she asked.

"That's Spelonk," I said. "It was built in 1910, before the advent of Loran or GPS, and marks the eastern edge of the island. It's been refurbished and still puts out a white flash every five seconds to aid in navigation."

"That sounds awesome," Tiffany said.

Lester walked over and glanced at the picture. "Where's it at?"

I snapped a gaze at him. He stared back at me.

"It's on the east side of the island," I said, shaking my head.

"I'll bet it has a great view," Tiffany said. "I'd like to see it. How do we get there, Roscoe?"

I tapped my fingers on the edge of the counter a few times then pulled a map from a drawer in the kitchen. Lester leaned over the map and scrutinized it as I pointed out the route to the lighthouse. Feigning ignorance, with eyebrows scrunched in concentration, he ran his fingers along the lines representing roads.

"Can I borrow this?" he asked.

"Think you need it?" I asked, hoping my sarcasm was palatable.

Lester slowly turned from the map to me. He lipped the words *fuck you.*

I laughed, folded the map, and handed it to him. "Keep it."

"What's so funny?" Tiffany asked.

"Nothing," Lester said. "Just your old boyfriend trying to be a comedian."

"Lester . . ." Tiffany said.

Lester raised an eyebrow and smiled at me in a way a barracuda might smile at a swarm of unsuspecting baitfish. Then, he put the map in his pocket and pointed to the corner of my living room. "Does that TV work?"

I hesitated, but with a shake of my head, gave in. "Sure does. It's pretty old, but all I ever watch is an hour or so of WGN in the evenings." WGN is the SuperStation out of Chicago and carried by the Bonaire cable provider. It's close enough to Rockford that I pick up some local news and Illinois issues in general.

Tiffany walked over to the counter, lifted the bottle of Baileys, and gave me a sideways look.

"I don't have coffee," I said. "Never touch the stuff."

"Then I'll take it straight up."

I set a clean glass on the counter and poured the Baileys. Tiffany picked up the cup with her left hand.

"You right- or left-handed?" I asked.

"Why do you ask?"

"Curiosity," I said and smiled. "Just call it a friendly survey."

"I'm a righty."

Lester was holding his beer in his right hand. I moved my head in his direction. "What about Lester?"

"He's a lefty. What's going on?"

Grabbing my third Bright from the fridge, I said, "Just a bet I have with Chuck. Drunk guys being stupid. Nothing serious."

I checked the wall clock and thought Arabella should've been back by now. Tiffany and I stood across the counter from each other, the smell of Baileys drifting my way.

She took another sip and fixed her eyes on mine. A half-smile broke across her face. "What?" she said.

Telling her about Bill and Marybeth was overdue. I'd procrastinated long enough and now was the time. Lester could listen in if he wanted, but I didn't plan to call him over. This was between Tiffany and me.

I sat my beer on the counter. "There's something I need to tell you."

"Okay." Her smile disappeared. "Why do you look so serious all of a sudden?"

As if on cue, my cell rang. I ignored it, instead focusing on breaking the news to Tiffany. "I have some bad news. It's about—"

My cell rang again. Thinking it might be Arabella, I looked at the number. Not Arabella. James Saragoza, her part-time patrol partner. He seldom called me, and never in the evening.

I held up a finger to Tiffany and answered the call.

"R . . . it is Arabella," James said, his breathing rapid. A chill traveled down my neck as his voice cracked. "She had an accident and is in an ambulance, on the way to hospital."

I ended the call and yelled a brief explanation to Tiffany as I headed for the stairs. She volunteered to come along, but I said no and that I'd call her later.

As I hit the first stair, the WGN anchor started a new story.

"And for an update, and some new developments, we go out to Rockford, and the murder, several days ago, of a retired police officer and his wife . . ."

CHAPTER 17

REGARDLESS OF MY ribs, I took the stairs two at a time. In the darkness, I tripped on the last one and almost fell on my face. An awkward stumble and I limped down the side of the building to my parking space in the back. A wave of distress overtook me, stopping me in my tracks.

My Wrangler was gone.

Arabella must've taken it. She had my spare key, and we sometimes shared vehicles, but usually told each other when we did.

I pounded my hand on top of her car. She didn't know about the brakes.

Fumbling in the darkness with my key chain, I eventually found the one to Arabella's car. I dropped into the Toyota's driver seat and slid it back as far as it'd go. The engine gauges sprang to life as I turned the ignition key, and I immediately understood why Arabella had taken my Wrangler.

The fuel gauge pointed at E.

Luckily, the engine caught, and I sped toward the hospital, located about two miles from my apartment. I leaned forward in the seat, slipping the clutch several times racing around corners and through intersections. James hadn't mentioned the severity of any injuries, so I didn't know what to expect but understood how it worked. Seldom was bad news delivered over the phone.

Arabella's sister, Ruth, lived on the island. I gave her a call, and she said she'd get to the hospital as soon as possible. Ruth's appearance anywhere always proved interesting.

Hospital San Francisco sits at the edge of Kralendijk, on a road called Kaya Soeur Bartola. The sixty-bed facility offered limited services, and severe cases went by air ambulance to the nearby island of Curacao.

I parked and made my way to the front receptionist desk, lower rib cage on fire, breaths shallow and labored. James waited in the lobby, and before the receptionist said anything, waved for me to follow him down the hall to the emergency room.

"Is she hurt badly?" I asked, gasping for air and holding my side as we hurried through the corridor.

"I do not think so. Looks like some cuts and bruises. She was still delirious when I arrived. The ambulance crew said she might have a slight concussion."

At the emergency room, a nurse instructed us to have a seat. "Someone will be with you shortly."

James sat down. I paced the floor.

"What happened?" I asked.

"She went through an intersection and into a building."

I closed my eyes. "Brakes?"

"Looks like they went out. She said something about the brake pedal not working and not able to slow down. She swerved to miss some people on the sidewalk."

The doors separating the waiting area from the examination rooms swung open, and a female doctor walked through.

"My name is Doctor Amanda Ingerbretzen," she said with a hint of German accent. "Miss Arabella is doing fine. We stitched some cuts, and she has some bruises on her face. She also has a slight concussion."

"Will she be alright?" I asked.

"She should make a full recovery. We will observe her overnight."

"Can I see her?"

"Yes, but we are currently moving her out of the emergency area and to a private room. She has an IV for pain medicine, so she will be sleepy." Doctor Ingerbretzen smiled, raised her eyebrows, and straightened her stance ever so slightly. "As you may know, since the hospital remodeled, all of the rooms now have air-conditioning."

That would suit Arabella just fine. Most Dutch I knew didn't use air-conditioning, not even when sleeping. Whenever I asked why, most of them responded with a grunt and a shrug. I guessed it had something to do with the extra electricity costs. Until she started spending nights at my apartment, Arabella hadn't used AC either. Now she was hooked on it—one of the few positive influences I'd had on her.

"I am leaving then," James said. "I will check with you tomorrow."

I shook his hand. "Thanks, James."

Doctor Ingerbretzen led me to Arabella's room. I walked through the door and stood by the bed a moment and stared.

A white, three-inch square bandage covered Arabella's right eyebrow and stretched to her temple, a patch of hair having been shaved to accommodate half a dozen stitches. Some scrapes and red blotches marred her right cheek, and, between her eyes, a large, blue-green bruise spoiled the beauty of her short, fleshy nose. An IV dripped clear liquid into her left arm.

This was my fault.

I pulled a big-armed, green upholstered chair close to the bed, sat in it, and took her by the hand. She opened her eyes and smiled. I stroked her hair.

"Hey, Conklin." Her voice was low and throaty, sounding as if it hurt to talk.

"Shhhh . . . Take it easy." I got out of the chair and sat on the edge of the bed. I moved some hair out of her eyes and looped it around her ear.

"Sorry about your Wrangler."

"Not an issue, but I'll have to borrow your car for a while."

"Not a problem." She tried to laugh. "You will need to buy some gas."

I smiled. "You need to rest. Close your eyes and get some sleep." I kissed her forehead. "I'm sorry, honey. I should be laying there, not you."

"An accident is an accident. It is not your fault."

I didn't argue but knew the truth.

With a slight head movement, she motioned for the cup of water on the nearby table. I grabbed it and held the straw in front of her. She sipped some water.

"Thank you," she said. "I do not remember much. Was anyone else hurt?"

"No. You swerved to miss some bystanders."

"Thank goodness . . ." Her voice trailed off as she slipped into slumber.

The chair creaked as I lowered myself onto the cushion and stretched out my legs. I took the remote and turned on the TV. The mute button worked, as did the closed caption.

Nothing on TV would hold my interest, not with Arabella lying in a hospital bed, but I flipped through the channels anyway. I stopped on a Dutch reality show, *Wie Is de Mol?* and smiled. Arabella watched *Who Is the Mole?* on a regular basis. As the name denotes, one of the ten contestants worked in conjunction with the producers to hinder the other contestants' ability to win money. The goal of the other nine players—and the viewers—was to identify the mole before time ran out. Arabella claimed watching the show and identifying the mole strengthened her deductive reasoning skills and forced her to think outside the box.

I wasn't concentrating on the episode but needed someplace to stare. Let my mind go a little. After numbing myself with the TV, I couldn't sit any longer and paced the room a few times, tucked in Arabella's covers, and checked her pillows. The displays and numbers on the equipment continued to change, and I felt hopeless not knowing what most of them meant. Regardless of the staff's approval or hospital policies, I was prepared to stay the night in this chair. It'd take an army to throw me out. I wanted to be here in case she needed anything.

I considered what the WGN anchor had reported as I ran out of my apartment—something about new developments in the case. Not sure how long the newscast ran or if it repeated stories on a regular basis. I flipped to that channel, sat back, and read the closed caption flashing along the bottom of the screen. The newscast came to an end with no re-mention of the case. Not interested in the Chicago weather or the sports report, I clicked the TV off and made a mental note to ask Penn about the new development.

From down the hall came the distinct staccato clicking of high heels striking the tiled floor, growing louder every second. The rhythm changed as the heels made a turn outside Arabella's room and sauntered through the door.

An overwhelming scent of perfume entered the room five seconds before the heels. No surprise who owned both. Arabella's older, red headed sister, Ruth, had arrived.

Now the fun would begin.

"Oh my God," Ruth said. "Is she alright?" She clicked over to the side of the bed.

Ruth fussed with the blankets and bedsheets as I explained what had happened and updated her on Arabella's condition. When I asked if she had any questions, she took the remote and turned on the TV, increasing the volume. She fluffed Arabella's pillow, sat in the big-armed chair, and held her sister's hand, remaining quiet for a moment and staring at the diagnostic machines.

I walked over to the TV and unplugged it, then stood on the other side of the bed from Ruth.

After a few minutes, without looking at me, Ruth asked, "Are you going to stay with her?"

I nodded, but it was a wasted motion. Ruth still wasn't paying me any attention, so I said, "Yes."

She stroked Arabella's arm and kissed her on the cheek. "When can she go home?"

"Tomorrow, hopefully."

"Tell her I was here, and I will pick her up tomorrow." She stood and pressed on the edge of a loose piece of tape along one of Arabella's bandages, then turned and headed toward the door.

"You're leaving?" I asked.

Without pausing, she said, "We are busy tonight. Since she is okay, I have to get back to work." She clicked out the door and started down the hallway.

I looked at the floor, bit my upper lip, and tried a ten count. I made it to three and walked into the hallway. Ruth strolled away, her heels echoing off the hard walls and tile floors.

"You know, if the situation were reversed, your sister wouldn't leave your side," I said, loud enough that a nurse behind a counter at the far end of the hall snapped her head in my direction.

Ruth didn't turn around or slow her stride. She put her hand in the air for a few seconds and turned down another hall leading to the exit.

The perfume lingered in the room, a not so gentle reminder of Ruth's temporary stopover. My shoulders slumped with guilt. Regardless of my feelings toward Ruth, Arabella would be hurt knowing her sister's visit was so short and meaningless.

I calmed myself and dropped into the chair, managing a full ten-count. The ache in my rib made it challenging to get comfortable, so I concentrated on the rhythmic beeping of the heart monitor, an electronic version of sheep counting. On the edge of slumber, Arabella's monitor beeped in unison with the pulsing of my heart. A romanticist might say we had two hearts beating as one.

And he—or she—might be right.

CHAPTER 18

I LEFT THE hospital at ten the next morning. James had called earlier and told me they towed my Wrangler to Richter's Garage, a mere four blocks from the hospital. I didn't trust the gas supply in Arabella's car, so I walked.

Kevin Richter stood in front of an open overhead door as I limped up the driveway to the five-bay service shop. Oil-stained fingers of one hand held a half-finished cigarette while the other cradled a cellphone to his ear. The sun shone over the top of the building and cast a long shadow down the front side. I put my back against the wall and savored the shade, the coolness of the concrete-brick exterior a welcome relief.

"Hello, R," he said, sliding the phone into a holder attached to his belt. "We have your Wrangler on the lift. I will show you what we found."

"Sounds good."

Kevin dragged the heels of his shoes along the concrete floor as he led me through the garage. The back cuffs of his long, baggy pants were torn, dirty, and partially worn away from being walked on and dragged underneath his shoes. I stepped over patches of dried oil and worked my way around filthy pieces of engine parts, transmissions, and radiators. My Wrangler, high atop a lift, rested a few inches below a sign that read Bay 3. All four of its tires were off and lay on the floor.

Walking a slow circle to the front of the lift, I examined the damage. Only a few bits and pieces of the front grill, broken in multiple places, were still attached. The lens and bulb of the right headlight were gone, and the housing hung out of its mounting bracket. It dangled a few inches above the bumper, held in place by a couple of small wires. A foot-long crease on the right portion of the front bumper caused it to poke out at an awkward angle. The other side of the bumper stuck out too far, and a significant dent ran from the front quarter panel all the way across the right side of the hood.

The damage to the Wrangler was frightening. I loved my Wrangler, but it didn't compare to my love for Arabella. The accident meant nothing. Arabella's recovery meant everything.

"Do you do bodywork, Kevin?" Knowing he didn't, I asked anyway with a half-laugh, trying to add some levity.

"No. You will need a body shop for that."

His face showed no humor, only concern. I had forgotten Kevin never joked about car repairs. It was a serious topic for him. Like a doctor touching the warm forehead of a young patient, he ran his skilled fingertips down the bent and misaligned bumper.

"But it's not that bad," he said, talking more to the vehicle than to me. "We'll bend you back into place, the best we can. You will be okay." He patted the bumper, then turned to me. "I can throw in a headlight. Should be okay to drive."

A mechanic in the next bay used a torch to cut through an old car's rusty exhaust system, the cloud of acetylene and molten steel stinging my throat. I coughed and tried to inhale as little of the noxious fumes as possible. Thick layers of dust and grime covered every shelf, bench, and otherwise flat surface in the shop, and I knew from experience not to touch or rub against anything. The filth seemed to sense human presence, yearning to jump out and embed itself in anyone who wandered too close. The soot hovered around me, and I couldn't breathe through my nose. I felt my life expectancy dwindle with every minute I stood in Bay 3, or, for that matter, anywhere else in the building.

Kevin pulled on a droplight from an overhead retractable reel and led me underneath the vehicle. He flipped the light on and pointed at the front driver's-side brake hose.

"The brake hose sprung a leak," he said. His greasy finger pointed at a pinhole in the rubber hose connected to the brake caliper. He followed a dark, wet stain that ran along the hose and onto the frame. The crimson trail continued along the metal, finding a low spot where it became a steady drip. On the floor, a small puddle of brake fluid had formed.

When it came to vehicles and keeping them functional, the extent of my knowledge ended just beyond keeping gas in the tank. I looked at the hose again and followed the trail of brake fluid to the floor. Before I managed to ask about the repairs, Kevin spoke.

"Someone tampered with the brakes," he said. Fine particles of soot and dust floated in the glow of the droplight.

"What?"

He motioned for me to step out from beneath the Wrangler. We walked to a workbench where random tools, rags, and a vehicle battery sat. I followed his lead and hunched over the dimly lit bench, peering at the battery, again careful not to touch anything.

"We took your battery out and checked for leaks," Kevin said.

I waited.

As if double-checking his work, he examined the exterior of the battery and tapped the hard-plastic shell with a screwdriver. "No leaks," he said.

"Okay." I had no idea where he was going with this.

Pointing at the manufacturer's label on top of the battery, he said, "Watch this." He peeled the label off the battery. Underneath was a round hole, about an inch in diameter. "I would say someone drilled a hole in your battery."

I leaned closer and touched the hole with my index finger. "What?"

"The acid level is low," he said.

"How does that happen?"

"Not sure."

I could've asked "What?" again but didn't see the point. Staring at the battery seemed appropriate. After a moment, I turned and studied the Wrangler. "Someone took acid from my battery?"

"Maybe. I would guess some type of siphon device through the hole?"

"Could that eat through a brake hose?"

"Not much is gone, but it would not take much. Over time, a little amount could do damage." Kevin took a deep breath and sighed, slowly shaking his head. "We see hoses with salt on them. 'Cause of the ocean. But salt on a rubber hose is random. There would be other places on the hose and truck that would look bad."

"So, someone siphoned acid out of my battery and squirted it on my brake hoses," I said, a statement, not a question. We walked back under the Wrangler, and Kevin pointed to the damaged hose.

"The one bad spot on your hose looks more like a burn, or something like that." He pointed at a white substance on the brake hose. "See this white, flaking stuff around the hole? It looks like corrosion, almost like dried sulfuric acid."

"Sulfuric acid?"

"Battery acid is about one-third sulfuric acid."

He walked me to the other side of the Wrangler and pointed at the brake hose on the front passenger side.

"This hose has the same burn marks and corrosion on it," he said. "Not failed yet, but close."

I pointed at the driver's-side brake hose, then back at the passenger side. "Both front brake hoses have the same burn pattern and corrosion on them?"

"Yes." Kevin inched up on his tiptoes, moved his head sideways, and placed his face near the brakes. He scrunched his nose and inhaled. "Put your nose close and smell."

I got on my tiptoes and took a whiff.

"Smell something?" he asked.

"Maybe," I said, which was a lie. Along with the cigarette smoke and brake dust, two large ceiling fans swirled oil, gas, and exhaust fumes into an invisible cloud engulfing every square foot of the shop. My nose might clear in a week or two.

"Smell a little like rotten eggs?" he asked.

It didn't, at least not to me. But I shrugged and said, "Possibly."

His eyes widened, and he bit his lower lip. "Sulfuric acid smells much like rotten eggs."

I walked to the open bay door but stopped before heading out into the sunlight and turned around. "Guess you shouldn't touch the Wrangler anymore. It's probably a crime scene now."

Lighting a cigarette, he sighed, released the safeties on the lift, and pressed a button. The Wrangler slowly slid down until it rested a few inches above the tires.

Not trying to do my Lieutenant Columbo impersonation, I said, "One last thing. This seems complicated. Wouldn't a person need specific training to know how to do this?"

Kevin blew smoke out his nose and glared at me as if I'd grown a dorsal fin. Auto repair might be easy and second nature to him, but I wondered how many people were knowledgeable enough to pull off something like this.

"Could the average person do this?" I asked.

"Maybe, maybe not. I guess it would depend on what they knew."

That sounded like something I'd say and couldn't tell if he were mocking me. Perhaps he'd picked up on my world-class interrogation techniques. I stared at him for a moment, then walked out the bay door and called James.

"James, it wasn't an accident."

CHAPTER 19

Before grabbing Arabella's car, I peeked into her hospital room. She slept soundly, and all the machines were flashing the same numbers and making the same noises.

After filling Arabella's car with gas, I headed to my apartment, the car dying twice before making it back to the YellowRock. It restarted both times on the first try, but the inconsistency alarmed me. Arabella hadn't mentioned anything about car troubles.

Erika sprang to her feet as I entered the office. "Miss Arabella is okay?"

I explained Arabella's condition and told Erika I needed to be back at the hospital by noon, Arabella's checkout time. Upstairs, I sat at my desk and punched the number for the Violent Crimes Division of the Rockford Police Department into the landline phone. Neither Traverso nor Penn answered.

Elbows on the desk, I cradled my head in my hands and rubbed my eyes. Between Ryberg, my attack, and Arabella's accident, I hadn't slept much the last three nights. I stood and dragged myself to the bathroom. It'd been days since my last shower and, although pressed for time, I let the water run down my body in a futile attempt to rejuvenate myself.

Retirement wasn't supposed to be like this.

I dressed—this time in a green Longtail T—and prepared to zip back to the hospital. The midday Bonaire sun was at full intensity and streamed through the sliding balcony door. I searched the apartment for my sunglasses but couldn't find them. They were always in one of two places: the Wrangler, or the kitchen counter. It was approaching noon, and I didn't have time to search further. Squinting, and with the sun visor down, I drove to the hospital.

Arabella and Ruth stood on the sidewalk alongside the parking lot. I pulled close, stopping with the car's passenger side in front of Arabella.

"Hey, Conklin," she said.

I walked around the car and gave her a peck on the lips. "Ready to go?" I put my hand on the door handle.

"Wait." Ruth jammed her hand against the door and held it closed. "She's going to my place."

"Sis, I need to go to Conklin's," Arabella said. "I cannot rest at your place."

Ruth tightened her lips and folded her arms across her chest. She clicked her toes on the concrete a couple of times. "She needs rest." She leaned forward, hands on her hips. "Make sure she gets it."

I held the door open as Ruth helped Arabella into the passenger seat.

"I'll take care of her, Blaze," I said.

Arabella threw her head back. "Conklin . . ."

I glanced at Ruth. Her jaw quivered, and her eyes narrowed. A crimson hue, similar in color to her red hair, crept across her face. I'd been calling her Blaze for two years, mainly because of her ridiculous red hair, but, also, because it annoyed her so much.

Dutch people are common on Bonaire, but I haven't seen many with red hair. Ruth's retina-burning, eye-popping, satanic shade struck me as over the top. I doubted it was her natural color.

Ruth stuck her head inside the window and kissed Arabella on the cheek. They mumbled back and forth in Dutch for a moment, then Ruth straightened and stung me with her eyes over the roof of the car. "You—" she said, cutting herself off mid-sentence. She continued in a lower, softer tone. "Let me know how she is doing, okay?"

"I'll call you tomorrow."

Luckily, the engine fired on the first try, and we made our escape, leaving Ruth standing at the edge of the parking lot. As we turned toward Richter's, I let out a deep sigh. Can't ever be far enough away from Ruth.

"What did she say back there?" I asked.

"Oh, Ruth thinks I am not well off at your apartment."

"Better there than her place."

"Yes, but you know how it is. She wants to control my life, make me live the way she thinks I should." She shook her head. "She just needs to let me be me."

"You should tell her that."

"Every time I try, she tells me I am wrong. She always knows best. Or she thinks she does."

We were both quiet a moment.

"You're tough," I said and put a hand on her knee. "You can handle her."

She covered my hand with hers. "We will see. Maybe someday." With her other hand, she shaded the sun from her eyes. "Where are your sunglasses?"

CHAPTER 20

THE CAR SPUTTERED and died as we pulled into Richter's front lot. Kevin came out one of the bay doors, motioned for me to pop the hood, and asked how long the vehicle had been dying like this. I suggested he talk to Arabella and went into the garage.

The police hadn't yet secured my Wrangler as a crime scene, so I searched it, hoping to find my sunglasses. I peered through the windows and, because the Wrangler might yet be evidence, didn't touch anything.

They weren't in the Wrangler.

Lost sunglasses shouldn't send me on a scavenger hunt across the island. Since every pair I've ever owned has either been lost, sat on, or somehow broken, five bucks was my price limit. For me, losing them was a minor inconvenience, remedied with a quick stop at the thrift store.

However, these were a nice pair of aviator glasses like Tom Cruise had worn in *Top Gun*. They were better than anything I'd buy for myself, and since they were a gift from Arabella, I needed to find them.

In the adjacent bay, a four-wheel-drive truck sat perched atop a hydraulic lift. The 4WD sticker glued to its front fender glared back at me. I was missing something but couldn't place what it was. Vague

images and concepts ricocheted off the edges of my brain but wouldn't
stick long enough for me to seize hold and formulate what they meant.

4WD. Shaking my head, I walked out of the garage.

Kevin still poked around under the hood of Arabella's car.

"Find anything, Kevin?" I asked.

He scratched the back of his head. "It could be a fuel pump going
bad, but I'm not sure." He closed the hood and took a pack of cigarettes from his shirt pocket. "Bring it in, and we can run some tests."

"Can't do that till I get my Wrangler back."

"Sure. Give us a call." He lit a cigarette. "When the pump fails, no
gas will get to the engine." He drew his index finger across his throat
as if slicing it open.

I got in the driver's seat, and stuck my head out the window. "Thanks,
Kev. Let me know when you get the go-ahead on the Wrangler, okay?"

Kevin gave a short wave and shuffle-dragged his feet through one of
the bay doors, back into the shop. I pulled out of the lot and headed
for the YellowRock.

We entered my apartment via the outside stairs. Arabella was doing
well, but tired. I led her to the bed, and within seconds, she was fast
asleep. I went downstairs to check on Erika and help take care of some
business.

Erika stood at the file cabinet. "How is Arabella doing?" she asked.

I headed to my desk across the room. "She's doing well. The doctor
is happy with her progress and said she could return to work tomorrow—depending on how she feels and if she gets a good night's sleep."

Erika closed the cabinet drawer and peered through the window.
"Tiffany is coming toward the office." With a wry smile, she turned in
my direction. "She looked for you this morning."

Tiffany flung the door open and marched toward my desk, lips
pursed. Her eyes seemed to emit an invisible laser, narrowing as she
approached, burrowing a hole through my body.

"Damn you, Roscoe." She hovered over me while I sat in the chair and punched my shoulder. It almost hurt. "Why didn't you tell me about Bill and Marybeth? I shouldn't find out from a news broadcast."

I glanced at Erika, and she quickly looked away.

"Yeah," Tiffany said. "Erika told me you knew. Damn you."

I stood and wrapped my arms around her. "You're right. I'm sorry. I didn't know how to tell you and hoped to have more information— something other than telling you they're dead. Lame, but I didn't want to ruin your vacation. At least not right away. Bill wouldn't have wanted that. Nor Marybeth."

We pulled apart, sat, and in the most reassuring voice possible, I told Tiffany and Erika what I knew. When finished, I paused a moment, then said, "We'll have to wait and see what develops." Based on their facial expressions, they weren't reassured.

Tiffany dried her eyes and placed a hand on my knee. "How is Arabella?"

I gave her the *Reader's Digest* version, leaving out the part about the possible sabotage.

"Anyway," I said, "did you get to do any diving this morning?"

"Yes," Tiffany said. She straightened in the chair and ran her hands across red cheeks, a small smile briefly brightening her face. "Erika put me in touch with her nephew, Rulio, a dive master. He invited me to go along with a group he took to Windsock."

"Good, so you had someone to buddy up with."

"Well, yeah, but I've never dived with any of them before. It's weird grouping up with people you don't know. Diving with strangers is almost like solo diving."

"I understand. But it's not solo diving, and it's a small price to pay for safety." I handed her a rogue napkin lying on my desk. "You have any dive plans this afternoon? Maybe hook up with Rulio again?"

"I was hoping to, but now I'm not so sure." She wiped a tear with the palm of her hand. "Not sure I feel like it."

"Maybe you should rest, let all of this soak in a little," I said.

"Yes," Erika said, "rest."

Tiffany sat quietly for a moment. "As you said, Roscoe, sad and shocked as I am, Bill and Marybeth wouldn't want me to ruin my vacation. They'd want me to enjoy myself."

"They would," I said. "But only when you've recovered."

Erika went back to filing. Tiffany rubbed her eyes, brushed away a few more tears, and turned to face the window. After a few moments, she said, "I was thinking about doing the Karpata dive from shore."

"With who?" I asked.

Her brows furrowed. "Like you're one to talk."

"Meaning?"

"Can you honestly say you don't solo dive?"

I folded my arms across my chest. "That's different."

"Yeah? How?"

I didn't respond.

"Tell me, Roscoe. How is that different?"

Erika turned from her filing. "Yes, how is it different?"

"Why is it okay for you to solo dive, but not me?" She waited for a response, and when I remained quiet, she continued. "You can't have it both ways."

I sighed heavily and puffed out my chest. "I'm more experienced."

My bluster didn't nudge her. She shook her head. "Yeah, that's it . . . C'mon, Roscoe. I can solo dive Karpata. It's a shallow reef, and I've done it a bunch of times. It's no harder than Tori's Reef." She leaned forward, smiling, her voice softening. "I promise not to go deep. If there's too much wave action on the surface, I'll come straight back."

"I can go with you." I leaned forward but aggravated my rib and winced in pain.

"In your condition?" She forced a laugh, slapped her leg, and forced more laughter. "I'd be safer carrying an old anchor. Besides, you need to stay here and take care of Arabella."

"No," Erika said as she slammed the filing cabinet shut, pumping a finger at me. "Solo diving is too dangerous. Even for Mister Roscoe." She held a gaze on me for a moment then focused on Tiffany. "You should not go."

"Maybe you shouldn't dive again today, even with someone else," I said. "Let things calm down a bit."

All three of us were quiet for a moment.

Finally, Tiffany sighed. "Okay, I'm just upset. You're both right. Probably best if I don't do any more dives today."

"You are promising?" Erika asked.

Just like before, Tiffany put a hand on her heart. "Yes, I promise."

"I'm going to hold you to that," I said.

"Please do."

I wasn't comfortable. Well-trained, experienced divers often take full advantage of solo diving. It's a significant part of Bonaire's *Diver's Paradise* mantra. Tiffany had command of her equipment, breathed well, and swam through the water in a relaxed way, confident of her training and abilities. But she still relied on others, as evident by her needing me to know she was clearing water from her mask. A highly skilled diver—one capable of self-reliance—would do what needed to be done and not seek the reassurance of another diver.

Tiffany's skills weren't at the solo diver level. Most vacation divers weren't.

Maybe Erika's authoritative demeanor had gotten through to her. Maybe she listened to her internal common sense. Regardless, I was happy she'd changed her mind.

"Tell you what," I said, "I'll buy you and Lester dinner tonight."

"You can buy me dinner *and* drinks." She checked the clock on the wall and stood. "I better go. I want to buy some cute T-shirts I found."

"Hey, where's Lester?" I asked before she left the office.

"Oh, I almost forgot." She turned and walked halfway back. "Lester and Mandy are driving out to Spelonk Lighthouse this afternoon. They talked and set it up last night."

"So, Mandy *did* stop by my apartment last night," I said.

"Yeah, sometime after you left. Who knows how long they'll be gone." She shook her head and was quiet for a moment. "Lester doesn't have one friend back home, but the first thing he does when we go on vacation is make a friend. Or, as he says, a *buddy*." Then, in a mocking tone, she added, "Don't worry about the things you can't change."

"What?" I asked.

"Just something Mandy says." She waved a hand and stared into space. "Wish I knew what was so great about *Mandy*."

I shrugged.

Tiffany needed to direct her anger toward Lester, not Mandy. I didn't know why, but she cared for Lester, and he knew it. So why would he spend so much time with this Mandy woman? It didn't add up. I wanted to squeeze my hands around his throat and get some answers.

But I knew better. Again, I convinced myself their relationship wasn't any of my business. Even though Tiffany was like a kid sister to me, I couldn't tell her who to fall in love with. Best for me to support her any way I could until she and Lester worked things out.

And I still hadn't met Mandy. I needed to make a point of introducing myself to her.

"Yeah, right," Tiffany said. "Well, can I borrow Arabella's car for the afternoon?"

I gazed out the window and considered her request, knowing full well Arabella wouldn't appreciate me loaning out her car. The Dutch didn't tend to be "loaners" of many things, and Arabella wasn't even close to the exception. Especially if it involved Tiffany.

"Most of the T-shirt shops are within walking distance," I said. "You shouldn't need a car."

"I want to take some pictures of the salt mounds before shopping."

Tiffany was an avid photographer, and the salt mounds, a trademark attraction on Bonaire, had filled the viewfinder of many a photographer. Their peaks were visible from many spots on the island.

The salt mounds—or White Mountains of Bonaire, as the tourism department referred to them—were a work product of the Cargill Company produced by opening gates that flooded Bonaire's southern lowlands with seawater. After the seawater evaporated, bulldozers pushed the salt into hills standing sixty to seventy feet high. When the snow-white pyramids of salt grew to a predetermined height, conveyors loaded it onto waiting cargo ships.

I almost said no, but then considered Arabella, upstairs, knocked out on pain meds, none the wiser if Tiffany borrowed her car for a few hours. Against my better judgment, my gut swirling with queasiness, I tossed Tiffany the keys. "It's having some issues and dies occasionally. If it does, you may have to try and start it a couple of times. It seems to kick over on the first or second try."

"Thanks. I'll be back by dark."

"You going to be alright?" I asked.

Her eyes watered a bit. "Yes, I think so."

She gave me a wave, kissed Erika on the cheek, and headed for the door.

"You're staying in town, right?" I said.

"Absolutely," she said, as she backed out the door.

No sooner had the door closed, when Erika said, "Why is Mr. Lester spending so much time with Mandy and not Tiffany? She is such a sweet girl."

"I don't know."

"Well, I am glad she is not solo diving. That scared me. I like that girl and do not want anything happening to her."

I didn't say anything.

Erika raised her voice. "She promised."

"Yes, she did," I said, remembering another promise she had made. Several days ago, on the water's surface at Tori's Reef.

"Promise?" I had asked. She'd flashed me the okay sign.

Then she went underwater for her mask.

CHAPTER 21

WHILE ARABELLA SLEPT, I ducked out to my lounger on the balcony, anxious for an afternoon nap. But after a sleepless hour, I decided a beer at Vinny's sounded better.

The sun was ablaze, and the breeze from the east swept out across the sea. I glanced at the deep blue sky as the palm trees rustled in the wind. Bonaire's weather was almost routine—sunny and eighty degrees every day, or more technically on Bonaire, twenty-seven degrees Celsius. A vacationer's dream. Postcards in the making. Three hundred and sixty-five days to forget life's problems and regrets.

Every day felt like the weekend. But when the island was home, problems and regrets weren't forgotten. Living on the island was *just another day.*

A group of tourists, their truck loaded with tanks and scuba gear, the red on their arms and necks telegraphing their overindulgence in the Caribbean sun, turned the corner in front of me. I stopped and watched them disappear down the street. All the license plates on the island had *Diver's Paradise* printed along the top, above the numbers. Part of that Paradise is allowing each person the freedom to establish their limitations and dive in a self-regulated manner. If a person wanted to go solo, they determined if their skill level warranted such a decision.

Recreational dive training preached against solo diving. Most vacation divers don't have the experience or currency to be self-reliant—best to dive in pairs or groups to help each other in case of an emergency.

A cruise ship had docked for the day, and the downtown streets swelled with people. On cruise ship days, many of the local merchants set up booths on the sidewalks and the one-block concrete mall, snagging additional sales from folks coming off the boat. One of the restaurants cooked chicken on an outside grill. The flame sparkled, and the meat sizzled, the smoke and aroma floating down the street before being pushed out over the sea. My mouth watered from two blocks away.

Locals and tourists comprised the crowd, neither one significantly outnumbering the other. Bonaire's population is a little over 18,000 but can swell above 20,000 based on the season and the number of tourists on-island. In town, the locals always had a purpose in mind. They weren't in a hurry and did what they needed to do. Relaxed and orderly, they took their time.

Tourists were a different story. They always appeared in a hurry, dashing from spot to spot in a blind pursuit to go somewhere—anywhere—and be the first one there.

Arabella swore she could smell the cruise boat people, or "cruisers" as she had termed them, from two kilometers away. "They smell like suntan lotion and sparkly T-shirts," she'd said. Doubtful I could smell a sparkly T-shirt, let alone from two kilometers away, but I was perfectly capable of identifying the cruisers in a crowd.

Vinny's was half full, a cruiser couple sitting on the far side of the bar, colorful drinks in front of them and a nearby stool overflowing with plastic souvenir-shop bags. Lobster-red skin, their floppy hats offering little protection from the afternoon sun.

Jan sat on a stool at the far end of the bar, flipping through TV channels at a rapid pace. He turned my way as I limped past the

Heineken sign above the front entrance and down the wooden stairs onto the plank floor. By the time I plopped onto Ole Blue along the seaside of the bar, Jan had a cold Bright waiting for me.

The wooden barstools were an assortment of colors. Scratches and dark grooves hinted to their years of service. I preferred a light blue one, the most tattered, its seat grooved perfectly for my butt cheeks. For some reason, Jan had named it Ole Blue.

"How is Arabella?" he asked.

Jan is Ruth's husband, so I wasn't surprised he knew about Arabella's accident.

"She's doing fine and sleeping right now." I took a hit of the beer and watched the TV, not noticing, or caring, what was on.

He shook his head. "I am glad."

"Me, too."

Jan flipped through more channels, stopping on a fishing show. He pointed at the screen with the remote. "We have not been fishing in a long time." He put his hands on the bar and leaned closer to me, eyebrows raised. "When do you want to go?"

"Sounds great . . . let me see." With my elbow on the bar, I drummed my fingers along my chin. "Hmm."

"We always have a good time. It has been too long." He imitated casting a fishing line out over the tables, hooking a big one, and reeling it in. "Besides, you are retired. Is that not what retirement is all about?"

I finished off the Bright and set the empty bottle on the bar. "Funny, I don't feel retired right now."

Jan opened another beer and placed it on the damp coaster in front of me. I looked out at the street, between the two six-foot-tall potted palm trees along the sidewalk, as Arabella's sometimes-partner, James Saragoza, passed through town in his patrol truck. He glanced my way but didn't return my wave. I made a mental note to call and update him on Arabella's condition.

"You okay?" Jan asked.

I threw back a swig of Bright and watched the TV again for a moment. I told Jan about the Rybergs, the ad, the weapon, and my mugging. Knowing the information would go straight to Ruth, I didn't dare mention the possible sabotage to my Wrangler. Arabella should know first, and I wanted to be the one to tell her.

Jan straightened and shook his head. "We should go fishing." We both laughed, and he walked to the other side of the bar where two newly arrived customers had saddled up to a couple of yellow stools.

Vinny's had a vaulted ceiling. Oscillating fans mounted on the edge of the rafters near the point where the pitched roof met the wall, pushed air down at the patrons. If it hadn't been for the green and yellow ribbons tied to the front of the fan guards, I wouldn't have known the fans were working. Above the central table area, suspended below the rafters on a long, thin rod mounted at the top peak of the ceiling, an eight-foot-diameter fan made slow revolutions.

I watched the cruisers on the other side of the bar. They ordered another round of tall, foamy blue concoctions, complete with random pieces of tropical fruit floating on top. Jan catered to the tourists only so far and refused to litter his drinks with bamboo umbrellas or fancy wood fish carvings.

The woman held her drink with her right hand. The man, his left. When it came time to settle the tab, the man signed the credit card receipt right-handed.

Not sure what any of this proved. Maybe it meant the position of the coffee cup at the Rybergs' was insignificant. Could've been set there by a right- *or* left-handed person.

I leaned back on the stool, placed my feet on the rail near the bottom of the bar, and admired the ceiling. For years, a loyal clan of customers, or Vinny's Vagrants as they called themselves, brought old U.S. license plates to the island and gave them to Jan. Most of these were vanity plates and from all over the country. Jan mounted them on the wood rafters.

A plate from Texas said BST HUGS. A Florida plate said DUVALL STRT and one from Wisconsin read EVR COOL. The Wisconsin people I knew weren't all that cool. Unless EVR COOL meant something about the weather, in which case, it might be true.

My favorite plate was an Illinois plate that read ME N RC. I had no idea if RC referred to the soda or a person. Since I had the same initials, I liked the idea of it being a person. Jan had mounted all the plates parallel to the top edge of the rafter. Except for the ME N RC plate. It was angled slightly, out of line with the others. Also, the Illinois plate didn't lay flat against the rafters as the rest did. It had a bent corner, which stuck straight out, almost as if it were waving at me, inviting me over. I liked having a beer sitting on Ole Blue, under the Illinois plate, as the mysterious RC person looked down, watching over me.

I dialed James's number on my cell. When he answered, I said, "Just wanted to let you know Arabella is doing fine. The doctor said that if she feels okay tomorrow, she can go back to limited duty."

"Good. She hates to sit around."

"Do me a favor, though. If she goes in tomorrow, make sure she doesn't overdo it for a couple of days. You know how she can be. She'll try to be back to full speed right away."

"No problem. I will keep an eye on her. Thanks for the call."

"One last thing—" James disconnected before I could ask about my Wrangler, whether they had inspected the damage, and if so, what they had found. Before I could dial him back, my phone rang. I recognized the number—Richter's Garage.

"R, the police are finished with your Wrangler," Kevin said. "They gave us the go-ahead to make the repairs."

"When can you do it?"

"Not today, but we should have the lines replaced by noon tomorrow."

"Will it be drivable, with the fender damage?"

"The body shop will need to repair that, but we can bend the fender out a bit, so it doesn't rub. You should be able to drive it."

"One more thing. Did the police say anything about what they found?"

He paused a minute, and I could hear him exhale what I guessed was cigarette smoke. "Not to me. They were not here long, maybe thirty minutes at most."

"Thanks, Kevin. See you tomorrow."

That sounded too quick. A thorough examination should've taken longer. Unless they found something right away. Like battery acid on the brake lines.

I took a piece of paper and a pen from behind the bar. I drew a vertical line down the middle and began making two lists—one for things I knew about the recent events, the other for things I didn't know. After a few minutes, the *didn't know* side was much longer than the *did know*. I studied both lists and tried to think of anything additional to add to either column. So as not to waste too much time thinking, I drank some more beer.

Downtown Kralendijk bristled with activity, folks piling into the restaurants and bars after a day in the sun and sea. Spontaneous laughter erupted from all directions and horns blared as vehicles passed on the one-way street. Jan asked if I wanted another beer. I hesitated but found the strength to decline.

I left plenty of money on the bar to pay my bill, gave Jan a quick wave, and stepped out of Vinny's, onto Kaya C.E.B. Hellmund. I stopped on the sidewalk and noticed a street cam perched atop one of the light poles. After a brutal attack on a cruise ship employee several years ago in downtown Kralendijk, the police department had installed street cams along the significant tourist thoroughfares. No idea whether someone continuously monitored the cams, but I liked waving at them. Don't know why, I just did. Probably had to do with my defiance of Big Brother watching.

I waved at the cam and started walking back to the YellowRock. After a few steps, I stopped, turned, and waved again. I smiled and turned toward home, satisfied with my show of insolence. Within the first block, a vehicle honked, and Lester pulled alongside me in his truck.

From the driver's side, he leaned across the passenger seat to the window. "Have you seen Tiff? I can't find her."

"No, I haven't."

"I'm getting worried. She said she'd be back by now."

I shrugged. "She said something about buying some shirts. Or maybe she stopped to pick up some grub for tonight," I said.

He shook his head. "No, no. She said we were to eat with you tonight."

"Well, maybe she's still out shopping and lost track of time."

"There are bags from several shops in the room." He leaned back and banged his head on the headrest several times, putting both hands on his face. "She shopped before she went diving."

"Diving?" My throat went dry. "What are you talking about?"

"She said she was going diving, that she talked it over with you."

My pulse quickened, and my gut did a summersault. I looked north, in the direction of Karpata.

"Please, we have to go find her," Lester said. "I'm worried. I would go myself, but I'm not sure where this Karpata place is."

I hoped Arabella's on-again-off-again car dying explained Tiffany's tardiness. Maybe she was walking back to the resort or sitting at a local bar killing time. She might be on the beach, somewhere, waiting for sunset, enjoying some alone time. Based on what I'd seen of Lester, she needed it. But Tiffany wasn't the type to make folks worry, and I had never known her to need a lot of alone time.

Only a sliver of orange shone above the horizon, casting a glow across the sea and the patchy, late afternoon clouds. Not much daylight remaining. I had no choice.

"Alright, but let me drive. I know where I'm going." Lester scooted over to the passenger seat as I jumped behind the wheel. "Why'd you wait so long to look for her?"

"Mandy borrowed my truck."

"Borrowed your truck?" What was it with Mandy and Lester? I shook my head and lowered my voice, getting control of myself and the situation. "Tiffany told me you and Mandy went out to Spelonk," I said.

Lester averted his eyes and looked out the window of the passenger-side door. "We did go to Spelonk, and then Mandy borrowed the truck. That's what happened."

"Okay, it doesn't matter." The sequence of events wasn't important, at least not right now. We needed to find Tiffany.

We made a quick stop at the YellowRock to check if Tiffany had returned, but she hadn't. Rib pain notwithstanding, I flew up the stairs to my apartment, grabbed a flashlight, and peeked into the bedroom to check on Arabella. She was still asleep, and I saw no reason to wake her.

We drove out of the parking lot and turned onto Kaya Grandi, the road that went north, toward Karpata. The engine revved nearly as fast as my heart.

My mind went back several hours.

"Yes, I promise," Tiffany had said.

CHAPTER 22

THE KARPATA DIVE site was at the northernmost end of the coastal road and had always been one of my favorites on the island. We sped north, passing small cacti dotting the roadside. To our left, the ground dropped off into the sea and to our right soared towering cliffs, ridged and grooved by the pounding of the sea millions of years ago.

The road was one lane, well maintained, and in excellent repair, but, as narrow as it was, handled two-way traffic. It wound back and forth, following the contours of the water's edge, many of the curves being blind to oncoming traffic. I sped along faster than usual, increasing the chance of a head-on collision. No choice.

I stepped on the gas after we passed the 1000-Steps dive site. Beyond there, the road became one way, lessening our chances of a head-on. Lester leaned forward and stared out the windshield. His left foot beat out a constant nervous rhythm, and his fingers dug into the dashboard. I had both hands on the steering wheel, focused on taking the curves as fast as possible. Several times, the right-side tires went onto the dirt shoulder, and the truck heaved sideways as I yanked left, forcing it back on the pavement. Neither of us spoke. Our bodies swayed in unison as the tires squealed around each curve.

The sun had fully set, and we still had several minutes of driving before reaching Karpata. Streetlights, houses, or any other light source didn't exist that far north on the coastal road, so our only sources of illumination would be the flashlight and the truck headlights.

The craziness of this whole trip raced through my mind. I doubted we'd find Tiffany still at Karpata. There had to be another, more reasonable explanation. Even if she *had* dived alone, she'd have been finished by now and be back in town.

Besides, she had promised.

We drove around the last curve and pulled into the small parking area at Karpata. Emptiness filled my gut as the headlights flashed across the side of Arabella's car—the only vehicle in the lot. After pulling alongside and killing the engine, I jumped out and swiveled my head in all directions searching for Tiffany, calling her name several times.

I walked over to a small ledge and looked out across the sea, at the spot Tiffany would've used to enter the slight surge. The rhythmic sound of the waves lapping the shore echoed off the rock cliffs, and a slight breeze rustled the trees. A crescent moon shone in a dark sky full of stars.

I cupped my hands around my mouth and called her name. No response. Only Lester's heavy breathing and the cadence of the sea along the shoreline. From our angle and distance, the flashlight beam wasn't powerful enough to penetrate the darkness to the shore, so we started toward the water's edge.

With Lester in tow, I headed for the concrete stairs that led from Karpata's parking lot to the edge of the water. The first twelve went toward the sea, then the staircase turned left and continued down eleven more steps. Near the bottom, two more stairs went to the right. They were wide and uneven, with a three-foot white-painted concrete wall that ran along the outside edge acting as a makeshift railing. I shone my light downward and moved as fast as possible.

Coral rubble and baseball-sized rocks composed most of the shoreline along that part of the island. In the dark, with only my flashlight and a sliver of moonlight reflecting off the water, I had to be careful navigating out to the shore. I yelled again for Tiffany. No answer. Not even an echo. The only sound being the slight hiss of the waves stirring small pebbles and sand along the water's edge before finding its way back to the sea.

I shone my light past Lester and peered into the blackness. He slowly walked the shoreline to the south, yelling, moving deeper into the darkness. I pointed the beam northward, in front of me, seeing only rocks, surge, and gloom.

Lester crunched along the coral rubble and continued his search, while I followed the shoreline in the opposite direction. I stumbled several times on the bigger rocks but maintained my vigil with the light and peered to the edge of its effectiveness.

After about twenty yards, the far edge of the light's beam shone on something. My pace quickened. The light bounced on and off the object as I moved faster along the shore.

"Lester, over here." My throat was dry, the yell softer than intended. A quick flash of the light behind me showed Lester striding in my direction as I hurried along the shore.

The reflection of a silver scuba tank halted me in my tracks. The object was indeed a body—a body decked out in full scuba attire, including pink fins and accents, swaying back and forth, in a slight rocking motion, as the surge hit the shore and retreated.

I did my best to run the last few yards but stumbled and fell, crawling over the last bit of rock and coral rubble. The diver lay on one side, back facing me.

I placed a nervous hand on one of the shoulders, the cold, moist wetsuit sending shivers slinking down my spine, goose bumps sprouting on my arms. On the edge of hyperventilating, I swallowed hard and closed my eyes. A couple of slow, deep exhales calmed me, and I opened my eyes. Terrified, I rolled the body over.

Lester kneeled beside me as I shone through the tinted glass of the mask, sitting sideways on the diver's face. The cloudy, opaque eyes showed no reaction to the light. I wasn't surprised. I'd seen this countless times before. The purple lips, the pale skin, the terror frozen on her face—she was dead.

Tiffany.

As if not believing my conclusions, I placed two fingers on her throat. No pulse. I bowed my head, deflated, unable to understand this nightmare. But a moment later, a shot of adrenaline pulsed through me.

I won't let this happen.

Not today.

"Lester," I said, unbuckling Tiffany's buoyancy compensator, the scuba vest that also doubled as a tank harness. "Help me get this gear out of the way."

For me to begin CPR, I needed her lying flat, and that couldn't happen with the tank strapped to her back. I unlatched the vest, and Lester dragged the gear and tank clear of Tiffany, allowing me to lay her as flat as possible on the rocks. Needing both hands for CPR, I gave the light to Lester and showed him where to point it.

Thoughts of preserving the scene never crossed my mind.

I tilted her head back and verified an unobstructed airway. Her chest rose and sank twice as I forced two breaths of air into her lungs. I put my hands on her sternum and did thirty chest compressions. As the rocks and coral rubble tore the skin off my knees, I continued the two-breath and thirty-chest-compression cycle hoping for a reaction, some sign that she was coming back to us.

I had almost convinced myself CPR might work, that Tiffany would take a deep breath and cough out the water in her lungs, her eyes returning to normal. She'd be her old self again, smiling and full of life. We'd all hug. Even Lester.

After five two-breaths-and-thirty-chest-compression cycles, I checked her pulse. Nothing. She remained unresponsive, but I continued.

Lester kneeled alongside me. "C'mon. C'mon," he repeated, over and over, his breaths as loud and rapid as mine. "Breathe!"

I maintained CPR and checked for a pulse every five cycles. Not sure how long I continued, but the more chest compressions, breathing, and hoping I did, the more it became clear Tiffany wasn't coming back. She was gone, and further effort seemed useless. By the time I gave up—by the time I had lost hope—a combination of sweat and tears ran off my nose and chin, falling onto the bloodstained rocks, my breathing quick and shallow.

One last check for a pulse, and one last time, nothing. I removed my fingers from her throat and slumped. Lester dropped the light, and it clicked off hitting the ground, leaving us in the quiet darkness. He moaned several times, bent over, and pounded the ground with his hands.

On the distant horizon, at a spot no map or GPS could pinpoint, the vast array of stars gave way to the black waters of the sea. Blurry-eyed, I glared at it for several moments. The waves continued their predictable lap against the shore, and somewhere in the darkness, a fish flopped.

As Lester moaned and pounded the rocks, I buried my face in my hands.

CHAPTER 23

I WHISPERED IN her ear, "I'm sorry."

Behind me, Lester stumbled over the coral rubble as he paced in all directions, screaming and crying, hands flailing. My emotions welled, and patience with him wore thin. He had ignored her most of the trip, treated her like crap, and spent time with someone else. Now he was upset and crying? Again, I considered grabbing him by the neck and squeezing, watching his eyes bulge out of their sockets.

But, instead, I stared at Tiffany and counted a slow ten.

The surge washed over her motionless body as I moved the light to her face and considered her lifeless eyes. I choked back bile, despair and sadness engulfing me for the second time in less than a week. Lester vomited. With the back of my hand, I wiped my cheek.

The air pressure gauge attached to her tank registered 1300 PSI—two hundred PSI less than half full. Air streamed out of the regulator as I pressed the purge valve, indicating it still worked correctly. Her dive computer displayed the surface interval—the elapsed time since her last dive—and showed two hours and thirteen minutes, which could indicate the time since she had died. Pressing one of the buttons on the console, I accessed the data for her most recent dive. It showed a shallow dive of only thirty feet, a duration of thirty-one minutes.

Tiffany was a good swimmer and comfortable in the water. With her gear in working condition and with plenty of air, something out of the ordinary had to have happened. Drowning didn't sound feasible.

Her body didn't show any visible indication of an attack—marine animal or otherwise—and no signs of trauma, such as a boat strike. A thorough examination was needed to determine the cause of death.

Stop it! Tiffany had just died, and I was going into detective mode—again. *Think like a civilian.*

I called the police.

Securing the scene was my next priority, but what was there to secure? Lester and I were the first to discover her and, as far as I could tell, the only people around. We'd already contaminated the scene some. Shouldn't do more.

Lester had walked over and sat on the bottom stair, elbows on his knees, head buried in his hands. Tears streaked down his face, but he seemed more controlled than he had been a few minutes ago.

I walked over, hesitated, then placed a hand on his shoulder. "You alright?"

He shook his head. "Of course I'm not *alright.*"

Like me, his emotions were also in high gear. I squeezed his shoulder.

After a moment, he looked at me. "How? Why?"

Same questions I had about Bill and Marybeth. *No answers. Not even guesses.* Same lousy answers, although I didn't say them out loud.

"Let's go sit in the truck," I said. He needed to get as far from Tiffany's body as possible. Plus, I wanted to examine Arabella's car.

I helped Lester into the passenger seat of his truck, leaving the door open to create some extra air flow. He grabbed a bottle of water, poured part of it over his head, and finished off the rest in one gulp.

"I need a drink," he said, "of something stronger than this." He threw the empty bottle on the floorboard. "Some scotch would be great."

I went to Arabella's car and shined the light through the windows. Not sure what I was expecting, but I needed to do something—couldn't sit and wait. I circled the Toyota twice and didn't see anything peculiar.

As much as I didn't want to admit it, Tiffany probably drowned. Although rare, it sometimes happened in scuba.

But it didn't feel right, and the circumstances didn't feel like a recipe for drowning.

I called Arabella.

"Did I wake you?" I asked.

"No, I have been up for a while," Arabella said. "I felt better and was about to make a small meal. Hey, where are you?"

"This is bad."

My voice cracked as I told her about Tiffany. The dryness in my throat and mouth made it difficult to talk, and my eyes watered over and over. Composure wasn't easy. I mentioned that her car would be at Karpata for a while. When she asked why, I told her. She went quiet.

Finally, in a low, controlled voice, she said, "I am sorry. Is there anything I can do?"

"I don't think so. As soon as I can, I'm bringing Lester back."

Her voice softened. "I will be waiting."

I put the phone back in my pocket. I needed a drink, too, but water would have to do for now. Reaching through the window of the truck and grabbing my water bottle, I noticed Lester had drifted off to sleep.

How could anyone sleep at a time like this? I took a deep breath and didn't wake him. He needed the rest. Besides, it made him easier to tolerate.

A small, one-story building painted in bright pastel colors, characteristic of many Caribbean structures, stood on the far side of the parking lot. Karpata was a frequent dive of mine, so I'd noticed the building before, but had never taken a serious interest in it.

Several tables and chairs stood scattered along one side underneath a modest-sized, dry thatched gazebo. Cacti, ranging in height from two to three feet, dotted the unplanned landscaping. The front of the building had a sliding window. I shone the light on the front. Hanging on the exterior, next to the window, was a handmade menu, and above the window was a sign that read *Cado Snack*.

According to the hours displayed on the outside of the window, the snack shop was open earlier today, closing at five o'clock. Using the surface interval of Tiffany's dive computer, and working backward, I guessed the place was open when she drowned.

Someone must've been here.

The only drowning case I had ever caught was years ago in Rockford. The details were a blur, but I remembered something about a jilted husband, recently divorced, jumping from a bridge. Bill and I investigated and ruled it a suicide. Every case was different, but something about that drowning and the recovery of the body gave me pause. I walked over to the concrete wall and looked at the shoreline in the direction of Tiffany. Two different drownings and two different bodies. I couldn't describe what it was, but something bothered me.

The sirens of approaching squads wailed behind me, and two police trucks pulled into the parking lot, their pulsating blue lights washing over the area. Two uniformed officers got out of one, and James stepped out of the other and walked toward me.

He took notes as I described what Lester and I had found. Before showing James Tiffany's body, I glanced at Lester, who was now awake and leaning on the hood of his truck. The other two officers began taping off the area as James and I headed for the stairs. I stopped halfway down.

"She's about thirty yards north of the entry point," I said, pointing. Seeing her body, lying lifeless on the rubble, wasn't going to happen. Not again. Not tonight.

"She was diving alone?" James asked.

I hesitated, blue lights bouncing across the shallow waves of the dark sea. Pursing my lips, I closed my eyes and nodded.

James sighed.

"Can I get Lester out of here?" I asked. Standard procedure called for James to confirm Lester's identity, verify the last time he'd seen Tiffany, ask him about their relationship, and a host of other investigative questions. In his current state, Lester wouldn't be able to answer any questions, so I hoped James would allow me to take him back to the YellowRock. "I'll be sure to bring him to the station tomorrow for a statement."

"Yes, go ahead. We will take care of this." He patted me on the shoulder.

"Thanks."

James went down the stairs, turned north at the water's edge, and began searching for Tiffany's body. I didn't flinch at the sound of the ambulance, sirens piercing the calm night, as it pulled into the lot. As James's flashlight beam approached Tiffany's body, two paramedics, carrying life support equipment and a light of their own, stumbled along the shore in the same direction. They'd take Tiffany's vitals and verify that she was dead. A few moments later, the ambulance crew fought the darkness and the uneven steps, working a gurney toward the dark shore. My nose tingled, and my face flushed. I couldn't bear the scene any longer. It would be etched in my mind forever—no way to un-see what I'd seen.

I ducked under the yellow crime scene tape as I walked back to the truck.

CHAPTER 24

"So, what happens now?" Lester asked, his voice barely audible. He slumped in the passenger seat and stared out the window as I drove us back to the YellowRock.

"They'll need statements from both of us." I hesitated and swallowed. "And you'll need to identify the body."

Lester turned to me, wide-eyed. "No! I can't do that. Why can't you do it?" His breathing was heavy, almost panicked. "Please."

I took a deep breath and sighed, returning my gaze out the windshield. "Okay, okay. I'll do it." I paused, not wanting to continue, but he had to know the next step. "Since no one was around when she died, and her death probably wasn't from natural causes, there'll have to be an autopsy."

He was quiet for a moment. "You mean they're going to cut her up?"

I didn't look at him, trying to focus as best I could on the dark road in front of us. "It's procedure. They have to rule out foul play." The instant I said it, I bit my lower lip and regretted my hastiness.

"Foul play?" He scrunched his eyebrows. "What are you talking about?"

I didn't say anything.

"As in murder?" he asked. "Who would do such a thing?"

I shook my head. "I doubt it's an issue. Just procedure." I concentrated on the windshield and driving. Anything to keep from falling apart myself.

We rode the rest of the way in silence. I wasn't eager to do the ID of Tiffany's body but knew Lester couldn't handle it. An autopsy didn't sit well with me either, but it'd confirm the cause of death, which I needed to know.

Something nagged at me, but I couldn't put a finger on it. Bill and Marybeth dead the same week as Tiffany felt like a huge coincidence.

Bill never believed in coincidences. I didn't either.

Lester also needed to consider the arrangements for getting Tiffany's remains back to the States. He'd need to coordinate with her parents, whom I'd forgotten about until that moment. Someone should call them.

It struck me how cold the word "remains" sounded.

Do the job while investing as little feeling as possible. I never dreamed that would apply to Tiffany.

And what about Tiffany's son, Ozzie? Two years old and orphaned. How tragic. What would happen to him? Who would he live with? Tiffany's folks? The father's identity was a mystery to me, so I didn't know how, or if, he figured into things.

Poor kid.

After a long night at Karpata and a long drive back, we pulled into the lot at the YellowRock. Arabella was on the balcony and walked to the rail as we parked. I waved and motioned for her to stay put. Lester walked down the path toward his unit, and I trailed a few steps behind.

"Do you need anything?" I asked.

He didn't turn around. "Leave me alone." I almost missed a step, his bluntness and resentment a distinct contrast to his earlier demeanor. He opened the door to his unit and walked in, closing it behind him with a resounding thud. Standing outside, six inches from the number five nailed to the doorframe, I considered going in and making sure he was okay but decided against it.

I wasn't his babysitter.

Arabella greeted me with a long, tight hug at the top of the stairs to my apartment. She pulled away and stroked my hair. "What happened?"

"Looks like a drowning." I went to the fridge and grabbed two Brights. "I can't believe it."

"Erika called looking for you. She is pretty upset."

"She knows already?" I opened the beers and handed one to Arabella.

"Surprise, it is a small island. She asked if Tiffany was solo diving."

"Thanks for reminding me. I feel bad enough already!"

She jerked her head back and blinked twice. "It is . . . well . . . it surprised me, that is all."

"I'm sorry. Tiffany and I discussed it, and she promised not to go." I let out a long, slow breath. "I never dreamed of anything like this." Arabella stepped up to hug me again. "Let's sit on the balcony. There's something I need to tell you." On the balcony, Arabella sat on one of the chairs; I settled on the end of the lounger. Leaning forward, I bit my lower lip in hesitation. "Please listen to me fully before you say anything."

She said okay, and I told her about the possible sabotage of my Wrangler. Afterward, neither of us said anything. Arabella stared at me. Finally, she set down her beer, stood, and walked back into the apartment.

"Where are you going?" I asked.

"I am going to call James and find out about your Wrangler."

I stood to follow her. "Please wait. It's late. I'll be at the station tomorrow to give a statement, anyway, so I'll talk to James then. Besides, if you're going to work tomorrow, you can nose around a little."

She stared at me, phone in hand. "It means someone is trying to hurt you. Possibly even kill you."

"We don't know that. Not yet, anyway." I took the phone and set it on the table. Taking her hand, I led her back to the balcony. When I sat, Arabella didn't join me.

"Three of your friends have died in the last week, you beat up, and your Wrangler sabotaged." She paced across the balcony as she spoke. "Do you not find that a little strange?"

Yeah, as a matter of fact, I did. I drank some beer and gazed at the sea, reminding myself I was retired. "A little. But we don't know if any of it is connected."

"But—"

"Nothing to base anything on. Bill and Marybeth murdered, and Tiffany drowned." Not sure who I was trying to convince. Me or her.

She folded her arms on her chest. "What about your Wrangler?"

Arabella was correct, but I didn't want to believe any of it. "Let's see what the autopsy results are before we get too crazy." I motioned with my head at the lounger next to mine. "Please, sit."

She didn't.

I lowered my voice and softened my tone. "Please."

She clenched her fists and let out a low moan, finally sitting. "How can you do nothing?"

"I *am* doing something." I set my beer on the table, laced my hands behind my head, and stretched my legs out. "I'm thinking."

"It looks like you are doing nothing."

"Well, it's harder than it looks."

"*Well*, I would hope so, because it looks easy." We both took a drink of our beers. "Do not hurt yourself, Einstein."

"Seriously." I stood to go for another beer, stopping after one step and pressing my side.

"Your rib?"

"Yeah. It must've stiffened up a little from sitting, plus all the excitement at Karpata tonight." I limped into the kitchen. "If Tiffany's death wasn't an accident, then there has to be some connection."

"A connection?" Arabella showed me her empty bottle, a signal I should bring her one, too.

"Yeah, there's always a connection between the victim, the motive, and the murderer." I walked back to the balcony and handed her a beer. "Bill always said, 'Find the connection, and you'll find the motive. Find the motive, and the murderer will be close by.'"

"So, we need to find the connection between Bill, Tiffany, and your Wrangler? Isn't that *you*?"

"Sure, seems that way." With care, I lowered myself back onto the lounger. "But first we need to find out what happened to Tiffany. Until we get more answers, we'll have to just sit and wait."

Talking this through with Arabella had helped, and the thing nagging me was becoming a bit clearer. I had ideas about the connection and the motive and what it all meant but needed evidence. It'd take more time to develop the picture.

"Well, we may have to wait, but we do not have to sit." She set down her beer, stood, and sauntered in my direction. Swinging a leg over the side of my lounger, she straddled my midsection and lowered herself on top of me, unzipping my shorts.

"I haven't had dinner yet," I said.

She kissed my neck, sending shivers rolling down my spine, and whispered in my ear, "Are you hungry?" She pressed her pelvis into my groin.

"Not right now." I wrapped my arms around her, and she moaned softly. I pressed my fingers into her spine and followed it down to the top of her shorts.

My bruised rib was all but forgotten, and Arabella didn't seem bothered by her concussion.

But the sight of Tiffany's dead body was still fresh in my mind.

CHAPTER 25

I AWOKE ON the veranda, sprawled sideways in the lounger with a stiff neck. I blinked the cobwebs from my eyes and tried to stand, only to crumble and fall back on the lounger. It felt like some of my internals had shifted in place as if my rib cage had ground against something. To my detriment, I'd ignored it the last few days.

Last night was a blur, but I remembered going to bed around two. Arabella went straight to sleep, her steady breathing muffling the pulse of the ceiling fan. My mind raced as I tossed and turned in bed, events of the last few days reeling through my mind like an old *Dragnet* episode. Unable to sleep, I went to the balcony.

Most of the night, I sat on the lounger. Different images of Tiffany's body lying along the shore filled my consciousness, the silence of the island interrupted only by the gentle lap of the sea from across the street.

I couldn't stop wondering about Ozzie. As he grew up, how much would he remember about Tiffany? How would her appearance change as he grew older and her image slowly faded? Perhaps he had a picture of her that he'd keep, watching it yellow and fade over time.

Did she have a favorite color? A favorite dress? What about the games they played together? Like mothers sometimes do, maybe she had a pet name for him. Would he remember her voice, how she talked? At two years old, I doubted he'd have many lasting memories.

She'd be a stranger—someone from his past who no one spoke of or about. To him, just a name.

Even though I'd never met Ozzie, his immediate future concerned me. I hoped he wouldn't get bumped from relative to relative. Or worse yet, thrown into foster care. As a silent promise to Tiffany, I vowed never to let that happen.

I was, in large part, responsible for Tiffany's death. I'd never be able to make up for that—not to me, Ozzie, or anyone else. Especially not to Tiffany. She had so much to offer, yet she was gone, and I was partly to blame. Maybe fully. Sadness and guilt had overwhelmed me as I eventually slipped into an uncomfortable sleep.

I limped into the bedroom at nine o'clock. Arabella had gone to work and left a note asking me to call her later. I borrowed some of her pain medication.

Downstairs in the office, Erika greeted me with tearful eyes and a hug. After she pulled away, she blew her nose and sat down. She shook her head and wiped her eyes with a tissue. "I'm going to miss her smile."

The desk chair squeaked as I sat. "So am I."

My stomach growled and reminded me I hadn't eaten since early yesterday. I reached into the small office refrigerator and pulled out a carton of yogurt and a small bottle of orange juice. Erika went back to whatever she was doing on the computer. I had lost track of any business concerns over the last few days and was grateful for her tenacity in keeping things straight. I had no doubt the resort—and me—would be lost without her.

I called Richter's Garage and asked Kevin about my Wrangler.

"It is ready, so stop anytime and pick it up," he said. "The keys are in it. I will send you a bill."

"Thanks, Kevin."

Next, I gave Arabella a call. She didn't answer so I left a message telling her I'd be at the station after picking up my Wrangler.

I leaned back in my chair. "I should check on Lester. See if he's alright."

"I do not believe he is in his room," Erika said. "At least not this morning. Housekeeping reported that his room needed no cleaning."

"What?"

"They said he had not slept the whole night in his bed." Erika stopped typing and looked at me. "Where would he be?"

"Don't know." I threw the empty yogurt container in the trash can.

"Should we be worried?" Her eyes widened, and she took a deep breath. "Would he hurt himself because of Tiffany?"

I shook my head. "Don't know that either. I should have a look."

Before I made it to the door, the office phone rang. Erika answered it, then held the receiver out to me. "It is Arabella."

I put the phone to my ear. "Hey."

"Conklin, some guy is at Ruth's causing problems," Arabella said. Her voice was loud, and she breathed heavy with each word.

"Do you want me to meet you there?" I asked.

"Yes. I am on my way now."

Reality struck—my Wrangler was at Richter's, and Arabella's car was still at Karpata. "Okay, I'll borrow Erika's car and be right there."

She took two breaths. "Conklin, we need to keep this quiet. One of Ruth's girls called me. Whoever this guy is, Ruth has Wilbur out and pointed at him."

CHAPTER 26

RUTH DID BUSINESS in a sprawling one-story structure on a dead-end street, nestled in a quiet residential area in the center of Kralendijk. The wrong attention is terrible for any business, but more so for hers. She prided herself on being a good neighbor, so the residents turned a blind eye to her trade, as did local law enforcement, and she wanted to keep it that way.

Five minutes after leaving the YellowRock, I pulled Erika's car onto the graveled edge of the road in front of Ruth's establishment. Arabella had not yet arrived. I didn't wait for her and hurried across the yard to where Ruth stood at the front of the carport. Huddled in a group, ten feet behind her, a group of five young women in various types of undergarments and see-through robes held each other tight.

At the back of the carport, wearing only a pair of boxer shorts, Lester Jeffrey had his arm wrapped around the neck of a naked woman no more than twenty years old. Both breathed heavily. Red-faced, eyes wide with terror, a stream of blood trickled from the young girl's nose. Sweat glistened off her light brown skin and tears rolled down her cheeks.

"Let her go, asshole," Ruth said. "Now!"

Ruth pointed a pistol—*Wilbur* as she referred to it—at Lester. Arabella had told me previously that Ruth owned a handgun, but until today, I had never seen it. She also said that Ruth had never fired it.

Wilbur was a Ruger model P89 semiautomatic with a four-and-a-half-inch barrel, chambered in nine-millimeter, identical to the first weapon I ever owned. But unlike the one I had owned, this P89 was well used and poorly maintained. Its finish was scuffed and scratched with traces of powder visible on the end of the barrel, indicating a lack of cleaning. The hammer was cocked, and I had to assume a round was chambered and ready to fire. The lack of proper safety knowledge and handling techniques are the prime causes of accidental weapon discharges. I doubted Ruth had much, if any, firearms training.

"Ruth, be careful," I said.

She ignored me, keeping the pistol pointed at Lester. "I said now."

"Hey," Lester said, kissing the girl's ear. "We're just having some fun." The girl closed her eyes and sobbed as he rubbed one of her breasts.

"Let me handle this, Blaze," I said.

She snapped her head at me. "Back off." She kept the weapon's barrel pointed at Lester.

We stared at each other for a few seconds as her eyes narrowed even further. She turned back toward Lester and the girl. "This is your last chance." She adjusted her grip on the old weapon and took a step closer to them.

Lester tightened his arm around the girl's neck and positioned her between himself and Ruth, acting as if he were daring Ruth to fire.

The situation was escalating out of control, and I was about to take the weapon from Ruth when a truck door slammed. Arabella ran across the yard and stopped beside me, her head swiveling from Ruth to Lester, and back to me. She shook her head and mumbled some Dutch, which I didn't understand. Must be a lesson I hadn't gotten to yet.

"This is your last chance!" yelled Ruth.

I fanned my arm, encompassing the entire scene. "It's all yours, *Inspector.*"

Arabella took a deep breath, walked over to Ruth, and took Wilbur away from her, holding the barrel pointed down and away from Lester and the bystanders.

To Ruth, she said, "*Geef het aan mij.*"

Ruth stared as Arabella dropped the magazine into her left hand and jacked the live round out of the chamber, catching it in midair. She laid the weapon on the front stoop and placed the magazine and spare cartridge alongside it.

She pointed at the Ruger as she moved her gaze across the crowd. "Nobody touches this weapon." She took two steps toward Ruth. "*Niemand.*"

Ruth opened her mouth, but before she could utter a word, Arabella stepped to the carport toward Lester and the girl.

Lester smiled. "No harm done, Officer." He nuzzled the girl's hair. "Right, honey?"

Arabella grabbed Lester by the throat and gave him a side jab to the kidneys. His eyes widened, he moaned, then gasped for air. The girl squirmed out of his grasp and ran to the comfort of her coworkers.

Still holding Lester's throat, Arabella yelled something in Dutch and shoved him backward. He tripped over a bench and fell on his back, his head slamming against the concrete driveway. Arabella maintained her grasp on Lester's throat and fell to the floor with him, landing in a kneeling position.

Ruth and I made our way to the back of the carport.

Arabella put her face close to Lester's, sweat dripping off her forehead onto his cheeks. "I am sorry for your loss, Mr. Jeffrey." Her teeth clenched and her voice low and throaty, she sounded like a mix of Uma Thurman and Linda Hamilton. "But this is not a way to handle it." Lester's head jerked back as Arabella tightened her grip on his throat. "Understand?"

Lester scraped his cheek across the concrete floor as he tried to nod his approval the best he could. Pain, oxygen deprivation, embarrassment, or a combination of all three had turned his face beet red.

"When I let you up, you will go stand by your truck." Arabella took a couple deep breaths. "Do not make me ass kick you another time."

Lester took a breath. "Okay!"

Arabella let go of Lester's throat. The color returned to his face as he raised his head from the concrete, waiting for Arabella to move away. After a moment, she got to her feet, which allowed him to stand.

So much for *light duty*.

I offered a hand to Lester, but he refused my help, standing on his own. Surprising he could stand, considering he reeked of booze.

He thrust his chest toward Arabella. "What about my clothes?"

Arabella pointed at his truck. With a scowl and pursed lips, she said, "Go."

With his chest still thrust forward, Lester started walking to his truck. Arabella wiped her face with the sleeve of her shirt and sighed deeply as she straightened her holster and belt. My mouth may have been open; I wasn't sure. She ran her fingers through her hair and looked at me.

I was speechless.

She jerked her head at Lester. "You want to talk to him for me?" Her voice and demeanor back to normal. "I will talk to Ruth. If we can, I want to keep this unofficial."

"Agreed."

Ruth had already gathered the girls and gone inside. Arabella turned and walked into the building, leaving me standing in the yard. I shook my head and watched Lester walk across the yard, then made my way over to his truck.

I mimicked Lester's lean against the fender of Ericka's car, waiting for him to speak. Why wasn't I fishing and enjoying my retirement?

"I didn't mean any harm," Lester finally said. "That wacky Dutch broad was going to shoot me."

Which one? I wanted to ask but decided against it. I crossed my arms and let out a long, slow breath. Helping Lester wasn't my responsibility. I was ready to give up on the jerk and let him fend for himself. His treatment of Tiffany had been deplorable, and he'd displayed nothing but hostility toward me. I owed him nothing and could easily walk away from all of this, never giving it a second thought. Maybe teach him a lesson.

But I decided to stay and help him work through it. Tiffany would've wanted it that way—me being there in Lester's time of need. Considering I was partly to blame for her death, I owed her that much. And then some.

"Lester, why are you here?"

"I don't know." The sun burned through the clear, early, Caribbean sky. Lester rubbed the back of his neck, sweat beading on his forehead. "I couldn't sleep last night. All I could do was think about Tiff. I drove around and ended up here." He rubbed his face with both hands. "Lonely, I guess."

I wasn't buying it. Something didn't make sense. The maid said he hadn't used his bed the previous night. Plus, he stunk of stale alcohol. I figured he was well past his way to a bender, although he gave no outward signs of being intoxicated.

Other than assaulting a young girl, that is.

"Lester, this isn't a place you happen to find. It's not like there's a big neon sign out front. You must've asked someone for directions."

"Honestly, I was driving around and saw this girl having a cigarette on the porch." He pointed at Ruth's front porch. "We started talking, and she invited me in. That's pretty much it."

"Why was she bleeding?"

He didn't answer.

"Did you hit her?"

"No!" He shifted his weight. "She fell off the bed."

I had reason not to believe him. Interrogating hundreds of people, I had learned that a terse, negative response usually indicated a lie. Also, he wouldn't look me in the eyes, and I could tell his blink rate had increased, all indicators of stress.

"Why didn't you leave?"

"I was about to when that redheaded Dutch bitch pulled a pistol on me." He stepped away from the truck and turned to me. He scratched his nose. In some people, lying causes the capillaries in the tip of the nose to expand creating an itching sensation. "Hey, what's with that pistol, anyway? Where'd she get it?"

A gun conversation with Lester wasn't territory I wanted to cover. No need for him to know anything more about Wilbur than he already did. It bothered me he had seen the weapon, and I wasn't about to volunteer anything more. Luckily, Arabella walked out the front door and down the driveway to Lester's truck.

"Here." She handed Lester his clothes. "You should never come back here."

I put my hand on Lester's shoulder. "Maybe you should go back to your room and get some rest. I'll check on you later."

He brushed my hand away and took the clothes from Arabella. "Would she have shot me?"

Arabella put her hands on her hips. "Maybe, maybe not."

"Really?" Lester asked.

With her eyes wide, Arabella made a single distinct nod. I held back a laugh.

"Lester," I said. "I'll see you back at the resort." I opened the driver's-side door and motioned for him to get in. Although he smelled of alcohol, he hadn't slurred any words or appeared intoxicated. He seemed normal. Jerk-normal, anyway. The YellowRock was five minutes away, and I'd be right behind him. "Drive careful."

He stared at Arabella for a moment, before getting in his truck and driving away.

Arabella and I watched until he turned the first corner, disappearing down a side road. We were still looking down the street when she spoke. "Ruth said that he knocked on the door late last night. He was with Tinkerbell when—"

"Tinkerbell?"

"Yeah, Tinkerbell, Julieta's professional name." She rolled her eyes before continuing. "Early this morning, one of the girls heard crying from Julieta's room. When Ruth went to check, Julieta said Lester was trying some rough stuff, so Ruth asked him to leave. That's when he went crazy, and Ruth went for Wilbur."

"That's not the way Lester told it."

"I believe Ruth," she said, an edge on her voice.

"Me, too," I said. "Who called you?"

She shrugged. "I didn't ask. All the girls have my number in case of something like this. Ruth has told them to call me anytime. I'm glad someone called this time."

"How are you going to handle this?"

"Well." She took a breath. "I explained who Lester is and what has happened. Julieta feels sorry for him, so she will not be pressing any charges."

"*Sorry for him?* He molested and assaulted her."

"What can I say? She is a romantic. To press charges is up to her. But I am glad she is not."

Regardless of the prostitution angle, Julieta deserved better. Lester should be arrested, put into the system, and made to pay for his disregard of the law and his disrespect for her. However, the Dutch take pride in toting tolerance as a cultural trait. They even have a word for it. *Gedogen* means to take a lenient stance or turn a blind eye.

But it wasn't my island, and I wasn't in charge. That responsibility fell to Arabella and, deep down, I agreed with her plan.

"Nice job," I said.

Arabella smiled. *"Dank je."* She surveyed the few houses lining the dead-end street. "But I hope none of the neighbors will say anything." She tossed her hands up and let them fall to her side. "If Wilbur is found out, I cannot help Ruth."

"You know, someday, someone will get hurt with that gun of hers."

"Yes, but what can I do? She feels safe having it."

"You never told me why she calls it Wilbur. I know one of her clients gave it to her, some old politician years ago. But why *Wilbur*?"

She laughed. "The guy's dog was named Wilbur."

"Seriously?"

"To tell the truth, the gun may not fire. It has not been cleaned or oiled in many years, and the firing pin is worn down. Plus, all of the cartridges have rust on them." She laughed and held up four fingers. "Ruth only has four of them."

"Good thing," I said and put my arm around her. We slowly strolled toward her police truck. "I wish Lester hadn't seen that gun. Something's bothering me about him."

"Quit thinking so much. The guy is a jerk. A drunk jerk." She got in her truck and talked through the open window. "What did Tiffany ever see in him?"

"I don't know. My grandma always said that every crooked pot has a crooked lid."

Her eyebrows scrunched. "But would that not mean Tiffany was like Lester? I did not think that was the case."

"No, it means that there's someone for everyone, and that . . ." I didn't finish the explanation. Arabella was right. It was wrong to consider Tiffany as the crooked lid to Lester. She was nothing like him. "True, never mind."

Her voice barely above a whisper, Arabella asked, "Are you going to the morgue?"

I hesitated, then said, "I'll be there shortly." She started to pull away. "Hey, wait a minute." She locked the brakes and skidded in the gravel, dust and small rocks pelting my sandals and feet. "Right before you threw Lester to the ground, you said something in Dutch."

"I did?"

"Yeah, you did. What was it?"

A thin, sultry smile crept across her face. "That will be part of your next Dutch lesson." She honked the horn as she pulled away.

I slid into the driver's seat of Erika's car and stared at the steering wheel for a moment. No doubt about it, Lester Jeffrey was a strange bird and came across as a total jerk. I agreed with Arabella, and for the life of me, couldn't comprehend what Tiffany had seen in him.

Lester's lies didn't surprise me. My experience had taught me that most people in a similar situation would lie, especially when confronted.

What did surprise me, though, was his appearance at a whorehouse, less than twenty-four hours after his girlfriend's sudden death. Especially when he appeared *so* devastated.

CHAPTER 27

I PARKED ERIKA'S car in its usual spot, behind the YellowRock near the garbage dumpster. Unwinding myself from the cramped confines of the driver's seat, a stab of pain pierced my side, reminding me of the mugging several nights ago at this exact spot.

I closed the door and leaned against the side of the car. The back parking lot was a mixture of crushed coral rubble and gravel with the dumpster positioned at the lot's edge, alongside the building. Most of the time, especially after Erika leaves work, my Wrangler was the only vehicle parked in the back. The guests preferred parking in front, closer to their rooms.

Several street lamps and a light on the exterior of the YellowRock building provided substantial nighttime visibility in the front. In contrast, the rear lot didn't have lighting, and the shadows generated by the surrounding buildings enhanced the darkness. Several times in the past, I had considered installing security cameras on all sides of the YellowRock but hadn't yet made it a priority. I needed to rethink that decision.

There was nothing of value in the back. No access doors, no room entries, no expensive cars. Nothing a thief would consider worthy of the effort—or worth the risk of capture.

Not much daytime traffic in the back, so if the mugger left anything behind, it might still be here. I turned a full circle and decided

to walk the area using a strip-search method. In my head, I divided
the lot into four-foot-wide sections running from end to end and
walked each one, head down, churning over bits of gravel with my
feet. When I got to the end of one strip, I turned and walked down
the next one, slowly, taking thirty minutes to examine the entire lot.

Nothing.

I checked along the edge of the building and behind the dumpster.

Again, nothing.

I stood in the middle of the lot and slowly turned in a circle, stopping when my eyes landed on the dumpster. Pickup day was tomorrow, so anything thrown into it over the last week should still be there.

With the hot Caribbean sun beating down on them, dumpsters on
Bonaire became big, dirty, steel crockpots, smoldering their contents
into a smelly, nausea-inducing pile of sludge. A paradise only rats,
flies, and mosquitoes would call home.

And I was about to jump right in.

But there might be a better way.

I went to my toolshed and brought back a stepladder and a broom.
I placed the ladder alongside the dumpster, and half limped, half
stepped to the second rung. After a few painful breaths, I threw open
the lid, banging it against the side of the building. It didn't smell as
bad as I had feared, at least not at first. The stench grew more toxic as
the wind whipped through the garbage and lifted the odor into the
air, straight into my nostrils.

Climbing to the third rung, I used the handle of the broom to re-
arrange the contents, moving the smelly bags, hoping to find something—anything—out of the ordinary. With every stir, the stench
became more intense. My eyes watered, and I covered my mouth, almost tasting the smell on my tongue. A layer of muck seemed to coat
the back of my throat.

Most of the contents were garbage bags, removed from the rooms
by the maid staff during their regular cleanings, along with many

wrappers and cups deposited by people walking past. I preferred the passersby using my dumpster as opposed to the trash finding its way onto the ground, or worse, into the sea. There were lots of empty Bright bottles, which should've given me pause and some needed reflection, but didn't.

Despite the noxious smell and near overwhelming impulse to close the lid, I couldn't stop searching. After fifteen more minutes, ready to concede and surrender to the stench, I moved one step down the ladder. Just before stepping off the bottom rung, I noticed something lying on top of a garbage bag, positioned off to my left, halfway deep, wedged in the corner. All the thrashing I'd done must've uncovered it.

It was a plastic tube-and-bubble turkey baster. Not a big baster, maybe more of a chicken baster, if such a thing existed. The transparent plastic tube section seemed to be the same diameter as the hole in the Wrangler battery.

My first impulse was to photograph the baster, the other contents, the dumpster, the parking lot, and everything else in the vicinity. Then put the baster in a clear plastic bag, label and date it, then take it to the police. Better yet, call the cops and get forensics people over here to do the work. Keep the chain of evidence intact.

But the cops weren't concerned about my Wrangler sabotage and had made their apathy quite clear. I decided to keep the baster and see what I could learn from it. I leaned over the edge—legs pointing skyward—and reached deep. I stretched, almost falling in, my rib pulsing with pain, and eventually grabbed it.

Standing on the ladder, I studied the baster as a wave of recognition gradually overtook me.

Along the back wall of each unit at the YellowRock is a small, basic kitchenette. In the cabinet drawers are cooking utensils, plates, pans, and lots of other gadgets used to prepare small meals. Because items were damaged, stolen, broken, lost, and sometimes moved between rooms, Erika had used a black marker to label everything in each kitchenette with that unit's number.

Some rooms have items that seem out of place, things a guest wouldn't use on a Caribbean vacation. Large baking trays, corn-on-the-cob holders, and rolling pins came to mind. Several units had small turkey basters buried in the drawers.

The one in my hand had a black 5 written on it.

Holding it to the bright sky and keeping it level, a small amount of clear liquid pooled in the tube section. I put my nose to the open end and sniffed, but my nose was still filled with garbage stink.

I held it level, trying not to spill the liquid, as I took it upstairs to my kitchen. I set it upright in a glass and squatted level with the edge of the counter. Drumming my hand on the nearby stove, I watched the clear liquid pool in the bottom of the glass. Not much—a total of only a few drops—but it'd have to be enough.

I removed the baster and placed a small saucer over the top of the glass, hoping to contain any odor released by the liquid.

My pulse quickened. I punched a number into my cellphone.

"Richter," said the voice on the other end.

"Kevin, do you still have the old brake hoses?"

He didn't answer immediately. In my mind, I imagined his bewildered expression, the memory gears turning in his head.

"They should be in the dumpster out back," he said.

"Can I have them?" It meant another dive, but I needed those hoses.

Kevin hesitated, then said, "Sure." It sounded more like a question than a statement. He probably didn't have many folks asking for old parts. I told him I was on my way and disconnected.

Before heading out the door, I leaned over the glass, raised the saucer, and inhaled deeply.

Nothing.

CHAPTER 28

I WALKED DOWNSTAIRS to the office and laid Erika's car keys on her desk. Without an acknowledgment, she scooped them into her purse.

Richter's Garage was about a mile from the YellowRock, but I refused to ask Erika for a ride or to borrow her car again. Besides, a walk would do me some good—my bruised rib notwithstanding.

"Is everything okay at Ruth's?" she asked.

No point in asking her what she meant or how she knew. "Yes, Bella handled everything."

She peered at me over the rim of her glasses. "It is good she was there."

"It's always good when she's around."

She smiled. "Yes, it is . . . For you."

I turned and headed for the door. "I'm going to Richter's. Be back shortly."

"Again, you are leaving me with all the work?"

"Yes, but only for a few minutes."

"I can drive you. Then you can be back sooner. Or you can borrow my car again and can use more of my gas."

"I think I'll walk. I need the exercise."

"Okay. I'll stay here and do the work."

Another beautiful day on Bonaire, perfect for walking. I cut across the parking lot of an adjoining business, making my way to Richter's.

Small drops of sweat sprinkled the back of my T-shirt, and my side ached as I walked through the shop door, held open by a rusty old muffler. The makeshift doorstop was a poor replacement for Kevin's lack of air-conditioning.

Kevin stood behind the counter. "Here." He held up the old brake hoses.

"Thanks. I was worried that I'd have to dig them out."

"I was out having a smoke and raised the lid. They were lying right on top, so I grabbed them." He laid a handwritten invoice on the counter and used a pen to point at a line on the bottom. I took the pen, signed the invoice, and handed him a debit card.

He gave me a carbon copy of the invoice and processed the card. "The keys are in it. It is parked around back."

"I'm surprised you still had these." My body rattled, and I flinched as an air-driven tool of some kind in the shop area blurted out a soul-jarring blast. I waited for the noise to subside before continuing. "I was sure the police would've taken them."

Kevin shook his head. "They took some pictures. That is about it."

"Did they say anything about their investigation?"

He lit a cigarette, held his breath a moment, and blew smoke out his nose. "They looked the inside over and also at the brake hoses. I showed them the battery and the hole." He took another drag and talked as he exhaled. "It was strange."

"How so?"

"They asked if this could happen by accident, you know, poor maintenance or something like that. I said it was possible, but not likely." He folded his arms across his chest. "I do not know . . ."

"What?"

"They were not interested. It seemed like they thought it was simply an accident? I think they *wanted* it to be an accident."

My earlier conversations with Kevin, and what I recently found in my dumpster, convinced me of the sabotage. I didn't know if the cops were dragging their feet or if they just weren't convinced yet. I placed my hands on the counter and leaned toward Kevin. "Be honest with me. What do you think?"

Kevin took a deep breath. Above us, the ceiling fan mixed the stale air with brake dust, exhaust grime, and cigarette smoke. I coughed. None of it bothered Kevin.

Finally, he said, "If it was an accident or poor maintenance, it was a big coincidence." He crushed out his cigarette, shaking his head. "Besides, how can the hole be explained?"

"Thanks, Kevin." I slapped the rolled-up invoice in my hand, grabbed the hoses, and left.

CHAPTER 29

JAMES CALLED MY cell as I pulled into the lot at the YellowRock. "R, when will you be able to identify the body?"

"Are Tiffany's parents on their way?"

"I understand that our department contacted them. They are looking for a flight."

"I'd prefer they do the ID. Besides, it might be something they feel they should do anyway."

"We would like to do this as soon as possible." He paused a moment and took a breath. "Inspector Schleper would like you to do it."

I'd been with many family members during body identifications and had seen firsthand the pain and agony they went through. The crying; the quivering; the realization that the body under the blanket was indeed their loved one. Or once had been.

Now I'd be on that side of the table.

"When?" I asked.

"Anytime, but sooner would be better."

Jeez, so much for *Island Time*. I looked down the row of vehicles. Lester's truck sat in front of his unit, the seahorse on the tailgate staring back at me. Hopefully, he was sleeping off the alcohol. He needed to. "Alright, I'll be there in a few minutes. I'll call you when I'm on my way."

I went into the office, brake hoses in hand. Erika sprang to her feet as I headed for the stairs leading to my apartment.

"I have some things to talk with you about." She moved in front of the stairs, blocking my way, lips pursed, her demeanor more pointed than earlier.

"Not now, Erika." I tried to move around her, but she stepped in front of me.

"You have a business to run." She shoved a stack of papers into my gut. I grabbed them. If I hadn't, she'd have let go, and they would've scattered across the floor.

"I cannot do it all," she said, still blocking my path to the stairs.

I flung the papers toward my desk. Some of them separated mid-flight, floating gently to the floor, while the rest landed atop other desk clutter already collecting dust. "Erika, I have to go to the morgue and identify Tiffany's body." I let the statement hang for a moment. "Can't this wait?"

A tear slid down her cheek, and she bowed her head as she returned to her desk. Guilt overtook me. Holding back a tear of my own, I put a hand on one of her shoulders and gently squeezed. She covered my hand with one of hers and sighed.

"Also, please call the police station," I said. "See if you can find out when Tiffany's folks will arrive on the island. Let's put them up in a vacant unit."

"Yes," she said, her voice cracking and stuttering. "I will be happy to do that."

"Thanks," I said before climbing the stairs to my apartment.

In the kitchen, I grabbed a plate from the overhead cabinet and placed it on the counter next to the glass containing the liquid. Stretching one of the brake hoses out as close to straight as possible, I laid it on the plate, the ends hanging over the edges.

I turned the hose until the hole—the spot where the brake fluid had leaked out—was facing straight up. Before pouring the liquid onto the hose, I removed the saucer that covered the glass and took a whiff.

Still nothing.

I eased the glass over and allowed half of the liquid to settle onto the brake hose, several inches from the existing hole. I anticipated a hissing or smoky smell, but, to my surprise—and disappointment— nothing happened. As the liquid settled onto the hose, a small portion penetrated the rubber, but most of it spilled off onto the plate.

Now the waiting began. Kevin had mentioned the acid wouldn't eat through the hose right away, but he hadn't said how long it might take. Nor the amount of acid needed. My limited supply might not be enough. If it was even acid at all. I didn't know for sure.

After a few moments of staring at the hose, I conceded that it might take several hours for the acid—if it truly was acid—to eat through the rubber. Something along the lines of a watched pot of water never boiling.

If I were lucky, this experiment would prove my suspicion. If not, it would be back to square one. While the acid simmered on the brake hose, I reached for some artificial courage.

A Bright.

One hard swig and I tossed the empty bottle in the recycle bin.

I drank the second one slower, taking nearly thirty minutes to finish. I strolled out to the balcony, mindful of my pending trip to the morgue, and tried to enjoy every swig, watching boats cutting across the sea.

After draining the last drop, I dialed James's number. "On my way." He muttered an acknowledgment, but I ended the call, cutting him off mid-sentence. I leaned on the railing and took in the view across the street. I could've had another beer—or two—and sat for hours on the veranda, hypnotized by the cadence of the sea, its waves lapping against the shore.

But that would have to wait.

I set the empty on the railing and rubbed my eyes with the heels of my palms. Couldn't avoid my next obligation any longer.

Time to identify Tiffany's body.

CHAPTER 30

THE BONAIRE MORGUE was located on Kaya Soeur Bartola, across the street from one of the island's large grocery stores. A small, unimposing building attached to the main hospital, with only two main rooms. Most island tourists were probably unaware of its purpose. A morgue situated across the street from the entrance to a major grocery store. Only in the islands.

I parked on the street and made my way to the entrance. James stepped out of the front foyer, holding the door open. I went inside and let out a deep sigh.

"Let's get this over with," I said.

James was quiet.

The configuration of the main room lent itself to modest memorial services, where many of the island funerals began. After the ceremony, the body is slowly driven to the large church in the center of Kralendijk with the mourners walking behind or alongside in procession. I'd never attended one of these services but had witnessed several.

A podium stood in one corner, adorned with beer-barrel-sized pots overflowing with flowers and greenery. Several semicircular rows of chairs faced the front. As would be expected, scattered amidst the seating were several boxes of tissue. At least they'd be easy to find later when I needed them.

James led me to a man standing at the back of the room dressed in a white lab coat. He was Antillean, either native Bonairian or from Curacao, and no more than five and a half feet tall. His lab coat hung loosely on his gaunt frame and black eyeglasses dangled around his skinny, overly long neck. A name tag clipped to the pocket of his lab coat read *Ruud Thode*. James didn't introduce us and Thode remained quiet, keeping his head bowed, eyes averted. He opened a large metal door and motioned for James and me to follow him through into the second room.

It had been a long time since I'd been in the cold storage room of a morgue, and my attire of shorts and a T-shirt didn't insulate me against the near-freezing air. The shock of the first few seconds eventually wore off, and the thirty-seven-degree temperature began to feel refreshing.

The putrid scent of decaying flesh, like that of a working butcher shop, clung to the air. Death has a particular smell, and a new detective discovers it early. One trip to the morgue is all it takes, and once learned, it's never forgotten. This one stung my olfactory glands worse than usual. It'd been a long time.

The lighting was bright and reflected off pale white floor tile. Gurneys lined all four walls, each with a beige blanket covering a motionless corpse. Only the feet of the bodies were exposed, and from a single toe of each hung a yellow tag.

Same view as in other morgues.

We walked toward a solitary gurney on the far side of the room, set along the back wall. The echo of Thode's hard-soled shoes was eerily out of sequence with the muted strikes of my sandals. James and Thode pulled the gurney away from the wall and stood along one side, me on the other. A blanket covered Tiffany's body; a yellow tag hung from her toe. I ignored the stares of the other two men as they waited for my signal. A signal I wasn't sure I'd be able to give.

Finally, I gave James the okay. He hesitated a second before pulling back the blanket, exposing the upper half of Tiffany's chalk-white, naked body. I grabbed the sheet, so he couldn't pull it down past her shoulders. Modesty had always been important to Tiffany, and even in death, I wanted to preserve some level of dignity for her.

Seeing her lifeless body a second time was harder than the first. Harder than I could've imagined. Her eyes open but empty, staring past me, head tilted my way. Chills ran down my spine. My face flushed; my heart palpitated. I took a deep breath, composing myself, and looked at the ceiling. A mixture of grief and guilt consumed me.

Once again, the anger rose.

"R?" James said, his tone soft.

I nodded at James. Thode began pulling the blanket over her head.

"Wait," I said.

Thode hesitated.

"What is it?" James asked.

Using a finger, I rolled her head the other way, exposing the part of her neck closest to me. I leaned in and examined it.

"What are these bruises on her neck?" I asked James. He shrugged. "I can see there hasn't been an autopsy yet. How much investigation has there been?"

"We are waiting for the medical examiner to fly over from Curacao. He is expected sometime this afternoon." James assisted Thode in pulling the blanket back over Tiffany's face. "It is a drowning. How much investigation would you expect us to do?"

I glared at James but didn't respond.

Thode gave me a mild body check as he moved to the center of the gurney on my side and shoved it back into place. He exerted more force than needed and it bounced off the wall.

"Hey! . . . Gentle." I slid the gurney against the wall and laid my hand on the section of the blanket covering Tiffany's arm. I closed my eyes and remained silent for a moment.

James put one arm on my shoulder, I opened my eyes, and he extended his other arm toward the large metal door, signaling that it was time for me to leave. "We have dealt with many drownings. I am sure we can handle this one as well."

We walked through the metal door, back into the first room. I had acclimated to the cooler temperatures of the storage room, and the heat of the memorial room hit me like a blast furnace. We continued toward the exit.

I stopped at the door. "What do you think about those bruises?" I had suspicions but was curious what James thought. Or might say.

He shrugged and shook his head. "I do not know, but I am sure the medical examiner will be able to find the cause." He opened the door and gestured for me to walk out.

"Can I get a look at the autopsy report, assuming it happens?" I asked.

James rested his right hand on the handle of his service weapon and shifted his weight to one side, the leather gun belt pulling tight across his waist, groaning from the movement. "If it will make you happy, I will talk to Inspector Schleper."

"Thanks." I didn't walk out. "What if this wasn't a drowning?"

James scrunched his eyebrows at me. "R, it was a drowning. Do not make more of this than it is. I know you had feelings for this young lady, but scuba has risks. Especially solo diving. Sometimes people drown."

"Let me know when the autopsy is done." I didn't need a lecture from James on diving and turned to leave.

James placed a hand on my shoulder. "R, we still need your official statement."

I didn't say anything, just giving him the once-over from the corner of my eye. He removed his hand, exhaled, and shifted his weight to the other leg, one hand still on the handle of his weapon.

"All right," I said. "I'll stop by the station on my way home."

"Ask for Inspector Schleper."

CHAPTER 31

JAMES DEFINITELY HAD a different take on this than me. Or maybe he was instructed to parrot the department's standard line. I didn't know but needed to find out.

The police station was a mere four blocks down the street, but I headed in the other direction. Something still rattled in my head about Tiffany having drowned. Unable to pinpoint what nagged me, I hoped to talk to someone more adept with the subject matter. Schleper wanted a statement immediately, but I didn't care. Not right now, anyway.

Arabella had told me the cops sent Tiffany's gear to Island Divers, one of the larger dive establishments on the island. If Schleper's team suspected drowning, they'd need to investigate and document the proper operation of Tiffany's scuba equipment. Island Divers had received top rankings in multiple customer surveys and five-star ratings by industry and certification agencies. The repair staff at Island Divers was the most qualified on the island.

Tiffany had dived with Erika's nephew, Rulio, who worked as a dive master for Island Divers. I called him and, reluctantly, he agreed to meet and discuss what they discovered. Not only was Rulio a certified dive master, but he also worked on the island's EMT squad. Trained in advanced underwater search and rescue, he had recovered the bodies of several drowning victims.

Island Divers was on the property of Captain John's Cove, the most upscale resort on the island, considered by many as the "Ritz-Carlton" of Bonaire. Rulio had suggested we meet at one of the resort's bars, The Green Iguana.

I pulled into the parking lot and heard the band, a local steel drum quartet, pinging out a familiar melody. Signs, carved from driftwood and painted in fluorescent colors, hung on poles along the sidewalks, helping guide would-be customers toward the bar. I ignored them. I'd been there before and knew where to go.

The maze of picturesque, palm-tree-lined sidewalks snaking through the property all culminated at The Green Iguana. It was an extensive, open-air joint offering a superb view of the Bonaire sunset. The place was spotless and smelled of coconut. Live music played every day, starting in the afternoon and continuing until the last tourist opted for bed and staggered back to their room. The bartenders were attractive youngsters, most of them native Bonairian, capable of concocting any of the foo-foo island drinks. They dressed in matching, brightly colored shirts and the women wore flower petals in their hair. Small bamboo umbrellas decorated the daily drink specials, most of which cost the same amount as an entire lunch at the Coral Reef Cafe. Of all the establishments on Bonaire, The Green Iguana was the epitome of a quintessential Caribbean Cantina.

Maybe that's why I despised the place so much.

Rulio sat at the end of the bar, nursing what appeared to be an iced tea, and gave me a friendly pat on the back as I sat on the stool next to him. He wore knee-length, loose-fitting, red swim trunks and a blue polo with his first name embroidered on the upper left breast. Flip-flops and sunglasses rounded out the basic "uniform" for dive masters working at Island Divers. Erika had mentioned previously that he was twenty-six years old. I'd spoken with him several times in the office of the YellowRock, and he came across very experienced and mature for his age.

The bartender, Nancy, according to the tag on her shirt, politely asked what she could get me. I ordered a Bright, and she served it with a lime wedge sticking out the top of the bottle. I smiled and pushed the lime down the neck into the beer.

Rulio spun himself on the stool to face me, and as he did, I caught a glimpse of the artwork just below the hem of his shorts. Rulio had a tattoo of Bonaire on his right thigh, a representation of the island any cartographer would be proud to claim. It had garnered significant attention, almost to the point of folklore. Even the island newspaper did a story about it. Rulio showed off the tattoo regularly and seemed to design his entire wardrobe around it.

"Before we talk," Rulio said, "you have to promise again that you will not tell anyone about this conversation."

"As I said on the phone, I need to know. I won't say anything."

"Thanks, I appreciate that."

"I can't afford to throw my friends under the bus." I chuckled. "Recently, I was told I don't have many friends."

"I don't understand."

I waved it off. "It's nothing. Please go on."

"Okay, but understand, we have sent this report to the police. They called and talked to my manager about it this morning. What I am telling you, the police already know."

"Understood. What do you have?"

He sipped his tea. "Not much. The gear was in excellent working condition and may have been brand new. The regulator still had replaceable factory parts in it. If it had ever been serviced, those would have been replaced."

I took a swig of beer, remembering my thought of price tags on Tiffany's gear. "Yeah, that sounds about right."

"The outside of the regulator was a little scratched, but that may have been caused by how the police handled it. They threw everything in a plastic tote and sent it to us." He pulled out his phone and scrolled through some pictures. "I took pictures if you want to look." He handed me his phone.

I studied each one as I sipped my beer. There were pictures of the tank and valve, the dive computer and its displays, and a few of her wetsuit, the one with the pink accents. He had numerous shots of the disassembled regulator, with its parts and some miscellaneous tools scattered on a workbench. For all I knew, it could've been random parts to a rocket ship or an electric toaster. To me, anything mechanical, be it cars or regulators, was far beyond my comprehension.

"What about the air?"

"We tested it before taking off the tank valve. It read as good air, no CO_2, moisture, or contaminants."

"Bad air would've been too easy."

"One thing, though," he said. "Water was slipping around the regulator diaphragm a little, causing a slight mist in the air she breathed. Maybe not a big issue, but in the right—or wrong—person it could cause a larynx spasm."

"What does that mean?"

"It's a reflex. The larynx spasms as water enters the throat and closes. Then, any water in the lungs is blocked from getting out."

"I assume air would be blocked from going *in* as well."

"Yes, that is the real problem."

I shook my head. "I've never heard of that."

"It is called dry drowning. If I understand correctly, it is a hereditary or genetics thing. Does not happen to everyone."

"Can this be seen on an autopsy?"

He shrugged.

I leaned back in the stool. "Not sure what I'm looking for, but you're saying her gear was working well."

"The larynx spasm would need to be identified by a doctor, but other than that, yes, the gear was good. I do not believe it to be the source of her drowning."

"So, what would cause her to drown?"

"You realize that, in a classic case of drowning, or dive injury, there's a triggering event, something that causes panic in the diver."

"Something unexpected happens."

"Exactly, like a flooded mask. The diver panics, and does something wrong, like heading for the surface."

An image of Tiffany's partially flooded mask and how calmly she had cleared it during our dive at Tori's Reef came to mind. Then I pictured Lester's bloody nose and his attempted jet toward the surface. The same type of event handled differently by two different divers. It would've taken a massive triggering event to panic Tiffany to the point of drowning.

I didn't buy it.

Neither of us spoke for a bit. The steel band played on, and a few tourists splashed in the nearby pool. It bewildered me why people came to a tropical island, with the Caribbean Sea at their doorstep, and spent time in a chlorine-filled pool.

"I don't understand how this happened," Rulio said. "When I took her diving, she seemed confident, especially for a vacation diver. Very comfortable in the water."

Rulio would know. Being a working dive master, he saw all levels of experience and diver capabilities. "Yes, she was. I thought so, too."

"Where was her dive buddy? What's their story?"

I hesitated but decided he should know. It might help with his analysis and how he answered further questions. "She was solo diving."

"What? How was that allowed?" he asked. "She was good, but I could tell she was not experienced enough for solo diving."

"No one knew about it." This would haunt me forever. "She went off on her own."

"That is sad. So preventable."

"Yes, it was."

"Can I ask who found her?"

"I did."

"How deep?"

I paused a moment. "What do you mean?"

"What depth did you find her at?"

"I found her on the shore."

"What?"

"Yeah, lying on her side along the coral rubble, north of the Karpata entry point."

He stared back, ran his tongue across the inside of his cheek.

I leaned closer to him. "What are you thinking?"

"I'm trying to understand. You found her soon after she drowned, correct?"

"That's right."

"Then how did she end up on shore?"

The gears in my head were clicking. Something was forming, but I didn't yet know what.

Rulio continued. "I'm sorry. You see, drowning victims always sink. The water fills their lungs, and they sink to the bottom—"

"Yes, now I remember," I said. The gears quit clicking and had stopped on the body. That was it. Drowning victims don't float, at least not initially.

"They come to the surface after the gases from the decomposition process bloats their cells," he said.

"Right and that takes . . . how long?"

He shrugged. "Usually from twenty-four to forty-eight hours. Depends on several things."

I took a swig of beer and sat for a moment. "She could've drowned near shore."

He shook his head and half smiled. "It has been my experience that not many people drown when the water is shallow enough to stand up." His smile disappeared. "Besides, the waves would have to be very strong to push her up on the rubble and keep her there. I don't believe they were that day."

"You said the regulator was scratched. That could've happened from dragging it along the coral and rocks."

"Maybe, but we think the police accidentally did that."

I took Rulio's phone and scrolled through the pictures, quickly finding the one I wanted.

"There." I pointed at the photo showing the side of Tiffany's wetsuit. I enlarged the photo and centered it on her right thigh. The pink accent running along the leg portion was scuffed and possibly torn. It was difficult to tell. "Does that look like a scuff and tear to you?"

Rulio studied the picture, enlarging and shrinking it several times. "Yes, maybe so."

"I think someone dragged her out of the water."

"You mean someone else found her?"

I said nothing and took a swig of beer.

"If so, why would they not report it to the police?" His eyes bulged. "Are you saying this was not an accident?"

"Maybe, maybe not." I patted him on the shoulder. "But you don't know that, okay?"

"Do you think the police know?"

I finished my beer and sat the empty on the bar.

"Yeah, I think they do."

CHAPTER 32

I PARKED ALONG the street in front of the police station and got out of the Wrangler. A car horn beeped, and Arabella pulled alongside me with her window down.

"Everything okay at Ruth's?" I asked.

"It will be fine. Nothing got reported, so we are clear."

Allowing Lester off the hook for assaulting Julieta, the young girl at Ruth's place, still gnawed me. But a report and investigation would nail Ruth for having a weapon and implicate Arabella for being complicit.

Arabella rubbed her temple. "But my head is hurting a little."

"How 'bout I cook dinner for you tonight?" I gestured toward the police building. "But right now, I have to talk to Schleper."

"Dinner sounds good." She bit her lower lip and swiveled her head from side to side. In a low voice, she said, "Be careful with Schleper."

"Thanks." We exchanged waves, and I entered the building.

A female officer sat behind the reception desk. In true island fashion, it took her a few moments to acknowledge me. "Can I help you, sir?"

"I'd like to see Inspector Schleper. I'm Roscoe Conklin."

She picked up a phone, punched a few numbers, and spoke Papiamentu into the handset. All I recognized was my name.

She hung up the phone. "The inspector will be out soon."

Three dilapidated plastic chairs that looked as though they had spent most of their lives in an old, inner-city laundromat lined the outside wall. One was yellow, one was orange, and one was blue. I chose the blue one. In the corner, a few old magazines and an empty coffeepot lay on a small table. A single fan moved the hot, stale air around the room doing little to prevent the sweat pooling on my brow.

A man appeared from a hallway behind the front desk and spoke to the female officer, who nodded and pointed in my direction. The man walked toward me, extending his hand as he approached. His shoes punched out a perfect four-beat cadence on the tile floor.

"Mr. Conklin, I am Inspector Schleper. Thank you for stopping by."

We shook hands. He wore a red tie and his long-sleeved, white shirt sported police markings. We stood eye to eye, but he was a few pounds lighter than me and maybe ten years younger. He had broad shoulders, and his biceps flexed as we shook hands. His haircut was paramilitary, "high and tight" as it's called.

"Glad to help," I said. "Please, call me R."

"Follow me, Mr. Conklin."

Schleper led me past the reception desk, down a short hallway, to a small room labeled Interview Room 1. I'd spent countless hours in similar rooms. The walls were beige, and the gray table sitting in the center could've come from the Rockford Police Department. Schleper plopped into a chair. Behind him, an old computer workstation sat idle on a wooden desk. A clear, plastic dust-cover laid over the mouse, monitor, and keyboard, and, judging by the thick layer of dust, hadn't been used in years. Money well spent on the dust protector.

Schleper motioned for me to have a seat at the table across from him. His chair had wheels, and he rolled over, switched on a corner fan, and returned.

A laptop computer lay closed on the table, and above it, a manila folder. Schleper opened the folder and positioned several sheets of paper across his side of the table. He gnawed on a pencil and didn't say anything as his eyes moved from sheet to sheet. I leaned back and crossed my legs, not sure how long this would take. The chairs in these rooms were designed to keep the occupant off balance and uncomfortable.

Kudos to the designers. They did their jobs well.

"So, Mr. Conklin, you found the body. Is that correct?" He began scribbling notes on a sheet of paper.

"Yes." I had decided to answer his questions as tersely as possible and not volunteer any additional information, at least not initially.

"In your own words, please describe how you came to find the body and its condition."

I took him through the entire event. He didn't ask any questions or interrupt, and as I talked, he continued to write. By the time I finished, my mouth was dry, and my T-shirt stuck to my back. The only sound was the predictable click of the oscillating fan.

Having filled the front side of one piece of paper, Schleper turned it over. "Your opinion is that she drowned. Is that correct?" His head hung down, toward his notes, but his eyes eased up, meeting mine.

"Looked that way to me. But I'm not an M.E. An autopsy would verify."

"Thank you for that opinion. Rest assured, I am fully aware of your qualifications and experience." He leaned back in the chair, hands resting on his stomach. He stared at me and rocked. "This is my investigation, Mr. Conklin, and we need some information, please, not commentary."

I returned his stare, but my chair wouldn't lean back or rock. "I told you what happened."

"We appreciate that."

"I have some questions for you."

He leaned forward, pointed his pencil at me. "Mr. Conklin, I will ask the questions."

"Tiffany was a longtime friend of mine."

"We are aware of that."

"Has her dive gear been checked out?"

"We are waiting for the report from the team examining the equipment."

I stared into his eyes. He stared back and didn't appear to know that I had caught him in a lie. "Explain how she ended up on shore if she drowned."

"Mr. Conklin—"

"Wouldn't she be underwater for at least twenty-four hours? Someone dragged her there. How is that an accidental drowning?"

"I have to warn you, Mr. Conklin, not to interfere with our investigation."

"Investigation? Do you really do investigations at this office? You haven't even tried to explain something as simple as the sabotage to my Wrangler. You know, the sabotage that put one of your officers in the hospital? Isn't that important—"

"Mr. Conklin!"

I wasn't about to let up. "You can't determine lung hemorrhaging or a larynx spasm unless you do an autopsy."

He shot out of his chair. With one hand on the table, he steadied himself and leaned as far into me as possible. With his other hand, he pointed a finger at me. "Stop these questions." Sweat dripped off his nose onto my cheek. "I do not need you compromising our work." After a moment, he sat back in the chair and glanced at his notes before facing me. "Besides, Mr. Conklin, you are retired." A thin smile worked its way across his face. "Go spend time at the beach."

I stayed seated, bit my lower lip, and counted to ten. "You done?"

Schleper straightened, repositioned his tie. "Yes, I am finished. If you are."

I slammed my hands on the arms of the chair, stood up, and hoped he'd respond in some outlandish fashion. But he didn't. He just continued to scribble his notes. He wrote small and flat, making it difficult for me to read. But at this point, I didn't care. There was more to say, ask, and talk about, but nothing civilized came to mind. The laptop remained closed and still sat near the edge of the table.

Arabella was right. Schleper was a prize-winning jerk.

Then, for some unknown reason, I considered the situation in reverse. If someone were poking his nose into my investigation and insinuating some level of ineptness, I might become a jerk, too. Had Schleper seen me as some big-city cop, proclaiming myself a know-it-all and inferring the small-town force couldn't do their jobs?

I shook my head and walked to the door.

"One more thing, Mr. Conklin," Schleper said before I left the room. "I have instructed Officer De Groot not to speak with you regarding this investigation."

CHAPTER 33

IT HAD BEEN a long day, but there was still time to drive to Karpata. If someone had been working the snack shop, they might have seen or heard something. I wasn't sure if the police had been there yet, so I called Arabella to ask, but the call went to voicemail.

Years ago, I had learned a little about drowning from the case in Rockford. Determining a drowning to be anything but an accidental death is difficult, given the nature of where a drowning occurs. Short of physical wounds on her body or a possible eyewitness, proving an unknown assailant had killed Tiffany would be an investigative challenge.

Fifteen minutes after my conversation with Schleper, I pulled into the parking lot at Karpata and walked toward Cado Snack hoping to find such a witness.

The sliding window was still open.

"Hi," I said, poking my head through the window, into the building.

The inside was small, I guessed twelve feet by ten feet, and didn't have electrical lighting. Ambient sunlight sneaking in through the window, along with the open back door, kept the area from being pitch dark. Shelves, stocked with packaged snacks and cans of beverages, lined one wall. Inside, the air was nearly motionless, stale, and hotter than outside. The only ventilation was a slight breeze flowing from the back door to the window. I didn't see a chair, stool, or any place to sit.

A short, stubby woman standing next to an ice cooler dried her hands on a damp towel. Her clothes, at least two sizes too small, had random tears and dirt smudges. She wore pants and a sweat-soaked long-sleeved shirt. Hard work, many cleanings, and lots of sun had faded the colors over the years. Perspiration reflected off her forehead as she stepped to the window, smiling, and greeted me.

"Hello. What can I get you?" Her voice was cheery with a heavy accent.

"A water, please?"

"Yes . . ." She reached down and retrieved a bottle of water from the cooler, bits of ice and water dripping onto the floor. She set it on a shelf that extended through the window. "Two dollars, please."

I paid her, opened the bottle, and took a swig. "My name is Roscoe Conklin, what's yours?"

"Malfena Cado."

"So, Malfena, you the owner?"

She nodded. "Yes, me and my husband, Ludson."

My Wrangler was the only vehicle in the lot.

"Slow day?" I asked.

"Not so much earlier. Now, yes. But it is late. Almost closing time." She removed the condiments, napkins, and other items from the counter and stacked them neatly on a shelf along one wall.

"Hey," I said, purposefully raising my eyebrows. "Didn't someone drown here the other day?"

"Yes, a young woman." She stopped what she was doing and shook her head. "Very sad."

"Yeah, it is." She went back to packing things up. "Were you here when it happened?"

She continued to work. "The drowning? Yes, I was here."

Bingo!

"What happened? Did you call the police?" She didn't answer, continuing to pack items into the cooler that she'd take with her when she left. I sipped the water, glancing around, acting as if I had nothing but time. "How long have you and your husband been the owners?"

"We opened one year ago."

"I'll bet the drowning is the most exciting thing to happen since you opened."

"Sure." She turned and met my eyes. "If you think a young girl drowning is exciting."

I bit my lower lip. Maybe the direct approach would be better. "Malfena, I—"

"Mr. Roscoe, I know who you are." She set the fully packed cooler near the rear door. "Just ask me what you want to know."

"You know me?"

"Ludson and I live in the next house to Erika. I meet you once at your office when I stop to see Erika."

Damn small island. I swore Erika was related to half the people on Bonaire and friends with everyone else. I couldn't possibly remember everyone. At least the air was clear between Malfena and me.

"I'm sorry. Do you mind if I ask you some questions? The woman who drowned, Tiffany, was a close friend of mine."

"Yes, I know. Me and Erika, we talk about it."

"I'm sure the police already asked you some of these questions."

She shook her head. "No, the police ask me nothing." She placed her hands on her hips, closed her eyes for a moment, and took a couple of deep breaths. "You can ask me what you want." She opened her eyes.

"You know I found the body."

"Yes, Erika tell me."

"By the time I got here, you were closed for the night."

"Yes, we have no electricity. We close and are gone before darkness."

Tiffany was dead by dark. If Malfena was here, she had to have seen something. "Please tell me what you did the last two hours you were open."

"I have lots of customers early in the day, but it slows down in the afternoon. I sell mostly soda, water, and chips and candy. And some hot dogs."

"The customers, any of them wearing gear with lots of pink on it?"

"My customers usually don't have on scuba gear. They come to me after they scuba dive and changed into clothes by their trucks."

"Okay, how about the divers walking past your window, headed to the stairs? Any of them have pink on?"

"Mr. Roscoe," she said shaking her head, "the diver people have all colors. I am sorry."

"Okay, I understand. Please go on."

"After I close, Ludson picks me up, and we drive home together. I not have a car." She laughed. "I not even have a driver license."

I smiled. "What time did Ludson pick you up that night?"

"I know Ludson will be late that night, so I take my time cleaning up. After I close, he still not here."

"Do you know what time that was?"

"No. I just know Ludson is late. So, I wait and rest in this hammock." She walked out the rear door to the side of the building. I walked around and met her in a small gravel patio area. A hammock swung in the breeze between two palm trees, near the edge of the cliff overlooking the water. A thatched wall, made of palm leaves and cactus, separated the stairs leading to the water from the patio. It also separated it from the parking lot. A person could be swinging in this hammock and never see anyone in the parking lot or on the stairs.

Of course, it worked the other way around, too.

"Did you see anything strange?"

"No. I fall asleep in the hammock right away. The breeze was nice, and I love the sound of the ocean."

"How long were you asleep?"

"I wake up right before Ludson come to get me. That was after darkness."

"Before you left, you didn't look at the sea, notice her having a problem or anything?"

"No, I am sorry. It was close to dark and seeing anything on the shore or in the water from here would not be easy. It gets dark dark."

Many of the locals repeat words. The sky is blue blue, and the parking lot is full full. Slow is poco poco. At first, I thought everyone on the island had a strange, localized form of stutter but soon learned it's their way of placing emphasis.

"Did you hear anything?" I asked.

She shook her head. "No."

Malfena wasn't much help, but maybe there wasn't any information to be had. I ran my hand over my face. "Well, that's about it. Thanks for your time." I looked down the street. "So Ludson will be picking you up soon, huh?"

"Yes, he will be here any minute."

"You sure you're okay here alone till Ludson arrives?"

"Yes, I will be fine," she called, walking away from me. After a few steps, she stopped and turned around. Her eyebrows scrunched, confusion on her face. "Mr. Roscoe, I thought of something. I did not just wake up that day."

I took a step closer to her. "You didn't?"

"No. Something woke me up." Her gaze fixed over my right shoulder, at a far distant point.

I took another step closer. "What do you mean something *woke* you up?"

"Yes, I remember now." She tapped her index finger on her chin. "I was asleep. Then I woke up from a noise."

"What kind of noise?"

"I think a car engine. I thought it to be Ludson, so I get out of the hammock and start walking to the building. I see a white truck go by." She paused and stared at me a moment. "Ludson has a black truck."

"Did you get a look at the driver?"

"Oh, no. It was already driving away. I only saw the back of it."

"Was it a rental?"

"Yes, it was."

"You sure?"

"Positive. It have a seahorse painted on the back."

CHAPTER 34

ABBY'S SEASIDE TRUCK Rental occupied the end unit of a side-by-side storefront building, located on the outside perimeter of the airport parking lot, housing a string of vehicle rental agencies. A service window at each business separated the employees on the inside with the customers on the outside. By the time I stepped up to the building, the young girl working at Abby's already peered out the opening.

"May I help you?" she asked. Her name tag read *Abby*, but she couldn't have been more than sixteen or seventeen years old—too young to be the owner. She was native Bonairian with dark brown eyes and wore a simple gold cross and chain around her neck. Her dark hair flowed over a pink sun visor. Hiding the upper portion of her white capris, an untucked red tank-top with a Nike swoosh draped almost to her knees. She was sockless and wore white, low-cut Converse tennis shoes.

"Abby?"

"That's me."

I smiled. "You the owner?"

She shook her head. "No, my grandfather is the owner. He named the business after me, though."

"Well, I have a few questions."

She raised her eyebrows. "Well, I have a few answers."

Touché. I liked this kid. Behind me, on the other side of the terminal, jet engines revved, and a Boeing aircraft began its takeoff roll down the runway.

"Your agency has the trucks with the painted sea creatures on the tailgate, correct?"

"Yes."

"How many do you have with a seahorse?"

"Three."

"You sure? That was a quick answer."

She bobbed her head back and forth. "I'm sure." She smiled and raised her chin slightly. "I do all the paintings."

"Nice job. They're good."

"Thanks. Why do you ask?"

"A friend of mine—"

"I don't have any available right now. Two are rented out, and one is in the repair shop."

"So only two driving around the island right now?"

"Yes, just the two."

"Any chance you could tell me where the renters are staying?"

"I'm sorry, but I can't."

"It'd help me out a lot. I'm not going to bother anyone and will only take a few pictures of your beautiful artwork."

"I'd like to help you, but I can't. Sorry."

One call to Arabella and she'd get all the information I needed.

"Okay, thanks." I turned to leave but stopped and turned back. Before Abby slid the window shut, I said, "By the way, your English is good."

She smiled and blushed. "Yeah, when my sister and I were young, we watched a lot of the Disney Channel. I guess it rubbed off."

"Imagine that."

CHAPTER 35

As I drove back from Abby's Seaside Truck Rental, another call to Arabella went to voicemail. I stormed into the office, grabbed my desk phone, and dialed her number, thinking she might answer a call from the office. No such luck. Voicemail, again.

My rib throbbed, and I leaned back and took a few deep breaths.

Erika came over and handed me a bottle of water. "Well?" she asked. "Are you going to tell me about Mr. Jeffrey's truck?"

I winced, repositioning, trying to alleviate the rib pain.

"You need to see a doctor," Erika said.

"Probably." I opened the water and drained half of it in one gulp. "What are you talking about? 'Mr. Jeffrey's truck?'"

She smacked her arms on the table and laid her glasses on a stack of papers. "Malfena called me as soon as you left Karpata. She lives in my neighborhood. You've met her."

I sighed. "Yeah, I know."

"Well, when she mentioned a white truck with a seahorse, I thought of Mr. Jeffrey. She said it looked important to you."

"Maybe. But don't say anything. I have to talk to the police."

"Of course. Who would I say something to?"

"Yeah, right. Probably half the island."

She smiled. A rarity. "Not quite half."

I sat in my desk chair and smiled to myself. "Isn't it time for you to leave for the night?"

"Yes, it is." She stood and stretched her back. "Oh, and I saw Mandy go to the beach. You should go and make an introduction."

She was right, but, at the moment, I didn't have the energy. "I'll see you tomorrow."

* * *

In my apartment, I popped open a Bright and stood in the middle of the room, staring at the phone, willing Arabella to call. No matter how hard I concentrated, neither the landline nor my cell rang. For backup, I grabbed another beer and walked out on the veranda.

Halfway through the second beer, my intense focus paid off.

"You called?" Arabella asked, after I answered my cell.

I told her what I had discovered from Malfena.

"*Je bent gek,*" she said. My Dutch was nearly as bad as my Papiamento, but the rough translation was something like *that's crazy*. Then she said, "I am on my way."

"Bring some food. I didn't cook."

"See you soon."

My cell rang again the instant Arabella hung up.

Chuck. "Hey, R," he said, "remember how we've always talked about landing on the road out by Spelonk Lighthouse?"

"What are you talking about?"

"I have a job, and it involves landing on that road."

"What kind of job?"

"Flying."

I closed my eyes and pinched the bridge of my nose. "I figured that. But why land there? Besides, you're not a bush pilot. How many off-airport landings have you ever done?"

"That's where the client wants to be picked up." When he continued, his voice sounded meeker, less confident. "It shouldn't be *too* tough. That's why I have the Tundras."

With everything percolating through my mind, this wasn't making any sense. I rested my head in my hand and leaned back in my lounge chair. I knew better than to ask the next question but did anyway. "Why not pick them up at the airport?"

"Don't know and I didn't ask. Ten thousand dollars keeps my mouth shut."

"Ten thousand dollars?"

Chuck giggled. "Yeah. This guy is paying me ten big ones to pick him up at Spelonk and fly him to Venezuela."

I sighed. "Think about it. Doesn't that sound a little fishy?"

"Hey, ten grand is ten grand. This trip is a cash cow. It's only about sixty miles, one way."

"One way is right. One way to the pen. Or maybe worse."

He paused a moment. "You want to go along?"

"Not even for a million bucks. Besides, if I'm in jail, who'll send you postcards?" I took a deep breath. "Think carefully about this. Who's the client, anyway?"

"Some guy I met at the bar a few nights ago. He wants to do this in a couple of days, maybe Friday. He's going to call and give me more info later."

"Who was this guy?"

"Don't know. Never seen him before."

"What'd he look like?"

"Pretty average, I guess. A little shorter than me . . . long blondish hair . . . sunglasses . . . hell, I don't know. I don't pay attention to guys."

"What color eyes?"

"I just said he had on sunglasses."

"How'd he find you?"

"Not sure, exactly. Maybe he saw one of my cards. Or he asked Jan."

"Did you ask him why he wants to do this?"

Chuck exhaled into the phone. "Well, *Mr. Detective with a thousand questions*, like I said, ten grand—"

"I know, I know. Ten grand is ten grand."

Arabella came into the apartment carrying two brown paper bags. "Do me a favor, call me before you do this. Don't go until you talk to me again, okay?"

"Alright already. I'll call before I go. Hey, one other thing."

"Yeah?"

"My neighbor said that the cops were looking for me."

I sighed. "What'd you do now?"

"I don't know." He paused. "Seriously, I have no idea. But if I get in a jam, I'm calling you."

"I'd expect no less." I hung up.

Arabella tossed me a small brown paper bag. Based on the smell and the grease spots soaking into the paper, I assumed it to be a burger and fries from the food truck near the police station, one of her favorite joints. Not good enough to pass for a Five Guys or an In-N-Out burger, but, in my opinion, the best on the island.

Watching her pull the burger and fries out of the bag, I almost questioned the healthiness of her menu choice but decided against it. Regardless of her diet, she was healthy. Much more so than me.

She propped herself against the railing with her meal and a Bright. "Who was that?" she asked as she squeezed mayonnaise onto her fries.

"Chuck," I said with a mouth full of burger.

She closed her eyes and paused a moment, then said, *"Ook dat nog."* Translation: "That's all I need."

"He says the cops are looking for him."

She shrugged. "I know nothing of that."

No point in telling her about Chuck's plan and ratting him out to the fuzz. Besides, maybe I could still talk him out of it. Or maybe "fix" his plane so it wouldn't start. Anything to stop him.

"Any news from Rockford?" she asked.

"Nothing. I think they're stonewalling me."

"What do you want to do?"

Beer sometimes helped me think. Not always, but sometimes. I took a sip.

"According to Abby's Truck Rental, there are only two seahorse trucks rented right now."

She stopped mid-chew. "Nice work, Detective."

I raised my beer bottle. "I have my moments." I leaned back in the lounger. "Lester was at Karpata. He had to be. No way the other seahorse truck just *happened* to be at Karpata the same time as Tiffany."

Arabella bit her upper lip and took a deep breath. She was quiet for a moment, then said, "We need to question Mr. Jeffrey."

In unison, we took a gander at the front parking lot. No sign of Lester's truck.

"We need to know who the driver of the other truck is. Rule them out," I said.

"I will get that information."

"Soon?"

"A soon as I am able." She munched a couple of fries. "Lester was spending time with Mandy, correct? Is that an issue?"

I snapped my fingers. "Hey, Erika said that Mandy was at the beach."

Arabella turned and looked across the street. "Well, the only person on the beach is some guy practicing karate."

I peeked over the railing. Tough to tell from this distance, but Karate Guy resembled the same guy I bumped into coming out of Vinny's the other night.

Mister Freckle Eye.

But Arabella was correct; no one else on the beach.

"Now what?" she asked and walked to the edge of the lounger, her eyes moving across my body.

CHAPTER 36

I WOKE EARLY, which for a retired guy living on a tropical island, meant sometime before nine in the morning, but never before eight. Except on run days with Arabella, which implied seven o'clock or earlier. Thankfully, this wasn't one of those days.

Before retiring, I'd never slept well. Bad dreams kept me tossing and turning all night. On the rare occasion I managed some sleep, the phone would ring in the early morning hours, jolting me from slumber, the person on the other end describing the next nightmare.

No nightmares on Bonaire. At least, not until recently, that is.

The photo labeled SCENE was open on my computer. A glass of Diet Coke with most of the ice melted sat next to the keyboard, along with half of a microwaved apple donut. I hadn't touched either for at least twenty minutes.

The picture of the blood-circled classified ad was enlarged two hundred percent. The increased size didn't reveal any hidden clues, but the larger letters made it easier for me to read. I had memorized it earlier, though. Not hard to do. *Four-wheel drive for sale. Call Bill.* My intense staring hadn't inspired an "Aha!" moment. Not yet, anyway.

On a piece of paper, I had scribbled every variation of *4WD, 4x4,* and *four-wheel drive* I could muster. A dozen internet searches followed; anyone within a hundred miles of Rockford named Bill selling a four-wheel-drive vehicle. Wasn't sure what good it'd do if I found someone, considering Bill's truck was a two-wheel drive.

Strike two.

Or was it strike three? Or maybe four, if that were possible. Was it possible?

Time to change gears. I hadn't seen Lester since the incident at Ruth's place and needed to find him, ask about him being at Karpata. Mandy had also disappeared. They might be together. If so, that could be bad.

I ate the last bite of the donut and drank the watered-down soda, then clicked off the computer. The brake hoses still sat on the counter. The acid from the baster—if that's what it indeed was—hadn't eaten a hole in the rubber as I had hoped. Nor was there any trace of a rotten egg smell like Richter claimed there should be. I bundled up the hoses and threw them in the trash. Next, I rinsed the saucer, plate, and glass, before laying them in the sink. The brake hose dead-end was at least strike four.

As I headed downstairs, my cell pinged with a text from Arabella.

It said she'd try to talk to Schleper today and get the info on the other seahorse truck as soon as possible. She'd be over this evening and should she bring food? I texted back "Okay, okay, and yes, please."

Sometimes, but not often, I'm a man of few words. Especially when it involved texting.

Before clicking off my phone, I noticed Arabella's previous text, the one she had sent after our run at Windsock. The words, not the picture, caught my attention.

Just 4 U.

I grabbed the sheet of paper and studied the 4WD scribble. That had to be it. The ad wasn't a real ad. It was a clue. A dare. A tease by the murderer. He had left a taunt aimed solely at me. After Bill's death, I'd be one of the few who could decipher and understand its meaning.

I called Penn and, surprisingly, he answered. I didn't bother to ask about the WGN News developments from several nights ago. My hunch trumped anything the WGN people thought they knew.

"Larry David, I have something for you," I said.

"What, no fifty questions today?"

"I need you to do some research."

"Should I pick up your laundry, too?"

"Just listen." I told him what I needed.

"That sounds familiar."

"It should. I'll do some internet searches of my own, but I need what you can get. I don't have those resources."

"This could be big, R. The link analysis wouldn't pull this."

"Might be what we needed. Maybe get some traction."

"Speaking of the ad, the circle around it was blood. Bill's."

I didn't know what to say.

Penn was already doing a lot for me, but I decided to go ahead and push more. "I also need background on one Lester Jeffrey." I spelled the name and gave a brief description of age, gender, and race. Arabella could also get this information, but since Penn was on the line, I might as well use him. "I know it's a lot. Thanks."

"Okay, I'll get on this, but you know I'll need to tell Traverso."

"That's fine. Maybe he can bring more to bear on it."

He paused a moment and spoke in a low voice. "Since we're sharing information, I have some news on the weapon."

"You mean the one you don't have?"

"Never said we didn't have it."

"Never said you did."

His voice went back to normal. "Do you want what I have or not?"

I sighed. "Yes."

"It was a .357 Magnum, an old Colt Trooper II model. Left at the scene, right on the kitchen table."

"I guessed that."

"Listen to me. I'm trying to do you a favor. Jeez . . . The ballistics aren't in the system. No criminal history on the gun and there weren't any prints."

"Well, that's *not* what I expected."

"But dig this. Four empty casings in the cylinder, a couple with partial prints on them."

"Four? The sketch only showed three shots."

"Yeah, I know. Based on powder, corrosion, and oxidation on the casing, it looks like the first one was fired long before the other three at Ryberg's place.

"That's strange."

"That it is."

"Get any DNA hits?"

"Nothing's come back yet."

"Anyone have any ideas why the weapon was left behind?"

"Not even a guess from anyone. Makes no sense."

"It does to someone."

"I'll see what I can do on this research and get back to you. There's a lot here, and I may have to go back some ways. Is email okay?"

"Yes, and thanks, Larry David."

I hung up and thought maybe I should take back a couple of those strikes.

CHAPTER 37

ERIKA WAS ON the phone when I went down to the office. I plopped in my chair, leaned back, and studied the ceiling, hoping the dirty tile would somehow tell me the next move. Nothing. Maybe clean ones would have more imagination.

"That was the police," Erika said, hanging up the phone. "Tiffany's parents arrive today."

A sinking feeling circled my body, shot into my heart, and settled deep in my chest. I couldn't look them in the face, at least not yet.

"Erika, can you please pick them up at the airport?" I asked in a low voice.

She shook her head. "Since you have so much to do, I guess I will have to."

"Thank you. I want to meet them. Later."

"Yes, I am sure you do."

"Seriously, I do." I remembered the unit Erika reserved for them only had a queen-sized bed. "Do we have a bed to move into their room, something for Ozzie to sleep on?"

"No need. Ozzie is not coming with them."

"No?"

"He is staying at a neighbor's house for a while."

I bounced a fist off my desk. Poor Ozzie, already getting shuffled around.

"The police came to my house last night," Erika said staring at her monitor.

"Why?"

She turned around. "Not sure. They asked questions about you and Tiffany."

"What kind of questions?"

"How long have you known her? Why was she on the island? What did I think?"

"What did you think about what?"

She paused a moment, shaking her head. "What did I think about you hurting her?"

"What?"

Erika's cellphone rang. I shrugged, gave a small nod. She answered it, and Papiamentu streamed from her mouth. I didn't understand any of it, but her facial expressions and the pitch of her voice gave me pause. She looked at me, tears welling in her eyes. I leaned forward and handed her a Kleenex.

"*Masha danki. Ayo*," she said, dropping the phone on the floor. Her cheeks flushed, and she buried her face in her hands, elbows resting on the desk.

I put a hand on her shoulder. "Erika, what happened? What is it?"

"It's my neighbor, Malfena." She removed her hands from her face, tears working their way down her red cheeks.

A knot balled in the pit of my stomach as my throat went dry. "Yes, Malfena Cado." I handed her another tissue. "What's going on?"

"She's dead." Her sobbing was frantic, and she put her face back into her hands.

My heart raced. I was speechless. The knot in my stomach grew to the size of a basketball. "How can that be? What happened?"

"That was my friend. He works at the fire department. They found a car on fire in the Playa Frans area." She controlled herself for a few seconds, her eyes becoming bloodshot. Her lower jaw fluttered, and the ends of her eyebrows sagged. "They found Malfena burned to death in the car." She lowered her head as tears continued to flow.

Erika cried, and I was silent, trying to absorb the news.

"Was it her car?" I asked.

"She did not have a car."

That's right. Nor a driver's license.

I gave Erika a hug. "Go home. Be with Malfena's family. They're going to need lots of friends right now."

"Probably so." She stood and gathered her things.

"You alright to drive?" I asked.

She stared at me a moment. "I am fine." She paused before walking out the door and half-turned back toward my desk. "First Tiffany. Now Malfena."

She was close. The correct order was Bill and Marybeth, *then* Tiffany, *now* Malfena, but I didn't correct her.

She wiped her eyes with the tissue. "What is happening?"

CHAPTER 38

I HATED LEAVING the office unattended during the day but needed to drive to the scene of Malfena's car fire. My cell number was posted on the outside of the building near the office door. If a guest needed me, they could call. I'd miss Penn if he checked in, but I had to chance it.

Outside the building, I took a quick glance at the parking lot, hoping to see the truck with a seahorse on the tailgate. No such luck, so I walked to Lester's unit and knocked. No answer. I used my passkey to open the door and call his name. No response.

Next, I went to Mandy's unit and knocked. No answer there either. Again, I used my passkey and opened the door, and, just like at Lester's place, no response when I called her name. I shut and locked the room door, then headed toward my Wrangler.

Sliding behind the steering wheel, I immediately froze. A drill lay on the passenger seat. It held a bit the size of the hole in my battery, the one Kevin had shown me.

Concrete dust and dirt covered the drill, along with multiple hand-prints, fingerprints, and dirt smudges. If it was the drill used to put a hole in my battery—and I believed it was—no attempt had been made to clean it or wipe away evidence. On the visible side of the drill, in bold black letters, was printed *M+M*.

I turned my head back and forth and peered through all the Wrangler's windows. Numerous people on the beach, random tourists meandering past, and a few customers sipping their expresso on the outdoor patio of the coffee shop a few doors down. Not a hint of anyone nearby who might've placed a dirty drill on my front seat. For whatever reason, the police department hadn't seen fit to install street cams this far south of the downtown district.

I could canvass the area and ask anyone nearby if they'd seen someone lurking around my Wrangler. Unlikely they would've. The windows were always open, so the Wrangler was an easy target. Who would notice someone walking by, reaching in, and putting an object on the seat? It'd only take a few seconds to do, and I had no idea when it happened—could've been any time this morning or last night.

The coffee shop down the street had a security camera mounted on the building over the front door. I doubted it viewed more than twenty-five to thirty feet out, just enough to watch and record activity on the front patio. The Wrangler was far outside its scope.

Again, my instincts—and training—told me to drive straight to the police station and turn the drill over to Schleper's team. However, I still wasn't convinced the cops were serious about the sabotage.

Marko Martijn hadn't attacked me, but that's not to say he hadn't coaxed one of his workers or buddies to do it. A visit would be the last thing he'd be expecting, and his reaction could prove interesting. I might get some answers. Or, depending on Marko's response, get the crap knocked out of me again.

Right now, though, I needed to get to the scene of the car fire. Confronting Marko would have to wait. I didn't touch the drill and pulled out of the lot, headed north.

Playa Frans was on the northernmost part of the island, well past the Karpata dive site. Remote and desolate, its only inhabitants were wild donkeys, roaming iguanas, and a few lonely fishermen. Cacti and sage grass comprised the hard landscaping, and the roads were a mixture of dirt, ruts, and rock—difficult driving, even on a good day. It wasn't the type of spot where a person would end up by accident.

I could take either of two routes. Both required the same amount of drive time, and I opted for the one that went past Karpata and Cado Snack, the same road Lester and I had used the night we discovered Tiffany's body. Not sure if I would stop, but a quick glance couldn't hurt.

Because it was before noon, an active time for tourists, the drive took longer than I had expected. The one-lane road winds north along the coast and is a primary thoroughfare for divers and snorkelers wanting access to the northern dive sites. As such, tourists crossing the road, slowing to park, or meandering along the roadside taking in the scenic vista and views slowed my progress several times.

I sped past Karpata, craning my neck to see as much as possible. The rear door to Cado Snack was open, swaying in the breeze, the place having every appearance of being vacant.

Farther north, I pulled onto a dirt road. Referring to it as a road, however, was generous and an insult to other roads. Comprised of hard-packed dirt and large sections of slate unearthed over time by wind and rain, it was more of a trail. Bumping up and down in first or second gear, the Wrangler was the perfect vehicle for this terrain, but I still needed to be careful. Concerned about hitting a large hole and bottoming out, possibly breaking an axle, I steered from side to side avoiding the deeper ruts and slabs of rock. It reminded me of the old show *Daktari*, except for not being in Africa and the side of my Wrangler not having zebra stripes.

The jarring eventually knocked everything to the floor, including the drill. Even the glove box sprung open; most of the contents spilling onto the floorboard. Glad to be in the Wrangler. An average car would be hard pressed to handle this road.

After ten minutes of bouncing, the road spilled into a clearing where, along the edge, two squads and a fire truck had parked. Worse than the smell of the dumpster and Richter's Garage combined, a thick, acrid odor enveloped the area, a combination of burned oil, gas, rubber, and plastic. Yellow barrier tape surrounded the charred remnants of a small vehicle, the ground black and sooty, soaked with water.

I drove around a large rut, slowing to a stop, and parked along the clearing's edge, as an ambulance eased past and headed in the other direction. That had to be a bumpy ride, considering the *Daktari* road they were headed toward. I considered the burned shell of the car and wondered how it had gotten here in the first place.

An officer I didn't recognize walked toward the Wrangler and held my door shut as I tried to open it. "Can I help you, sir?"

Arabella came alongside him. "It is okay. He is with me." The officer gave me a quick glance, shrugged, and walked back to one of the squads.

As I opened the door and stepped out, Arabella grabbed me by the shoulder and turned me away from the scene. "Conklin, what are you doing here?"

"I wanted to see what happened."

Arabella checked over her shoulder at the other officers, then turned back to me. She talked in a low voice, almost a whisper. I barely heard her over the commotion of the scene. "You should not be here. This does not concern you."

"Bella, I talked to Malfena yesterday, and now she's dead."

"I was told to say nothing to you about police business. Schleper is pissed at me right now. He will think I called you."

I turned sideways and leaned against the door. "What was she doing way up here anyway?" I motioned toward the smoldering hunk of metal. "Whose car is that?"

Arabella shook her head. "I cannot tell you anything. Now, please leave."

"You know Malfena didn't have a license."

Arabella folded her arms across her chest. "Of course we know that."

"Then how does this happen? I spoke to her yesterday, and now she's in a car dead, with no driver's license, in the middle of nowhere."

"Conklin!"

Our eyes locked. After a short moment, I realized she was right. Schleper would blame her for my presence. For her sake, I needed to leave. I opened the door, but before getting in, turned to ask one final question. "Did you tell Schleper what we discovered last night?"

She hesitated, pursed her lips. "Yes. But he has a theory of his own."

"So, what is *his* theory?"

"Look, Conklin, I need you to—"

"Mr. Conklin." Schleper had snuck up on us and stood in front of the Wrangler, hands on his hips. "You should leave. We do not need your assistance here. This is a police matter, and Officer De Groot has no information for you." He folded his arms across his chest and narrowed his eyes at Arabella. "Is that correct?"

Arabella shot her own laser eyes at Schleper, but after a second, relaxed and hesitantly nodded.

I turned full around to face Schleper. "Don't be a jerk, Schleper. This is bigger than you realize. You think this car spontaneously burst into flames? Up here, in the middle of nowhere?"

Jaw clenched, he walked around to the driver's side and faced off with me, the open door between us. "Do I have to put you in jail?"

His less-than-fresh breath made me consider sending him a toothbrush next Christmas. Refusing to back down or be pushed around any longer, I took a half-step forward and breathed through my mouth. If going to jail proved my point, so be it.

Arabella stepped closer to me. "Conklin, it is not worth it."

In my peripheral vision, I saw two officers walking our way. I took a deep breath, nodded at Arabella, and, retreating a step, lowered my shoulders.

"Just answer one thing, Inspector, and I'll leave," I said.

Stern-faced, he said, "Go ahead, ask your question."

"What was she doing up here?"

He let out a sigh. "We believe it was suicide."

"Suicide? You've got to be joking. Suicide by car fire?"

"Conklin, we found a note," Arabella said.

Schleper snapped his head at her, his scowl as demeaning as his attitude. "That is right." He looked back at me. "We found a note that claims she did this to herself."

I let out a short laugh, not because any of this was funny, but because I didn't know what else to do. Tension, I guessed. This conversation was ridiculous. "She didn't have a license, for God's sake. Who drove her? And whose car is it?"

"That will be part of our investigation," Schleper said.

He motioned for me to get in the Wrangler. I got in but wasn't ready to leave, not quite yet anyway. "Did Bella—I mean, Officer De Groot—explain to you what we discovered last night?"

"Yes, the officer and I talked this morning."

Again, I laughed. "That's not important to you?"

"Mr. Conklin, leave the investigating to us. You are retired. Start acting like it." He tapped his hand twice on the roof of the Wrangler. "Now . . . leave." He backed away and pointed toward the road.

Arabella looked away from me. I slapped the transmission into drive, made a small half circle, and headed back down the *Daktari* road. Leaving was best. For Arabella and for me. And for Schleper—I was ready to explode at him and that wouldn't have been good. More problems for everyone.

Halfway back to Karpata, knowing I should wait, I phoned Arabella. She didn't answer. No surprise. I disconnected when the call went to voicemail and redialed her number. Patience during an investigation had never been one of my virtues. "C'mon," I yelled into the phone. She answered on the second ring.

"What!" Her voice pointed, but low. "You are going to get me in trouble."

"Do you think it was suicide?" The question tumbled out, my mind working faster than my mouth.

"Conklin, we found a note."

"What position was the body? How could she sit still and let herself be burned alive? It doesn't add up."

"Look, I will tell you something, but you have to promise not to call back."

"Agreed."

She sighed. "The body was found locked in the trunk."

"What?"

She hung up, and I didn't call back.

Suicide by fire, while locked in the trunk of a car that wasn't hers.

I shook my head and pressed the accelerator. Going too fast for the conditions, it took a two-handed death grip on the wheel to keep the Wrangler under control. Priority one was getting back to Cado Snack. Turning off the dirt road onto the pavement, I increased my speed, tires squealing as I took the last curve and skidded to a stop in the gravel parking lot at Karpata.

Walking a full circle around the building, I didn't see anything unusual. The rock and gravel landscape prevented footprints. I peered inside the door a few moments, allowing my eyes to adjust to the darkness. Nothing strewn about or out of place; everything stacked and neatly arranged on the shelves, same as the previous day. Boxes and supplies were stacked neatly against the walls. There were visible broom marks in the fine layer of dust on the wooden floor. I pulled on the front sliding window. Shut and locked.

The warm breeze rocked the door back and forth, never fully penetrating the opening. I used the front of my shirt to wipe the sweat from my brow and stood in the middle of the swept floor and organized shelves. I didn't know what to make of the situation.

Malfena's cooler contained two unopened bags of ice. I tipped it from side to side and noticed only a small amount of water move along the bottom. Tapping one bag with my fist, the hard edges of ice cubes poked at my skin. Malfena *must've* been here this morning. Yesterday, during her cleaning ritual, she emptied the ice water from the cooler and packed items in it to take with her. Those items were now on the shelves.

Suicides have a certain feel, and this one didn't have that feel. How, after arriving to open her business for the day, did she get to Playa Frans? And what about the suicide note Schleper claimed to have?

Drumming my fingers on the counter, I stared out the open door into the sunlight. This couldn't be a coincidence. Malfena's death had something to do with either Tiffany or yesterday's conversation with me. Had she seen more than she thought or could remember? Or was it simply a case of talking to me?

Either way, guilt swam through me, along with anger, thinking of Lester doing this to Malfena *and* Tiffany. I pounded my fist on the wall and leaned my head against the sliding window. I wanted all of this to have never happened.

After a moment, I straightened myself, took a deep breath, and headed for the doorway. An examination of the jamb showed no recent scrapes or pry marks and twisting the knob in my hand proved the mechanism worked correctly. The dead bolt was in the unlock position, and a key was needed to move it back and forth. Two more walks around the perimeter of the building revealed nothing of interest.

The sun beat down as I stood in front of the building staring at the hand-painted menu, as if by staring long enough some form of divine intervention would force an answer to materialize beneath the words "Amstel Beer 4$USD."

A truckload of divers pulled into the parking lot, their laughs and yells bringing me back to the moment. I made sure none of them approached the building and disturbed anything. They were interested only in the sea and headed straight for the water with their gear.

I leaned against the hood of my Wrangler, pulled out my phone, and displayed Arabella's number from the directory. Just before I pressed the call button, she and James pulled into the lot and parked.

James got out of the passenger side and stood behind the open door. I couldn't see his gun hand but imagined it—as he had done at the morgue—resting on the handle of his weapon. Arabella got out of the driver's side and walked over to me.

"Conklin," she said with a deep sigh. "What are you doing here?"

I held my hands in a surrender fashion. "Just leaving." I pocketed my phone and opened the Wrangler's door. "Doubt you'll find anything. The place is pretty clean."

Arabella put her hands on her hips. James lowered his head.

"But you know," I said, "I'd love to see that suicide note."

James slammed the door and the truck rocked back and forth twice. Arabella folded her arms across her chest.

I drove away thinking about Malfena committing suicide by car fire.

Maybe now I *had* seen it all.

CHAPTER 39

I WAS SURE Malfena had seen Lester's truck at Karpata but needed proof. Thoroughness required the other seahorse truck be excluded. I needed to talk with the renter and determine if they had been to Karpata lately. Arabella hadn't given me the rental information yet, and I doubted she would anytime soon. I wasn't brave enough to call her and ask, at least not for a few more hours. Her annoyance with me would pass. It always did.

Marko's drill still lay on the Wrangler's floorboard, and like Lester's truck, was part of this mess. Bill had kept a wooden sign on his desk that read "Follow every lead, no matter how small." I wanted to close the loop on the drill but considered the truck lead more critical. My confrontation with Marko would have to wait.

It took a little over an hour to drive through the parking lots of the major resorts and hotels. Remaining in first gear, the truck seemed to crawl along as I scrutinized the tailgates of white pickup trucks. In some instances, I had to get out and walk around to the back of each vehicle. It was the busy season on the island and, considering the significant number of open stalls in the lots, I assumed most of the guests were out and about.

I didn't find the seahorse truck at any of the major hotels. I could continue my search at the smaller establishments, places similar in size to the YellowRock, or I could search the dive sites. It'd take hours to explore the parking lots of numerous small hotels scattered around the island. A search of the dive sites—dozens of them—along the coast would take nearly as long. But, I rationalized, if people were away from their rooms doing what they came to Bonaire to do—scuba dive—then the dive sites were the next logical places to check.

I drove south, along the southern coastal road, which gave access to many of the popular dive sites. The salt mounds loomed in the distance. Hopefully, Tiffany took some pictures of them and hadn't played me. I hated the thought of her story being a ruse to borrow Arabella's car and drive to Karpata, ultimately, it seemed, to break a promise.

White trucks, loaded with divers and equipment, passed me every few seconds going in the opposite direction. I studied them as they approached and glanced in my rearview mirror as they passed.

Most of the sites didn't have defined parking spots, so drivers parked haphazardly along the shoreline or road. Some sites didn't have any vehicles; some were overflowing. At the ones that did have trucks, I exited my jeep and checked the tailgates. Divers typically parked with the back end facing the sea. Much easier to drop the tailgate, gear up, and walk into the water.

After visiting half the sites along the southern road with no luck, I became frustrated. This hunt-and-search operation might be a waste of time. No guarantee the person was at a dive site right now. They could be driving around the island, eating at a restaurant, drunk at a bar, or in transit, maybe to a dive site I'd already marked off my list. Or they might be headed back to one of the resorts I'd already checked. Maybe parked at a marina, having gone out on a boat.

The proverbial needle in a haystack came to mind. But at least I was doing *something*. Forward movement, albeit marginally.

Or was I kidding myself?

I searched two more sites, ending with the same results. It was late, and I decided to head back to the YellowRock and develop a different approach. My method was too hit or miss, and, so far, all misses.

Still too soon to call Arabella, so I was on my own.

As I drove past a dive site called Pink Beach, a white truck passed going the opposite way. I checked my rearview mirror and saw a seahorse on the tailgate. I did a quick three-point turn and followed it to where it stopped at a site called Margate Bay.

The occupants, a man and a woman, got out, leaned against the side of the truck, and faced the sea, each holding a water bottle. The man was topless and wore a knee-length flowered swimsuit, while the woman wore a black-with-blue-accented lycra jumpsuit known as a dive skin. Both had on sunglasses and hats.

Even before speaking to them, I knew they were either American or Canadian. After a while, it became easy to tell the Americans and Canadians from the English, Dutch, Germans, and Scandinavians. Haircuts, clothing, make of dive gear, even posture were all tells. But language would make it definitive.

They appeared to be in their mid-sixties, which in the past I might've referred to as elderly. But with my next milestone birthday approaching fast, I had decided that "elderly" was far beyond mid-sixties.

I reached onto the floor, where the contents of my glove compartment had spilled, and grabbed some flyers about the YellowRock that I always carried to pass out to prospective clients. Not that I needed the business, but some folks, when they discovered I owned a resort, asked for information about the place.

Some companies left flyers and various advertisements on the windshields of vehicles at the dive sites, trying to entice the divers to visit their establishments. Not me. Most of those flyers eventually found their way to the ground. Or worse yet, the sea.

The flyers did, however, offer a good excuse to approach the couple leaning against the truck.

"Hi there," I said, as I handed each of them a flyer. "Here's some information on a hotel."

Neither said anything, and they dropped their heads to scan the material.

After a quick moment, the man looked up. "No thanks," he said. He gathered both flyers and handed them back to me. "We're happy where we're at."

Americans, upper Midwest.

"Where you folks from?" I asked. Best to ask mundane questions first, followed by more serious ones.

"Grand Forks," the woman said. "North Dakota." She accentuated and drew out the *ko* part of the word.

"Enjoying your stay?" I asked.

The man took a swig of water and stared at me. He had a large USMC tattoo on his left arm and a Harley-Davidson one on his right.

The woman smiled and said, "Oh, ya, we've been all over the island. Bonaire is the best dive trip we've ever done, ya know."

"Have you done any north dives?" I asked.

"Oh, sure," the man said. He walked to the other side of the truck, leaned into the bed, and fiddled with some dive gear.

"We've done several up north," the woman said, "but we more than prefer the southern ones."

"Have you done Karpata?"

She scrunched her eyebrows. "Ya know, we have done Karpata. Nice dive. Lots of soft corals."

"Do you know which day?"

She yelled over her shoulder at the man. "Hey der, hon, you know which day we did Karpata?"

He quit fiddling with the equipment for a moment. "What in the hell is this?" he asked. "Fifty questions?"

"I'm sorry," I said. "Just being friendly."

The woman turned back to me and put a finger on her chin. "To be honest, we've done it more than once."

"What's it to you, eh?" asked the man, continuing to focus on the dive gear.

"Nothing, I'm just a curious guy, I guess."

"Well, then, how about every day. Yeah, that's it. Every day."

The woman nodded. "Ya, well, Ben's right, kind of. We've dived Karpata a lot. No, not every day, mind you, but close to it. I couldn't say exactly which days we did or didn't."

"I'm actually helping a friend of mine. She lost some dive gear and we're trying to find it. When you were there, did you see a young girl with pink gear, fins, and mask? A wetsuit with pink accents on the sides?" I ran my hand down the side of my body.

They eyeballed each other a moment. He shrugged and she turned back to me.

"Nope, don't remember anyone like that," she said.

"Anything else, there?" the man said. He dropped the tailgate and pulled some tanks out of the truck bed. "Speaking of diving, that's what we're about to do." Without looking at his wife, he said, "You ready, Sophie?"

"Karpata is such a beautiful dive. We'll do it again, more than likely before we go home," the woman said. She went to the rear of the truck bed and began assembling her gear.

Trucks drove past, some going north; some south. The sun was high off the horizon, with lots of daylight remaining, and up the shore, vehicles entered and left various dive sites. None of them had a seahorse on the tailgate. I had found my needle in the haystack, but was it any help?

Across the street, a small, knee-high cyclone spiraled dirt and small pieces of gravel a few yards down the shoulder before dying out.

Bonaire has a constant wind from east to west, and it had gained strength over the last few days.

The man and woman stood at the tailgate, fiddling with their dive gear. "Nice talking to you. Have a good day."

"Thank you," she said. "We will. Tomorrow, we plan to visit the park and do some diving there."

She referred to Washington-Slagbaaii National Park, a preserve on the north end of Bonaire that covers almost one-fifth of the island. Several secluded beaches and dive spots are within its boundaries, along with numerous hiking and nature trails.

I walked toward my Wrangler but couldn't resist the urge to offer some advice. I turned, and said to the woman, "Be careful if you go to Karpata again."

They both stopped what they were doing.

"Oh, yeah?" the man asked.

"The wind has picked up. Heavier wind can make the entry a little difficult."

"Not from a boat," he said.

"What?"

The man shook his head.

"We do Karpata from a boat," the woman said. "We'd never do it from shore." Her eyes widened. "We'd never chance Ben's bad knee on those stairs, ya know."

CHAPTER 40

I TOOK A chance and drove to Marko Martijn's building hoping he'd be there and not working at a job site. The drill was a lead, but, at best, a long shot. I doubted any chance of tying it to the truck sabotage, but the loose end bothered me and needed following to its finish. Not sure how Marko would take seeing me. Maybe he'd consider the return of his drill a peace offering and welcome me with open arms.

I needed to do something.

Marko ran his operation from a dilapidated metal building situated on a rock-filled lot on a side street off Kaya Nikiboko Zuid. The corrugated metal curved at the top forming a half-cylindrical roof, reminding me of an old World War II aircraft hangar. Sometime in the distant past, the metal had been gray, but now rust covered nearly the entire surface.

Random lumber and concrete blocks were stacked on both sides of the building and along the dirt driveway. In the middle of the rocky yard, an old concrete mixer, rusted and scorched by the sun, leaned sideways on broken legs, its working days long gone. An old truck with flat tires, no doors, and a shattered windshield sat at the lot's edge next to the wall separating Marko's property from the building next door.

I parked midway up the driveway, grabbed the drill off the front floorboard, and walked toward the open, double-wide overhead door.

Two men, cigarettes dangling from their mouths, were loading tools and cement bags into the bed of a dented, faded blue dually pickup truck. They stopped working as I approached and stared at me. I asked if Martijn was around, and they both pointed toward the inside of the building. I strolled through the door.

The temperature inside was ten degrees cooler than outside. The length of the building, coupled with the open front door and back doors, caused a wind tunnel effect. Large, round lights hung from the ceiling rafters and swayed rhythmically in the breeze. None of the bulbs worked. Not sure if they were switched off or burned out.

My eyes adjusted to the darkness and I saw Marko walking in my direction. He wore an identical outfit to the one from a few days ago, and cement dust still covered his clothes and exposed skin. His dread-locks needed a good shampoo as well. Wiping his dirty hands on a dirty white cloth towel, we stopped two feet apart.

He balled the towel and tossed it to the side, at a trash can over-flowing with garbage and construction debris, falling two feet short of the pile.

He folded his arms across his chest and took a deep breath. "What do you want?"

So much for the warm, open-arms greeting.

I raised my hands in a surrender fashion. "I come bearing gifts." I handed him the drill. He held it in one grungy hand, while wiping off some of the dust and dirt with his other grungy hand. He pressed the trigger and the motor hummed for a moment.

"Where did you find this?" he asked.

"You tell me."

"What does that mean?"

"I found it this morning in my jeep. I thought you might know how it got there."

Head shaking, his arm dropped to his side. "It was stolen."

"When?"

"I do not know for sure. We noticed it missing a couple of days ago."

We were both quiet for a minute. A mangy black mutt walked over and sniffed my sandals and feet. It wagged its tail and raised its nose at me, but after a moment, disappointed in my lack of response, wandered off through the door into the sunlight.

"I think it was used to sabotage my jeep and cause an accident," I said. "An accident that put a police officer in the hospital."

He slowly smiled. "Your woman cop, maybe?"

I squirmed a bit and said, "Yeah, my woman cop." I had never referred to Arabella in those terms before. I took a deep breath, thankful she wasn't here.

"I do not know anything about that. Why did you bring it to me? If it is part of a crime, the police should have it, no?"

"I don't know." I laid my best smile on him. "Shame to see a good tool go to waste."

"Thank you." No smile. His face remained stern. "I thought you might be here to cause trouble with me."

"Marko," I said, shaking my head. "I thought we were friends." I spread my hands in front of me, palms up.

One of the guys from outside yelled something in Papiamento. Marko waved at them, never taking his eyes from me.

"I heard you were beat up," he said.

Damn small island.

I didn't like the term "beat up" especially when it applied to me. It may have been accurate, but that doesn't mean I accepted it. Or liked it.

"Yeah, a couple of nights ago." I pointed at the drill. "About the same time someone used that drill on my jeep."

"It was not me," he said, fixing me with a blank stare, bewildered.

"I know."

"If I beat you up, you would not be walking now."

I knew that, too, but didn't admit it. "Any idea who?"

His body tightened, and he stuck out his jaw. He took a step forward. "How would I know that?" He held the drill up. "Just like how would I know about the drill?"

"People talk, maybe you heard something."

He stood there.

I sighed. "If you do, I'd appreciate you letting me know."

He yelled something in Papiamento to the guys outside, and a moment later an engine fired to life. I walked out the overhead door and past the two guys with the cigarettes hanging from their mouths, still loading tools and cement bags into the bed of the idling, faded blue dually. A moment later the door hinges creaked as someone got into the driver's side of the truck. Within a few seconds, as I walked toward my Wrangler, the truck pulled alongside me.

Out the driver's-side window, Martijn said, "I still want my money."

"I still want the work done. Finish the work, and you'll get the money."

He hit the gas and sped up, driving around the Wrangler and onto the road.

CHAPTER 41

HEADED SOUTH TOWARD the YellowRock on the one-way through the business district, I sat, idling, in the Wrangler on Kaya C.E.B. Hellmund. Three trucks, lined up one after the other, were stopped ahead of me causing a mild traffic jam.

The one directly in front of me had four people in the cab and two in the bed. Arms hung out all the windows, and the guys in the back were shirtless, turning a crispy red, assisted by spray-on tanning lotion, which they applied at each stop. The drivers crept forward a few feet every minute or so, stopping to allow everyone a look at the sea or to point at one of the restaurants.

I'd driven this road countless times and was familiar with all the sights but still enjoyed the scenery. The sea was on my right with sailboats and fishing boats moored at the reef's edge. Fishermen cleaned their catch on the piers, pelicans and sandpipers swooping down at the sea to gobble the guts and other discards. The birds shrieked and squealed either in triumph or defeat, depending on the success of their swoop.

Restaurants, T-shirt shops, and bars lined the left side of the road supplying every consumable, trinket, or beverage a tourist or cruiser desired. Most of the restaurants were open-air, so the aromas swirled and meshed together as they filtered across the street.

I peered into Vinny's. The place was nearly empty, except for a few customers occupying the tables near the sea rail, and Jan sitting at the end of the bar watching the TV screen. I honked and Jan waved, not bothering to turn around. Everyone honked at Jan. He quit turning around years ago.

Chuck's apartment was to my left on the second floor. His balcony was a jumble of drying laundry, a couple of lawn chairs, and an old, rusted barbeque grill, which he hadn't used since the Wright brothers' first flight. No sign of Chuck, but two cops strolled out the street-level door that led to his apartment stairs. I didn't recognize either of them.

Traffic finally moved, and I turned on the next side road and parked. I doubled back to Chuck's and up the stairs. He answered the door after my first hard knock.

"What'd they want?" I asked.

Chuck motioned me inside. He hadn't shaved; unusual for him. He wore a gray Budweiser T-shirt with a dark stain down the front and blue workout-type shorts with a faded, peeling USAF emblem.

A young Bonairian woman, wearing nothing but a large white T-shirt, leaned against the kitchen counter holding a glass of red wine. I recognized her as a bartender, but I couldn't remember where. Her name might've been Anna. When I walked further into the apartment, she finished her wine and went into the bedroom.

"You busy?" I asked.

Chuck shook his head. "She wants to hang out for a while." He shrugged. "Did you get a good look? Hell, I'm not going to argue."

The apartment was a mess. My place would never win the Good Housekeeping Seal of Approval, but at least I occasionally picked up dirty clothes and cleaned the dishes. Old food containers and empty beer bottles cluttered the kitchen counter and coffee table. Dirty, torn sheets hung over the windows employed as makeshift curtains, and a bead of dark mold adorned the seam where the tile floor met the plaster walls. Streams of sunlight, sneaking in through the filthy sliding doors leading to the balcony, illuminated the dust particles suspended in the air, thrashed around by the dust-caked ceiling fan.

Chuck went to the fridge and grabbed two beers, handed me one and said, "They asked about you."

We ventured through the dust to the balcony and sat in the lawn chairs.

"Like what?" I asked.

"About you and that Tiffany chick."

"What about Tiffany?"

"I didn't even know she was on the island." He shook his head and drank some beer. "I told them I only met her once, maybe two years ago. Which was the truth."

Unlike mine, Chuck's balcony didn't have a cover to provide shade and protection from the sun. For a moment, I worried my beer might boil. Luckily, Chuck had placed the beers in koozies to help keep them cold. I wore a hat and sunglasses. Chuck had neither.

"They kept asking about you," he said.

"What about me?"

"Shit like why Tiffany came to see you. How long you've known her. How long I've known you. Crap like that."

"What'd you tell them?"

Chuck looked at me and hesitated a moment. "I told them the truth. What'd you expect?"

I nodded. "Good, that's what I'd expect."

"They asked where you were when she died."

"What'd you say?"

"I said I didn't even know she was dead. I can't remember where I was that afternoon, let alone where you were."

"Anything else?"

"They asked about some guy at the bar the other night. I think it was the night you brought me home, the night Jasmine came over."

"Lester?"

"They didn't mention anyone by name, at least I don't think so. I told them I was drunk and didn't remember shit."

"They ask you anything you didn't know?"

"Yeah, they did." Chuck wiped moisture off the upper part of his beer can, the section not covered by the coolie. "They asked if I knew anything about you being the father of her kid." He took a swig. "Hell, I didn't even know she had a kid."

"A little boy."

"Fuck, that's bad. I feel terrible about it."

"I'm not the father."

"That's what I figured, and I told 'em that. Not sure they believed me, though."

I stretched my legs out in front of me. The balcony was narrow, so my feet touched the outside rail even though my chair was against the wall of the building. "This is ridiculous."

We were both quiet for a minute.

The woman came out of the apartment with a fresh glass of wine and leaned against the railing. She had ditched the white T-shirt for a pair of capris and a button-down shirt tied at the waist.

"Anna," Chuck said, "this is a private conversation. Can you go watch TV or something?"

She just stared at Chuck.

"Please?" Chuck said.

"Why do I not just leave?" she said.

A hint of a smile crossed Chuck's face. "Okay."

She gulped the remainder of her wine and walked into the apartment. A glass broke in the sink, and a door slammed.

"I'm guessing you have one less glass," I said, half-smiling.

Chuck shrugged. "She'll be back."

"Maybe. Maybe not."

Chuck leaned forward and placed his elbows on his knees. "Seriously, R," he said, glancing at me, "be careful. I think they believe you killed that girl."

"Schleper can't be serious. It's got to be a game."

"What does Arabella think? Does she know what's going on?"

I sighed. "Not sure. But I need to find out."

CHAPTER 42

AFTER LEAVING CHUCK'S, I considered walking across the street and having a beer at Vinny's, let go of some stress. Maybe two beers. But I needed to get back to the office and see if the Rockford folks had checked in with any new information.

I fired up the Wrangler and continued down Kaya C.E.B. Hellmund. A side street one building past the YellowRock gave access to an alley that flowed into my rear parking lot, which is where I planned to park, as usual. Several units on the north side of the YellowRock were visible as I passed, including number five—Lester and Tiffany's—and seven—Mandy Driver's.

A guy walked out of Mandy's door, strolling down the path in the direction of Lester's unit. The hairs on the back of my neck tingled when I noticed the orange Chicago Bears hat and the same NIU T-shirt from the other night.

Freckle Eye.

It was time for me to find out who this guy was and why he was in Mandy's room. Maybe meet her in the process, which was long overdue.

No parking spots were available on the street or in the front lot. If I stopped to get out and run toward unit five, I'd block traffic on the one-lane road all the way to downtown. My only choice was to park out back and double around on foot. It seemed like an eternity but was less than five minutes from the time Freckle Eye walked out of Mandy's unit, and I knocked on unit five's door.

No answer, so I knocked again.

Lester's truck wasn't parked out front, and I couldn't remember seeing it when I passed earlier. He didn't answer my third set of knocks, and I debated using my passkey. I had already used it once to enter his room without permission, and I didn't want to abuse my privileges.

No answer when I knocked on Mandy's door either. I knocked again, harder, and yelled her name. Still nothing. The lights were off, and the drapes were pulled shut, preventing me from peeping through the windows. Using my passkey in this situation was different and possibly warranted. An unknown man had left less than ten minutes ago, and now Mandy didn't answer or respond. In my opinion, that constituted probable cause. A bit shaky, but it'd have to do.

I unlocked the door and eased it open a few inches, calling her name. When she didn't answer, I slid my hand inside the door, flipped the light switch, and entered.

All the YellowRock units had the same basic layout. The main room was the combination living/bedroom area situated at the front with a kitchenette along the side. A small wall indentation served as a makeshift closet. Tucked far in the rear of the unit was the bathroom. They are all-over plaster, painted in whatever pastel color I found on sale at the hardware store. The floors were white ceramic tile. The ceiling fan over the bed rotated on the slow setting and needed a new bearing, making a clinking sound with every turn. The smell—a persistent odor, accrued over the years—was a combination of seawater-wet swimwear, fast-food grease, and alcohol. Possibly some Pine-Sol in the mix, as well.

No sign of Mandy.

The bathroom door was partially open, so I walked over and called Mandy's name again. When she didn't answer, I pushed the door fully open and hit the light switch. The bathroom was empty.

It was also incredibly sparse.

At first glance, the lack of items in the bathroom jolted me, made me wonder if I were in the right room. Many tourists use the shower rod to hang swimsuits and wet clothing, but there wasn't anything drying in this bathroom. Not many toiletries, either. Lying on the vanity was a comb, a toothbrush, a tube of toothpaste, and a half-bar of hand soap.

Arabella traveled lighter than most women, but Mandy was the master. No makeup, hairspray, fancy conditioners, oils, or any other feminine products. A partial bottle of complimentary shampoo from the YellowRock sat on the shelf in the shower stall.

I turned out the light and left the bathroom door as I found it.

Not much of a wardrobe, either, only a few T-shirts and a pair of gym shorts hanging on the rod in the small closet. No clothes lying on the bed, the chair, or the floor and no food containers or empty beer bottles on the small counter. Both wastebaskets were empty. The unit felt barely lived in, almost vacant.

Sometimes, what *isn't* found can be as interesting as what *is* found.

I took a piece of paper and a pen from the drawer of the small corner desk and wrote a note asking Mandy to please stop by the office. I turned off the light, locked the door, and left.

CHAPTER 43

NEITHER PENN NOR Traverso had left any messages or emails. I had expected Traverso to call after Penn chatted with him about my requests, but maybe they didn't have anything yet. Or they had decided to go dark. Nothing would surprise me right now.

Regardless of some mysterious note Schleper claimed to have, I didn't buy the whole suicide-by-car-fire story and didn't see how anyone ever would. It appeared to have been a regular workday for Malfena, and the condition of the snack shop didn't lead to the thought of suicide. Nothing to suggest she had decided to stop living. Yesterday, she was full of energy. Her death, hours after our discussion, was a big coincidence to ignore.

But Schleper and his team were doing just that.

The internet search function was a marvelous invention, and I had used it more in the last few days than in the previous year. I prepared to up that tally.

My search for "suicide by car fire" generated several relevant hits. I read several case studies of people who committed suicide in this fashion. They'd start the car on fire then lock themselves in the trunk. Once the lid slammed shut, the commitment made, the person couldn't back out, which the article claimed, "strengthened their resolve." One piece stated that the *commitment* is lightened by most modern cars because the back seats fold out, allowing someone trapped in the trunk to escape. Also, since 2002, models manufactured in the USA were required to have a release handle located inside the trunk. If trapped, pull the handle and the trunk pops open.

I didn't know the year and model of the car Malfena burned in, let alone if it was manufactured in the States. Vehicles destined for other countries didn't always require the same safety devices as U.S. models, so it became a crapshoot whether Malfena was "trapped" or not. The VIN, or Vehicle Identification Number, could tell a lot about the car, including safety packages and place of origin. But I didn't have the VIN, nor did I ever expect to get it.

Regardless, the victims in those studies all exhibited signs of being suicidal, unlike Malfena's demeanor. One article included quotes from a psychologist who specialized in suicides and made mention that women preferred methods that weren't disfiguring. No specifics, but I'd put car fires in the disfiguring category, as I bet most people would.

I leaned back in my chair and took stock of what displayed on the monitor. My unscientific, twenty-minute search of the internet confirmed my suspicion.

Malfena hadn't committed suicide.

I grabbed a water bottle from the fridge at the same time two police officers sauntered through the office door. It's a small island, but I didn't recognize either of them. One, the larger of the two, walked toward my desk leaving his partner standing by the door, guarding the exit.

Drat! My escape foiled.

"Mr. Conklin?" he asked.

I leaned back in my chair and put my feet up.

"Sir, Inspector Schleper wants you to come to the station."

I looked at the cop guarding the door, then back at the one standing over me.

"Why?" I asked. "Kind of late in the day, isn't it?"

He shrugged and shifted his weight from one leg to the other. He glanced over his shoulder at his partner and turned back toward me to resume his glare. Some people can't get enough of me.

I'd given up being shoved around by a police department at retirement and counted to ten. Another chat with Schleper was needed, but I wanted it to be on my terms, not his. "Tell the inspector I'll stop by in about an hour." I turned up the water bottle, downing several swallows, and looked at the office wall clock, making a point of comparing its time to the display on my cellphone. "Make that"—referring to the wall clock again, and then my cellphone— "an hour and fifteen minutes." For no reason, I studied my phone a moment, then tossed it on my desk. "That'll give me enough time for a few beers."

The cop frowned and put his hands on the desk, leaning toward me. "The inspector told us to escort you to the station." He leaned further over the desk, closer to me. "Now."

I ran a hand over my face, applying pressure to my forehead. My nap was past due. I opened the fridge, and grabbed a Bright, opting for a can instead of a bottle. I drank it in one upturn. After crushing the empty in my hands and throwing it in the bin, I stood and headed for the door.

The officer at the door led the way as the other one followed me. The bigger cop, the one behind me, grabbed my arm before I got to the Wrangler. I twisted at the waist and yanked free, as the other cop put his hand on his weapon, taking a defensive stance.

"Seriously?" I said to Big Cop.

Big Cop shook his head at Small Cop, then turned to me. "The inspector told us to give you a ride." He motioned with his head toward their police truck.

At least they hadn't cuffed me.

Big Cop opened one of the back doors and closed it after I climbed in. A single breath reminded me that every cop vehicle I'd ever been in had a distinct smell, and it wasn't pleasant. It's the smell of being lived in sixteen to twenty-four hours a day. Cops hastily eating fast food between runs and spilling coffee during long stakeouts. Drunks and unwashed perps sprawled across the back seat. Most of all, it smelled of discharged bodily fluids. Exactly where I sat.

To a veteran cop, it smelled normal, like home. But not to me. Not anymore. It reminded me of a sewer. Or my dumpster.

None of us made small talk on the ride to the station. I held my head out the window and breathed through my mouth as much as possible. The radio blared several times, for the most part in Papiamentu or Dutch, but on one transmission I recognized Malfena's name. During another, a chill slithered down my spine when I heard my name.

We parked behind the station and went in the back door. Big Cop and Small Cop escorted me up a set of stairs to the second floor. Only a couple of the officers watched us as we walked through a large open room, past mostly empty desks, and down a narrow hallway. Big Cop opened the door to a small, windowless room, and motioned me in.

"Please have a seat," he said and left, shutting the door behind him.

The room smelled musty, like the place in the basement of my hundred-year-old former house in Rockford that stored all my useless crap.

The walls in this interview room were a similar faded beige as the previous one, and an identical gray desk and two brown chairs, one with wheels, sat in the center. A large mirror occupied the majority of one wall, presumably the wall behind where Schleper would sit. I'd sit facing the mirror, and anyone on the other side could see me.

But I couldn't see them.

CHAPTER 44

SCHLEPER EXPECTED ME to sit facing the mirror. Not my first choice. I knew the other chair better; the one with wheels; the one Schleper would sit in. People of suspicion—convicts, criminals, suspects—occupied the one facing the mirror.

Today, that felt like me.

Leaning back in the wheel-less, uncomfortable chair, I put my feet on the table, laced my fingers behind my head, and took a deep breath. I fought the temptation to steal a glance at the mirror. My jaw tightened, and I counted to ten.

People stared, watching me. I didn't like it.

Schleper strolled in about fifteen minutes later, a clear indicator that his time was more valuable than mine. He laid his notebook on the table, flipped on the fan, and sat in the chair with wheels, his back to the mirror. He didn't acknowledge me, instead, taking his pencil and jotting some notes.

I waited.

After a few minutes, he raised his head. "Mr. Conklin, there are a few things to clear up."

Difficult as it was, I continued to ignore the one-way glass. "Clear up? Like what?"

Schleper exhaled. "I'll ask the questions."

I lowered my feet and rested my arms on the table. "Ask away." I hesitated then added, "Inspector." An instant after saying it, I wished I hadn't and leaned back again.

He glared at me, rubbed the side of his nose with the pencil. "Tell me again, who found the body and how."

He knew the story, so I made a point of drawing out a long, slow sigh before starting. "Lester and I found her, north of the entry point at Karpata."

"It was you *and* Mr. Jeffrey who found the body?" He poised his pencil at the paper, ready to write as if waiting for a starter's pistol to be fired.

"Well . . . no."

Schleper's head didn't move, but his eyes slowly raised to meet mine. He laid down the pencil and rolled up his sleeves. I wore a T-shirt and didn't have sleeves to roll up. I felt cheated.

"We went down the stairs, and I told Lester to go south. I went north. She was a few yards up the north shore."

"*You* found the body." He made a few notes. I waited, continuing to resist the urge to peek at the glass, my resolve dwindling. "How did you know which way to go?"

"What do you mean?"

"You sent Mr. Jeffrey in the other direction."

My heart pounded in my chest, and I jumped to my feet, the chair falling behind me. I didn't bother counting to ten. "What is this?" Unable to control the urge any longer, I glanced at the one-way glass and wiped several beads of sweat from my face. "What are you imply-ing, *Inspector.*"

A vein in Schleper's forehead pulsed. For a moment, neither of us said anything. I calmed myself and got my breathing under control, then picked up the chair and sat. This conversation needed to go my way, and thus far it hadn't. I needed to turn it around, keep Schleper from having control.

Schleper leaned back and placed his hands on his lap, a non-confrontational posture taught during Interrogation 101.

The door opened, and an officer walked in. Schleper waved him over to the table and extended his hand. The officer handed Schleper a plastic bag and walked back to the door but didn't leave. He shut the door and remained standing near it—on the inside of the room.

Another escape blocked.

I jerked a thumb at the officer. "You think I'm dangerous?"

"Officer Pasik should remain here with us." He leaned over and placed the bag on the table, inches in front of me. "What can you tell me about this?" He tapped his finger twice on the table near the bag, then leaned back again, waiting for my reaction.

The bag was a plastic evidence bag like thousands I'd seen before. No doubt it held a surprise, but I didn't reach for it right away. I braced myself and didn't move for several seconds.

Most days, I liked surprises. But based on Schleper's cocky demeanor, this wasn't one of those days.

I took the bag off the table. Inside was a pair of sunglasses. I examined the sunglasses and moved them around behind the plastic using my index fingers and thumbs. The screw in the right-side hinge was a slightly different color than the left one, and a scratch was visible on the head. I had replaced the screw a few weeks ago after drinking too many beers and using a screwdriver that was too large.

"It's a pair of sunglasses," I said, tossing the bag into Schleper's lap.

"Do they look familiar?"

I shrugged.

Schleper picked up the bag. "We found these in the rocks near Miss Wilcox's body." He fingered the glasses through the plastic. "Would you be surprised if I told you we found fingerprints on the glasses?"

"No. I would expect prints or at least partials."

"What if I told you the fingerprints were yours?"

Something dawned on me. Just as easy as laying a drill on the seat of my Wrangler, someone could've reached in through the window and taken my sunglasses. Or, without me noticing—when I wasn't home, possibly at the hospital with Arabella—the sunglasses could've been swiped from my kitchen counter.

"Would you not find that interesting?" he asked.

I stayed silent.

"You knew where the body was, and your sunglasses were found at the scene."

"I had a fifty-fifty shot on the direction. Prove I dropped the glasses at that time." After saying it, I wished I hadn't used the word prove. "Someone else might've put them there."

Schleper smiled. "I cannot prove anything . . . yet." He rocked in his chair and made a point of examining the glasses again. He looked at me. "Did you drop them when you *found* Miss Wilcox?" He placed the glasses on the table and forced a chuckle. "Or do you think someone on the island wants to frame you?"

My silence was all the answer he needed.

"Where were you the afternoon Miss Wilcox drowned?" he asked.

"Vinny's, having a couple of beers."

"Good, then you must have a debit card slip."

I didn't say anything.

"No? Bar receipt, then?" he asked.

I sighed.

"I see." He continued with his notes.

"This is ridiculous. Check the cam outside of Vinny's. I waved at it. Twice."

Big Brother is watching.

"Yes, we will check that cam." He stopped with the notes and touched his chin with the pencil. "Mr. Conklin, we need to explore all leads."

Follow every lead, no matter how small. Maybe Schleper and Bill had the same desk signs.

"What about the truck?" I asked. "The truck Malfena talked about."

"Mr. Conklin, do you know how many trucks are on this island?"

"But only three with a seahorse painted on the tailgate." I paused for effect, then continued. "And one is in the repair shop."

"We are aware of that. You see, Mr. Jeffrey came in and spoke to us, voluntarily. He was very cooperative."

I couldn't hold back a short laugh. "What did he say?"

"I do not think laughter is advised at this time, Mr. Conklin. Besides, you of all people should know I cannot talk about an interview with someone else."

"Motive. That's what I used to dig for. What's mine?"

Schleper leaned back in his chair, this time folding his arms across his chest. He rocked a few times, then straightened and leafed through his notes, shuffling a couple of pages. "Well, Mr. Conklin, it seems Mr. Jeffrey was helpful. He gave us some interesting information." He raised his eyebrows. "He told us that you are the father of Miss Wilcox's child."

For an instant, the world stopped spinning. Then spun out of control. Sweat rolled down my back as his words echoed through the room. I folded my hands on the table and looked at the floor.

"Oh, that is right," he said. "You are unaware."

He had maneuvered me right to where he wanted me; as if I were a hooked tuna he needed to pull onto the boat. Schleper laid down his pencil, stood, and walked around to my side of the desk, plopping his butt on the edge in front of me.

"I believe Mr. Jeffrey said that Miss Wilcox wanted to tell you," he said. "That is why she came to the island."

"Impossible."

"Oh?"

"Yes. Impossible."

"Or maybe she told you, and you were not happy. Maybe the responsibility of a child would destroy your little paradise life on this island." He jumped off the desk and put a hand on each arm of my chair, leaning in so close I could almost taste his bad breath. I maintained my composure and started a ten count. "Maybe the idea of being a parent was too much for you to handle. Before you know it, you lose it." His eyes widened. "Sound about right?"

I made it to five when my patience broke. I sprang to my feet, putting a fist in Schleper's chest, driving him back and onto the desk. Pasik's shoes clicked against the concrete floor as he approached me from behind. I took a step backward to close the distance and spun, delivering an elbow to his nose. His head snapped back, and he staggered. He shook his head trying to clear the cobwebs and grabbed for his weapon. He cleared the holster as another officer ran into the room armed with a Taser.

Schleper stood and waved everyone off. "Stop," he said. "Hold everything." He walked over to the door and said something in Papiamentu to Pasik, who then left the room. Schleper closed the door. He motioned for the other officer, the one holding the Taser, to stay put and walked over to me.

"Innocent, huh? Not the kind of behavior I would expect," Schleper said.

As my muscles relaxed and the adrenaline subsided, it dawned on me what I had just done. Expecting handcuffs, a cellmate everyone called Tiny, and a monthly postcard from Chuck, I didn't say anything and waited for what came next. Probably a trip to the Big House. Shaking my head, I finally stole another glace at the mirror.

But only for a moment.

"I do not know what's going on, but I will get to the bottom of it," Schleper said.

Throat dry, my voice cracked as I said, "I truly hope so."

To my surprise, Schleper walked over to the desk and barked some Papiamentu to the officer, who left immediately. He looked at me for a second then flipped through his notes. "We are finished, Mr. Conklin. That is, for now."

I was speechless. My actions over the last couple of minutes made me look foolish, if not guilty, and I couldn't take them back. Hard to call Schleper the jerk this time. I should be processed and jailed.

"Schleper, there's no way that child—"

"That is all, Mr. Conklin." Lips pursed, he waved me toward the door. "Or should I call in some officers and, how do you say . . . throw the book at you?"

I turned and walked out of the room. Several cops mulled and watched me limp down the narrow hallway, their eyes penetrating my body like nine-millimeter rounds on a range target. I stared straight ahead and resisted the urge to ask any of them for a ride.

How could Lester think I was the father? Tiffany knew I wasn't, and she wouldn't have told him otherwise. Did he assume on his own? If so, that could explain his hostility toward me. In his warped view of reality, maybe he saw me as neglecting my responsibilities to Tiffany and Ozzy.

Or, maybe, he was lying to Schleper. But if so, why?

The sky was clear and blue and the blazing Caribbean heat greeted me as I left the police station. I shook my head in disbelief. Schleper's *investigation* was out of control.

As I walked back to the YellowRock, I couldn't help wondering who was behind the one-way glass.

And how all of this would affect our relationship.

CHAPTER 45

THE NEXT AFTERNOON a police squad car was parked across the street from the YellowRock. The two officers in the front seat were the same two who had previously escorted me to the station. Small Cop snoozed while Big Cop held his hand out the window dangling a cigarette.

Still hadn't heard from Penn. I considered calling him again but knew it wouldn't do any good. My cell rang; Chuck calling. I sighed and plopped into my chair, letting the phone ring four or five times before answering it.

"Any more talks with the cops?" I asked.

"No, but last night, Jan told me they talked to him."

"Same questions?"

"Pretty much."

"Jeez . . . Anyway, what's up?"

"Tomorrow's the big day."

"The big day?"

"Yeah, flying that guy off the island. Ten thousand big ones."

"Chuck . . ."

"I'll cut you in if you want to go along."

"If I were to go, I'd fly. You can ride shotgun."

"Fine with me, so long as I get the same cut. Does that mean you're going?" I could almost see the glee on his face.

"No, I'm not going."

"Oh, c'mon."

"Not going to happen. I suggest you don't go either."

"I need the money. Besides, it's a short, easy trip."

I leaned over and grabbed a beer from the office fridge and opened it.

"Did you open a beer?" Chuck asked.

"Yes." I took a sip. "Who's your client anyway?"

"Can't say."

"Can't or won't?"

"I'm sworn to secrecy. Client's request."

Arabella walked into the office, and I motioned for her to lock the door. She twisted the dead bolt, and I waved for her to follow me up the stairs to my apartment.

"Do me one favor, buddy," I said. "Think this over tonight and call me before you leave tomorrow."

"Give you another chance to talk me out of it?"

I smiled at Arabella. She wore a T-shirt that happened to be my favorite. It was black and had a white banjo on the front. In white lettering above the banjo, it read, *Feel Safe at Night, Sleep with a Banjo Player.*

"Go to Vinny's and get smashed," I said to Chuck. "You'll be too hungover to fly."

Chuck released a deep breath into the phone. "Okay, call you tomorrow." He hung up.

Arabella sat on a counter stool and didn't stretch up to meet me as I gave her a peck on the lips.

"You want a beer?" I asked.

She shook her head.

"You notice the squad outside?"

She furrowed her brow.

"Yeah, I guess Schleper wants me watched." I walked out on the veranda and checked for the police truck across the street. "Yup, they're still there." I raised my beer to them. "Going to be a long night, fellas."

I walked over to Arabella and put a hand on her shoulder. "Okay, what's wrong?"

She bit her lower lip and looked at the floor.

"Sorry if I got you in trouble," I said. "You know that wasn't my intention. I need to figure this thing out."

"I do not think the squad is watching for you."

"They're not?"

She shook her head. "I believe they are watching for one of your guests."

"So Schleper does believe us."

"Or at least part. I believe he is covering his butt. He wants to eliminate you as a suspect."

"'Covering his butt'? Is that a new technical police term?"

She didn't smile.

"What's wrong?"

She wiped her eye, took a deep breath, and said, "I did not come here to talk about the case."

I waited.

"I came here to talk about us."

"What . . . about . . . us?"

"I heard your talk with Schleper. Yes, I was on the other side of the glass." She stood and paced in front of the couch. "I heard why Tiffany came to the island. I always teased you about her being your girlfriend, but I never meant it."

"Bella, you can't possibly think that I—"

She stopped her pacing and focused deep into my eyes. "That you what? Killed Tiffany?" She shook her head. "Not in a million years do I believe that."

"Then what's the problem?"

"Are you the father of her child? I need to know."

"No, I'm not."

"Then why would Lester say such a thing?"

"I don't know."

She was quiet.

"Seriously," I said.

She brushed several strands of hair away from her face and hooked them around her ear. "Did you sleep with her?"

"No, never. She'd always been like a kid sister to me. You have to believe that."

She went to the fridge and got a Bright. She took a drink, then another. I waited. "I was not alone on the other side, you know. There were others. As soon as Schleper mentioned you and the child, everyone looked at me. It was embarrassing."

"I'm sorry, Bella. Schleper's a jerk, and he shouldn't have said that. Please believe that there's no truth to anything he said."

Arabella collapsed into my arms. I held her, and we swayed to an internal rhythm for several minutes. I kissed her on the head, and she pulled away.

"There is something else," she said.

"What?"

"It's about the suicide."

"Malfena's?"

"Yes, Malfena's . . . Anyway, it was not suicide. First, Schleper has not let anyone see the note. He claims to have it, but no one else has seen it." She jabbed her finger at me. "And, Roberto, the first officer there, never saw it. Schleper found it when *he* arrived."

"Interesting."

"Wait, I have more." She took a drink of beer. "By accident, I saw a report—"

"By accident?"

"Conklin, let me finish. The report said that she was shot, in the head."

"What?"

"Yes. A bullet was found under the car. She was shot in the trunk, and the bullet went through to the ground." Her eyes widened. "Guess what caliber."

"Nine-millimeter."

"Exactly."

If I could whistle, I'd have done so. "Has Ruth mentioned anything about Wilbur being missing?"

"She has not said."

"You should ask her."

"I will. As far as I know, no one knows about Wilbur except you and me."

"And all the girls in her front yard the other day."

"Yes." Her shoulders slumped. "And Lester."

"Yes, and Lester."

"Can they trace it back to Ruth?"

"Maybe, maybe not. It would most likely have her fingerprints on it."

We both took a drink of beer.

"By the way," I said, "how did the fire department find the car fire?"

"A call from an unknown cell. We could not trace it."

Anonymous call. We couldn't trace it so probably a burner phone. Just like Bill and Marybeth.

"I'm guessing the car was stolen," I said.

"Yes, it is a rental. Damn tourist left a key in the ignition. It was parked at a resort so no street cams. The resort has security cameras so Schleper will request them."

"Good. That could point to whoever is behind all of this."

She smiled. "*Ja hoor.*"

"I have something for you, too," I said. "Things have spun out of control so bad lately that I haven't had a chance to run this past you."

"Before you start, I have something to give you." She walked over and reached into the leather bag that she sometimes carried and pulled out a revolver. She opened the cylinder, eyed the cartridges, and closed it. "I want you to have this for a while." She gripped the weapon around the middle and handed it to me in such a way that the muzzle was pointed down and away, the handle toward me. "With everything that has happened lately, I need you to be safe."

She wanted me to take her backup weapon, an older Smith and Wesson snub-nosed revolver, chambered in a .38 Special. I doubted I'd need it but nodded and said, "Thanks."

"Be careful," she said, as I opened the cylinder and verified six cartridges. "It's fully loaded."

"I hope so. Hate to think you'd loan me an empty weapon." I smiled and, because Arabella was a stickler for maintenance and proper weapon care, made a point of gently closing the cylinder. TV shows depict people snapping revolver cylinders shut with a flip of their wrist. In reality, that technique causes damage to the cylinder crane and over time can create a loose fit between the cylinder and the body of the weapon. "If Schleper finds out about this, your career is over."

She bit her lower lip momentarily. "Probably, but I need you to be safe."

"Okay." I went to the bedroom and placed the .38 in my top dresser drawer, on top of a pair of socks I hadn't worn in months. Before shutting the drawer, I ran a finger across the brown, wood-simulated grip.

Her backup piece. Not sure I'd ever loved someone enough to hand over my secondary weapon. Let alone risk my career.

I left the bedroom and walked back to Arabella. "Schleper and your career aside, I feel guilty taking your backup piece. What if you need it?"

"Do not worry, I have yet another weapon I can use."

Three firearms? Wasn't sure I realized that.

She smiled. "Always have as much firepower as possible."

I considered her shirt again. Maybe I should have one made that said, *Feel Safe at Night, Sleep with Arabella.*

She looked at me, eyes wide. "Okay, now what do you have for me?"

"This is big. Penn, in Rockford, is doing some research for me, so we'll see what he comes back with, but—"

"Conklin, I can research for you."

"I know, but I had him on the phone, so I asked."

She sighed and waited for me to start.

"You may want to sit for this," I said.

She sat. I took a long hit on my beer.

"Ten years or so before I retired, Bill and I worked a case involving a murder at the local city dump, located ten miles south of Rockford in a small town called New Milford. New Milford doesn't have a detective force, so they asked RPD for help.

"Well, a body was found at the dump. But not out in the sludge and garbage. It was laying on one of the main dirt roads that the trucks use. No attempt to hide it. In fact, the first truck of the day almost ran over it. Two gunshots to the head, from behind. Turned out to be .22s. No wallet or driver's license, so we used fingerprints to ID the body. It turned out the victim was the brother of a city alderman. Everyone knew this alderman was on the take and as crooked as the day is long."

I had never gone into detail about any of my old cases. Arabella liked talking shop and sat forward in her lounger, hanging on every word. Wide-eyed with a faint smile, she listened like a six-year-old hearing a bedtime story.

"We didn't have much to go on, so we had uniforms ask around the area. The dump is in a rural area on a secondary road, so the houses are pretty scattered. No one saw or heard anything. After two weeks, I was ready to let it go cold, but Bill wasn't. He said we needed to push a little longer and something would spring."

"Was he right?"

"Yeah, kind of. Bill always said, 'Work from the end,' so we went back to the dump one afternoon. We stood on the dirt road, nosed around a bit, and bounced ideas off each other. But we didn't get anywhere."

"What did you do?"

"We left. But, on the way back, we stopped at a convenience store in New Milford. Bill claimed the place made the best hot dogs in the county, and he was hungry. Well, anyway, it was a good thing we stopped.

"The girl working the register saw our badges and asked if we were investigating the murder at the dump. It was big news in a town the size of New Milford. She said she was working the night of the killing and was still freaked out—her words—by the whole thing. Bill showed her a picture of the victim, and she said she thought he had been in the store.

"We checked the security video for several weeks before and after the murder, and sure enough, he *had* been in the store. Several times. He even stopped on the night of the murder. But he wasn't alone. Two other guys were with him. We used the video to get a mug shot of his companions and circulate it around the department."

"Did someone know them?"

"Yeah, one of them. He was a petty thug, in and out of county a dozen times. We tracked him down and brought him in. He claimed his innocence, big surprise. We had an eyewitness placing him with the victim the night of the murder. But that's all. Nothing else. No weapon, no motive, no blood or trace evidence. Circumstantial at best.

"Bill thought we might have at least one of the guys. We couldn't ID the other guy, and the one we had wouldn't give up his buddy."

"So?"

"The alderman puts pressure on us to make this guy as his brother's killer. I didn't bite. No way this is a case. Bill is on the fence. So, the alderman goes to the DA's office. Suddenly, the DA says to lean hard on the guy, so Bill does. Real hard. I wasn't so sure. So, two goofballs know each other. Big deal. Doesn't prove murder."

Arabella shook her head. "No, it does not."

"Bill had never been in such a hurry with so little to go on. I kept telling him to slow down, let's make sure. But Bill kept forging ahead. I was the odd man out on this one. Usually, Bill was telling *me* to slow down."

"Wow." She smiled wide, almost laughing in disbelief.

"The guy finally pleaded out. It stunk, but the die was cast. Part of the plea was that he didn't have to rat out his friend. Everyone was happy. The DA closed the case, and the alderman strung up his brother's killer." I swallowed some beer, glanced away for a moment, and shook my head. "Bill was never the same after that. Neither was I. It was disappointing and not our best work. It went against everything I thought Bill stood for and what I believed.

"After that, all he wanted to do was retire, which he did about two years later. That was the one case we never talked about." I finished my beer and stared at Arabella.

"What?"

"Tiffany was the witness, the girl at the register that night."

She scrunched her eyebrows and glared at me. "Oh, Conklin—"

"She was all we had."

"You had the video, no?"

"Not really. The video only showed a couple of guys at a gas station. Circumstantial at best. If not for Tiffany, Bill and the DA couldn't have pressed so hard. The plea wouldn't have happened."

"But you became friends with her."

"I know. Unethical, to say the least. But there wasn't a trial. It just happened. She met Marybeth and considered her a mother figure. I don't know . . . We all became friends."

Arabella slowly shook her head.

"Like I said, not my proudest moment."

We were both quiet for a moment. Arabella straightened her back. "Seems you are the only one left."

She was right, again. I *was* the last one left, and hearing it out loud drove the point home, which may have been her intent.

"So how does all of this help us?" she asked. "What should we do?"

"That's the second half of what I have for you."

I went to my desk and brought back a pencil and a piece of paper. I wrote out the words *four-wheel drive* and *4WD*.

"See this?" I said, pointing at the words *four-wheel drive.*

"Yes, that is from the ad."

"It doesn't mean four, as in the number four," I said.

She hadn't gotten it yet.

"It means for as in f. o. r." I crossed out the *4* in *4WD* and replaced it with *for.* I showed her the paper. "What does this mean to you?"

"It could mean *for* someone with the initials W and D."

"The guy that took the plea, and went to prison?"

"Yes?"

"His name was Wayne Dow."

She pored over the paper for a moment, eyes widening. "For Wayne Dow! *Heilig shit!*"

"To say the least."

CHAPTER 46

I STOOD ON the veranda and watched the morning rain drench the island. With an average rainfall of fewer than twenty inches per year, precipitation was a rare event on Bonaire. But when it came, it did so in a deluge. The intense downpours lasted only fifteen minutes or less and caused large standing puddles and flooded roads. I sipped a Diet Coke, munched on the last microwaved apple donut, and watched cars drive past the YellowRock throwing large columns of water across the sidewalks.

The surveillance team was gone. I scanned the street in both directions and leaned out beyond the railing to check the nearby side street. I also checked the parking lot. No sign of the squad or the truck with a seahorse on the tailgate. Lester had to be somewhere with Mandy, which could be bad for Mandy. Bonaire was a small island. A person—or persons—couldn't hide forever.

Tiffany came to mind as I held the last bite of donut between my forefinger and thumb. I couldn't bring myself to finish it and broke it into several pieces, lying them on the far side of the railing. A few small yellow and black birds called chibi-chibis braved the rain and converged on the remnants. They're known on Bonaire as "the Sugar Thief" because they like all things sweet, even many-days-old, microwaved apple donuts. They devoured the morsels in a matter of seconds and stood on the railing screeching at me. One lost patience and flew away.

I held up my hands. "Sorry, guys, that's all there is."

The gray clouds moved across the island at a steady pace, and I self-ishly hoped the bad weather would last most of the day. The low ceiling and poor visibility would make it impossible for Chuck to fly over to Spelonk and carry out his planned trip.

A boat from one of the dive operators sped across the water, headed south with a full load of divers. Rain never stopped the diving. The term *Dive into the Weekend* had a very literal meaning on Bonaire. The sun peeked through the overcast in the south, bringing with it the trademark blue sky of Bonaire. The weather would soon return to normal, back to perfect.

My rib didn't hurt as much as it had the last few days but still ached whenever I shifted my weight to the right. Any attempt to run or swim was at least a week or more away. I finished my soda and tossed the empty can in the bin, but before I could head downstairs, Arabella called my cell.

"You're up early," I said.

"Morning, Conklin. I have been up most of last night and early this morning researching Wayne Dow."

"What'd you get?"

"I was able to get stuff from the NCIC and—"

"The NCIC? How'd you get access?" She referred to the National Crime Informational Center, a multiple database criminal records system owned and operated by the FBI.

"I have friends in The Netherlands who helped. But some of this I got from doing internet searches. My friends in Holland even got information from your old department."

I had no idea who she, or her Holland friends, had talked to in Rockford or how they had tapped into NCIC, but it didn't matter. I was eager to listen. Her voice rang with excitement and I hoped the new intel would create some forward momentum.

"That Wayne Dow stuff," she said. "Wow, it sure was a messy hell."

"Yeah, I told you."

"They found him dead in his cell a few years ago. The case said *mysterious circumstances*, whatever that means. Earlier, they had moved him to a place called Big Muddy River Correctional Center, in Ina, Illinois. Doesn't say why." She said the "s" at the end of Illinois.

"Yeah, I know the place. Does it say—"

"Hold on, Conklin, there is more," she said. "Dow had a wife and son."

"I remember."

"Seems after Dow dies, the wife commits suicide. She shot herself in the head. Residue on her hand, stippling on the temple, handwritten note—verified by a writing expert. No doubt she did it."

She paused.

"But?" I said.

"Strange thing, though, no gun was recovered."

"Don't tell me."

"Medium caliber," she said. "Seems there was never ballistics testing with the wife's suicide, so nothing was in the system."

"Penn had mentioned partial prints on some of the cartridges. I'm betting they're Dow's, loaded back before he went to prison."

"Would make sense, but I do not have any information on that."

"What about the son?"

"Report says Dow Junior found his mom's body. Swears there was no gun. No one believed him, but they could not prove otherwise."

"He took it."

"That would be a good working theory, but, again, how to prove it."

"Anyone talk to him?"

"Looks like no one knows where he is."

"What?"

"Yeah, it is like he vanished. He was an adult when all this happened, and it seems he disappeared, right after his mother's suicide."

"Job?"

"Nothing currently. It looks like his last job was at Jay's Automotive in Rockford, Illinois."

A hollow sensation stung me as my mouth went dry.

"There was an insurance policy on his mom, Dow's wife."

I swallowed what saliva I could muster and said, "How much?"

"No information."

"How about Lester Jeffrey?"

"He is twenty-eight, graduated from Rockford High School East, and went to Rock Valley Junior College, has a two-year degree in criminal justice. Clean record . . . Get this. He works for a private security company. Doing what exactly, I do not know. Lives in Madison, Wisconsin."

The license plate at Vinny's came to mind. *EVR COOL.*

"Bella, is it possible—"

"Conklin, I do not see any connection between him, the Rybergs, or Dow."

We were both quiet for a moment. Lester was a weird cookie, but that didn't mean he was a murderer. Or in any way mixed up with this. But everything kept coming back to him.

"I'm checking island immigration," she said, "to see if they processed someone named Wayne Dow Jr. I should rule it out."

"Agreed. Have you spoken with Schleper?"

"Ha! I do not think he wants to hear our leads. Besides, I was told not to talk to you about this. I am on his shit list right now and need to lightly tread."

"Okay. Good work and thanks. Thanks for the weapon last night, too."

"Please be careful. Speaking of shit lists, I think you are the last one on his—whoever this Wayne Dow Junior person is."

"Yeah, I think you're right."

"Oh, and I forgot to tell you. When I left last night, my car would not start again. I took your Wrangler."

CHAPTER 47

Erika sat at her desk, typing away on the keyboard. I hadn't expected her back to work until after Malfena's funeral, which was still two days away. A man had walked out of the office as I came down the last stair. I did a double take, noticing his orange Chicago Bears hat.

"What are you doing here?" I asked Erika.

"Working." She continued fingering her keyboard. "That is what you pay me for?"

"I thought you'd be with Cado. At least until after the funeral."

She leaned back in the chair, eyes fixated on the monitor. "Ludson has a lot of family right now. Besides, I need to get away from all the sadness. Work takes my mind off it." She straightened and shuffled through stacks of papers on her desk. "When I am not here, no work gets done."

I bit my lower lip, shook my head, and held back a grin. She needed to win this one, so I kept quiet. Besides, I agreed with her.

I sat for a few moments and considered the conversation with Arabella. She had given me a lot of useful information on Dow, stuff I didn't previously know. But the info on Lester left me stumped. I'd have bet a new banjo on Lester being my man. It all added up. His attitude this week, him being at Ruth's after Tiffany died, his truck at

Karpata, his lies to Schleper. Bill would say it was all circumstantial and he'd be right. I had nothing tying Lester to any of the crimes. The facts needed to stand on their own and not be manipulated to fit *my* prejudicial vision.

I didn't like Lester and didn't like the way he had treated Tiffany. She deserved better, and I'd never understand why she stayed with him. My disdain for him had encouraged me to mold reality to implicate him. His relationship with Mandy was also unsettling. Why would he bring his girlfriend to a tropical island, then spend time with another woman?

Mandy *W.* Driver.

I stared at the dirty ceiling tile again for inspiration and considered the guy who had earlier walked out of the office.

"Hey, Erika, who was the guy that left as I came down the stairs?" I asked.

She continued with her work for a moment, but eventually said, "That was Mandy."

I hadn't met Mandy, but that didn't make sense. Maybe Erika hadn't heard me correctly. "No, I mean the *guy.*"

She laid her glasses on the desk and turned to face me. "Mandy Driver, one of our guests. He said someone left a note for him to stop by the office. I did not know what he was talking about."

"Mandy is a *man?*"

She stared at me and leaned forward. "Did you not hear what I said? Yes, that was Mandy." She turned back to her computer and put her glasses on. "So, yes, Mandy is a man, and he is not happy that someone—" she glanced over her shoulder in my direction "—went into his room with no permission."

A guy. A *guy!*

That explained the lack of toiletries and clothing.

Follow every lead, no matter how small.

I called Arabella and when she answered, I asked, "Can you do a little more research for me?"

"Sure, I will try. What do you need?"

"Find out what you can on Mandy Driver . . . Mandy *W.* Driver."

"Yes, I can find out about her."

"Not *her.*"

"What?"

"Yeah, I just ran into Mandy." I avoided Erika's gloat, my face burning with embarrassment. "*She* is *he.*"

"What? Mandy is a man?" Arabella said.

"Yup."

"Wow. I will call you back."

Arabella would provide information on Mandy, but I didn't need to sit and wait. No reason I couldn't do searches of my own. After all, over the past few days, I'd developed into an internet guru.

First, I searched on Wayne Dow. Should've done this earlier, but I didn't need to with Penn pulling the information. Or at least I thought he was. Thankfully, Arabella came to the rescue.

The effort yielded results for white pages, Facebook pages, and LinkedIn profiles. I read them all but didn't discover anything of value. I discerned most of the listings and links didn't pertain to *my* Wayne Dow—different spellings, ages, locations, and in one case, even an incorrect gender. Lots of bogus information on the net.

I found several obituaries and a photo. One of the obits was for Wayne Dow, Sr. It mentioned he died in his cell at Big Muddy River Correctional Center, as Arabella had said, and left behind a wife, Shelly, and a son, Wayne Jr.

Along the side of my screen were several links regarding the name Wayne. If so inclined, I could discover the meaning, where it came from, and the definition.

Being an in-depth investigator and a world-class detective, I clicked on the link about the meaning. Things like a craftsman, wagon-wright, and wagon driver were listed. It noted John Wayne as a famous bearer of the name. Interesting, possibly.

Next, I found the obituary for Shelly Dow, maiden name: Mandel. She was preceded in death by her husband and left behind a son, Wayne Jr. No surprise.

I went back and clicked on the photo of Dow, enlarging it as much as possible. The resolution was weak, and the picture was old, taken at least twenty years ago. It showed Dow standing against a brick wall in an orange prison suit, probably taken during one of his many incarcerations, before the one that caused his death.

Even with the poor picture quality, his brown and glossy eyes held me in a trance, trying to pierce through me. No doubt about it—a dark spot in the white of his left eye.

I paged back through all the search data. The link was there, and like an ember igniting a roaring fire, the pieces fell into place. My heart skipped a beat. My mouth went dry. Compared to this, discovering Bigfoot or finding life on Mars seemed insignificant.

"Aha!" I said, and to make sure I was right, said "Aha!" again. Erika glanced over her shoulder and stared at me. I smiled and gave a thumbs-up gesture in her direction. It wasn't yet noon, but I reached into the fridge and grabbed a beer.

However, before too much celebrating, I had a little more sleuthing to do. Erika maintained the reservations and payment methods in a spreadsheet stored on our office server. When I clicked the file open, I was prompted for a password.

"Erika, what's the password for the spreadsheet with the payment info?"

"Don't you know it?"

"I wouldn't be asking if I did."

She folded her arms across her chest and swiveled her chair in my direction. "Why do I have to tell you each time?"

"Erika!" She flinched. I softened my tone and asked again. "What's the password?"

She recited the password and I opened the file. Among other things, the spreadsheet listed the current guests, arrival and departure dates, and payment methods. As was typical, everyone checked in had paid in advance with a credit card. Every guest, that is, except one. That person had paid with a direct money transfer. To accurately determine who had initiated the wire transfer, I used the transaction ID listed in the spreadsheet and, with Erika's begrudging assistance, logged into the bank website.

After a few clicks and a couple of page loads, there it was. The name. No Senior or Junior listed. Just Wayne Dow. Reinforcement of my earlier "Aha!" moment.

I pulled out a piece of paper and wrote *Mandel Wagon Driver*.

Then crossed it out and wrote *Mandy W. Driver*.

CHAPTER 48

BEFORE I COULD grab my phone and call Arabella to tell her what I had discovered, she called me. Much sooner than I had anticipated.

"Bella, you won't believe what I figured out."

"Conklin, listen to me. I was right. They were not watching you." Her voice went soft. "Something is up. I heard Schleper is on his way to talk to you."

"Over here?"

"Uh-huh."

I drummed my fingers on the desktop. "Any idea when?"

Before she could answer, the office door opened and in marched Schleper. He greeted Erika and walked in my direction. I abruptly ended the call without another word to Arabella and placed the phone on a small stack of papers near the corner of my desk.

I leaned back and put my feet up. "Hello, Inspector."

He grabbed the spare chair against the wall, set it in front of my desk, and sat. "Are you not surprised to see me?" He looked at my cellphone, then back at me.

I put my hands behind my head and interlaced my fingers, pointing my elbows straight out.

"I think we need to talk," he said.

"Here?"

He smiled. "Mr. Conklin, this is not an official visit. I would call it . . . a friendly chat."

"Okay." I straightened and rested my arms in front of me on the desk. "Why do you have men watching me?"

He glanced over his shoulder at Erika. Turning back to me, he whispered, "Do not be a fool, they were not watching you. They were watching for one of your guests." He reached into his pants pocket, took out an evidence bag, and held it out for me to see before dropping it on the desk.

I picked up the bag and removed the sunglasses from the inside. The right-side hinge screw was still scratched and still a slightly different color than the left-side one. I nodded and set the glasses and bag off to the side.

"How's Officer Pasik?" I asked.

"Yes, well, his nose is bruised, but not broken."

"I'm not proud of what happened. Do you think he'd accept my apologies?"

"He is young and tough. He will recover." Schleper pointed at my open beer. "He drinks regular Amstel."

I glanced at the beer, and back at Schleper. "Understood."

"I think you know who we are watching."

"Tell me anyway."

He motioned a thumb toward Erika.

I took a deep breath. "Erika, could you step outside for a few minutes?"

She stopped what she was doing and sat motionless for a moment. Standing, she laid her glasses on her keyboard and gathered some envelopes lying on the desk. "I need to take these to the post office." She grabbed her car keys but then placed them back in her purse. "I will walk to give you *men* more time."

After Erika had closed the door behind her, Schleper pulled a picture from his shirt pocket and handed it to me. It didn't require a detailed look. Long blond hair, pointed nose, and a dark spot in the white of his left eye. I handed the picture back to Schleper.

"I'm betting he's the same guy who tampered with my Wrangler, put Arabella in the hospital," I said.

"I agree but cannot prove it. We have no physical evidence."

My mouth went dry. *You mean like a cordless drill or a turkey baster? Or a set of brake hoses?* "Have you found him?" My voice cracked on the first two words, the realization of my evidence tampering hitting me harder than a rogue wave against a rowboat.

"No, not yet." He put the picture back in his shirt pocket. "We think he killed Miss Wilcox and Mrs. Cado."

I felt my chest muscles tighten. "So, you agree with me after all. Those were both murders."

"Yes. The autopsy showed seawater in Miss Wilcox's lungs and nasal passages."

My stomach churned, bile raising in my throat, at the thought of Tiffany trying to breathe underwater.

"Remember those marks on her neck?" Schleper asked.

My voice cracked as I responded. "You mean the ones I pointed out to your people?"

He leaned back and smiled. "Mr. Conklin, we did not miss those marks. They were part of our investigation. The medical examiner determined that fingertips and thumbs most probably made the bruises." He put his hands around his neck.

"Someone held her under."

"Yes." He raised a finger. "She was not strangled. There were no blood vessel bursts behind her eyes or inside her mouth or nose. None on her face or any pressure marks. No indication of petechial hemorrhaging whatsoever. We believe someone dragged her out of the water after drowning her. We found some DNA under a fingernail."

"The water didn't wash it away?"

"All but one of her thumbs. We faxed a DNA report to your friend Mr. Traverso."

As much as I tried to show no reaction, my expression must've given me away.

"Officer De Groot told us about him and the murder of your friend Mr. Ryberg." The office was quiet for a few moments then Schleper continued. "Mrs. Cado's death was not a suicide."

In faked surprise, I raised my eyes to meet his.

"We could not tell the truth," he said. "Two murders in one week. This island could not handle that kind of news. We had to buy ourselves some time."

"What happened?"

He let out a breath. "A bullet wound to the skull. There was no ash or soot in her air passages."

"She was dead before the fire."

"Yes, but we cannot connect our suspect to her death. We believe it was him, maybe tying up loose ends, but we have no proof. Maybe he was afraid of what she saw."

"The sad part is, she didn't see anything."

"All of it is sad."

He was right. I leaned back in my chair, ran my fingers across my forehead. "Do you know where he is?"

"My team saw him come to your hotel last night. But he got away before they could apprehend him. They lost him through town."

My jaw dropped. "You lost him? On Bonaire? This isn't New York or . . ." I waved my hand. "Amsterdam."

"Mr. Conklin, as you have been so gracious to point out, it is a small island. We will find him."

"I think there is another person with him."

"According to my officers, he was alone last night. But if someone else is with him, they could be in danger."

"Okay, so where do we go from here?"

He stood. "*We* do not go anywhere. You will need to let my department do its job."

I stood. "I have some skin in this, too. Three of my friends are dead, and he tried to kill me once already. Who knows when he'll try again."

"Oh, yes, Mr. Conklin, we are *very* anxious about your safety." He raised his eyebrows. "If you like, we can place an officer to guard you." A thin smile crept across his face. "Maybe Officer Pasik will volunteer."

"Keep it. I haven't needed your help so far."

"No, you have not, and things have worked out so well for everyone around you, including Mr. and Mrs. Larsen."

My neck hairs bristled. "What about them?"

"Oh, that is right, you don't know," he said. "Mr. and Mrs. Larsen. Seems they had a truck with a seahorse on the tailgate. You were looking for such a truck?" He had a look of confusion—obviously faked. "Well, this morning, we found their bodies at the bottom of a cliff at Washington-Slagbaai Park. We are not sure what happened."

I didn't have a response. My stomach knotted. Ben and Sophie. From Dakota. All I could do was stare at the wall. Mandy was killing everyone I came in contact with.

He started out the door but hesitated. Maybe he felt bad about dropping that bombshell on me. Wasn't sure Schleper could feel bad about anything.

"Although I do not need to tell you this," he said. "Your hunch was correct. Mr. Wayne Dow Junior is on the island. An immigration lieutenant called me this morning. Without my knowledge, it seems Officer De Groot requested a search of incoming passports. Mr. Dow arrived last Saturday." Before leaving, he pointed a finger at me. "Even so, I warn you again, Mr. Conklin, stay out of this."

He left and didn't bother to shut the door on his way out.

CHAPTER 49

IF SCHLEPER AND his force couldn't locate Mandy, maybe I could. Someone had to find him before anyone else got hurt. Including me. I headed for the door but got a text message before making it out of the office.

Arabella had configured my cellphone with unique ringtones for people in my address book—her, Jan, Erika, Chuck. This ringtone was the generic one, signaling the message was from an unknown caller. I considered ignoring it but decided to take a quick glance.

It read, *Conklin, come to my room ASAP. Lester.*

A message from Lester was the last thing I expected. Especially one asking me to come to his room. I froze for a moment, peered down the path toward unit five, then at the text message again. Something didn't feel right. Was I expected to just waltz into Lester's room?

I turned and bounded up the stairs to my apartment, into my bedroom, and opened my dresser drawer. The snub-nose .38 lay where I had left it. I opened the cylinder, verified it was still fully loaded with six cartridges, and shut it—gently again, not with a wrist flip—hearing a click as it locked into position. Old habits are hard to break, and I extended my arms, holding the pistol out straight, lining up the sights. I hadn't fired a weapon in many years, so I took a few moments to acquaint myself with the grip and its balance characteristics before sliding it inside the belt on my left hip.

I ran down the path to unit five and knocked. No answer.

"Lester!" I shouted, knocking again.

Still no answer. I grabbed the door handle, and, to my surprise, it turned. Standing on the threshold, I nudged open the door.

Drapes closed, lights off, darkness engulfed the room, the only noise being that of the ceiling fan, clicking with every rotation. I pushed the door open further, casting a ray of sunlight across part of the room, and waited for my eyes to adjust. I made out a person lying on the bed. My heart sank as an all too familiar odor took hold of me.

Death has a particular smell.

I switched on the light and walked to the bed. Lester Jeffrey lay naked on his back in a muddle of blood-soaked covers, sheets, and pillows. His face was pale white, his lifeless eyes staring at the ceiling. A gash stretched from ear to ear across his throat, and the blade of his scuba knife stuck halfway out of his sternum. Blood stained his skin and ran down the bedsheets.

Held to his chest by the knife was a map of Bonaire, pierced at the exact location of Spelonk Lighthouse. The same map I had given Lester several nights ago in my apartment. Below it, pinched up close to the map, was a bloodstained picture.

To see the picture, I'd need to remove the knife from Lester's chest or tear the map off the blade. Doing either would be altering evidence at a murder scene. Not a trivial offense. Over the last few days, I had tampered with evidence, but the baster, brake hoses, and drill were related to the Wrangler's sabotage. A murder scene was more serious and, given a chance, Schleper would gladly "throw the book" at me.

But I had to do one or the other. The elaborate staging of this crime scene was a message. The piercing of the map at Spelonk was the first part, and the picture was the second. I needed to see it.

Lester's chest was a crimson-colored mess. Dried blood had acted as a glue of sorts, sticking the picture and map together. I didn't have time to devise a way to separate the two and maintain the evidence, so I decided to disturb as little as possible.

I retrieved a debit card from my wallet, knelt by the side of the bed, and slipped it between the picture and the map, gently separating them. Using the flashlight feature on my phone—a feature I thought I'd never use—I shone a small bead of light in the gap.

My heart pounded. The picture—one of Arabella and me having lunch at the Coral Reef Café, taken without my knowledge—was sliced through Arabella's face. In the dark, hands and eyes soaked with sweat, I fumbled with my phone and called her. It went straight to voicemail. I put the phone in my pocket and took a few deep breaths.

Only one option.

I ran out of the room, back up the stairs to my apartment, and grabbed my running shoes sitting on the floor in the bedroom corner. The rough terrain at Spelonk made sandals a poor choice for footwear. Time was critical, and I strapped on my Nikes, sockless.

I went to the office and told Erika to call the police and send them to unit five.

"But don't go in yourself," I said.

I ran out the door, but before getting to the back parking lot and Arabella's car, a man on the front sidewalk called my name.

"Sorry," I said, rushing past him, "I'm in a hurry."

"Please," he said from behind me. "It's about my wife, Malfena."

I stopped in my tracks and stood for a moment. He walked up behind me, his feet striking the sidewalk in an uneven, lopsided manner. I turned and saw a skinny, short man in tattered blue jeans and a gray T-shirt. A simple black baseball cap covered his head, wisps of gray hair poking out under the edges. Eyes swollen and sagging, jaw quivering, he languished in front of me for several long moments. Neither of us moved. He held a cane in his right hand and used it to support his diminutive body weight.

Three young men and a woman, none of whom I recognized, leaned against a car parked on the far side of the street. They watched us intently but didn't approach.

"I'm sorry for your loss," I said.

Ludson's eyes watered. "Sorry? That is all you can say?"

His voice was low, and I looked away, shame preventing me from maintaining eye contact with him.

"She did not deserve this," he said.

"No, sir, she didn't."

He shifted his body weight to his other leg and pointed the cane at me. "It is your fault. She would still be alive if it were not for you."

Hard for me to argue and I didn't know what to say. "I'm truly sorry."

He limped forward and poked me in the chest with his cane. The three men leaning against the car stood and began crossing the street. "Why did you come to this island? You should not be here. You had no right."

I took the poke and half-stepped backward. Ludson moved forward and poked me a second time, and, again, I did nothing except move back. The three men arrived, two of them each taking one of Ludson's arms and the third stepping between Ludson and me. I raised my hands in a surrender fashion and shook my head. The guy nodded and turned to face Ludson.

"I am a Christian man, Mr. Roscoe," Ludson said, the ends of his mouth curved down, his eyes sunken. "I . . . I should forgive you, but I cannot. I will never forgive you."

"Let's go, Papa," the guy said to Ludson. "Nothing more to do here." The guy turned to me. "*Mr. Roscoe* doesn't care." He spoke in English, as opposed to Papiamento, I assumed, so I'd know what he said.

Message delivered, loud and clear.

The other two men helped turn Ludson around and began moving him toward the car. After two slow strides, Ludson turned back to me. With tears streaming down his cheeks, he said, "What am I supposed to do now?"

Nothing I could say. I watched the five of them squeeze into their car and drive away. Ludson was right—although someone else pulled the trigger, Malfena's death was on me. Whether I lived on Bonaire or back in Rockford, Mandy may have still killed Bill, Marybeth, Tiffany, and possibly even Lester. But if I hadn't come to Bonaire, Malfena wouldn't have been involved. She'd still be alive.

As would the Larsens.

None of this was fair, but I couldn't dwell on it now. I had to compartmentalize, get my mind straight. Arabella was in trouble, and she needed my help.

Cycling between an adrenaline high and a guilty conscience, I crammed myself into the driver's seat of Arabella's car, turned the ignition key, and sighed with relief as the engine fired to life. I backed out of the parking spot and headed for Kaminda Lagun, the road that leads to Spelonk.

Traffic was light, and I sped through town, making good time. Several minutes outside of Kralendijk, as I approached the east side of the island, the sea appeared in front of me. The blacktop ended, and I pulled onto the three-mile rock and dirt road leading to Spelonk Lighthouse. I swerved the car from side to side, bypassing large ruts my Wrangler could've driven through with ease.

As I maneuvered to miss one rock, I hit an even larger one. The car jerked and bounced hard, slamming my head off the roof. Things blurred for a moment, and I shook off some dizziness but continued to push forward. Then, a short moment later, for no apparent reason, the car shut down and coasted to a stop. Silence engulfed the cab, the only sound being the whistling of the wind as it blew through the open windows.

My mind raced as I sat in horror, muscles stiffening more and more with every passing second. I turned the key several times while pumping the gas. The car didn't start. I slammed my fist off the steering wheel as my face flushed and I tried in vain to control my breathing. I put an ear close to the steering column. Not sure what a fuel pump sounded like—if it even made a noise—but turning the key generated a slight clicking noise. Nothing else.

I got out and hit Chuck's speed-dial number on my cell, ending the call with a shake of my head as it went to voicemail.

I was on my own.

No point in opening the hood and nosing around underneath. I couldn't describe what a fuel pump looked like, let alone where to find it on a vehicle. Car repairs had never been my bag. Being a grease monkey was something I scrapped halfway through my first semester of high school auto mechanics.

Spelonk lay two miles ahead on a dusty dirt road. Only a few random puddles remained from the morning's rain. The ground on Bonaire was so consistently dry, the water disappeared quickly, soaking into the earth like a dry sponge. Within minutes of a shower, everything was dry and dusty again.

But I had to get there. I *would* get there. I sighed, knelt, and cinched the laces on my Nikes.

I ran along the road, the midday sun beating down on me, draining my energy. Sweat soaked my face, back, and chest. My forehead ached, pulsing like a bass drum with every rapid heartbeat. On a typical run or swim, I controlled my pace for maximum endurance. But this was no ordinary run. I dug deep and pushed myself harder than I had in years, as close to an all-out sprint as I could manage. I hadn't sprinted in a long time and never with a bruised rib or a .38 Special tucked between my belt and shorts. I found it easier to run carrying the weapon in my hand.

My chest heaved more and more with every stride as my lungs worked hard to supply oxygen to my aching muscles. I focused on shoving one leg out in front of the other and fought the urge to collapse. A fine layer of brown earth covered my shoes, and grit had found its way to the bottom of my feet. Within a half mile, blisters formed. I pushed forward, knowing they'd soon bleed.

I hadn't driven out to Spelonk in several years but remembered three roads branched to the left off the main one, none of them leading to the lighthouse. I had passed two of them before the car died and had jogged past the third a few minutes ago.

What I didn't remember was the Y in the road. I stopped, bent at the waist, and put my hands on my knees. My chest heaved. Go right or go left. With my eyesight blurred from sweat and heat, I squinted and tried to visualize where each road led.

Two roads diverged in a yellow wood. I imagined Robert Frost having a good laugh. But this was no laughing matter. *And both that morning did* not *equally lay.*

The road to the left continued north, and I needed to go easterly. Regardless of the one less traveled by, I chose the one that went right, took a few more breaths, and started running again. After a few strides, lightning bolts of pain shot through my side, spreading to my chest and back. I leaned to one side as I ran.

A half a mile later, the road went over a small ridge and ended, fifty yards from Spelonk Lighthouse. Every stitch of my clothing was soaked and sticking to my skin, and the insides of my shoes were slick with blood. My lounger, the sunset, and a beer sounded good right now.

But saving Arabella sounded better; more important than anything else.

The ground, from the end of the road to the lighthouse and beyond, all the way to the coast, was comprised of cooled volcanic rock, formed millions of years ago. The edges stuck up and sideways, and were jagged, sharp, and uneven, thick with crevasses. I had to be careful. It'd be easy to catch a foot and break an ankle. Basket-sized pockets of thickets and thorn bushes grew randomly in the rocky surface.

The ruins of the abandoned caretaker's residence, a square, two-story stone building, sat thirty yards apart from the lighthouse. All the windows and doors had long ago been torn out. Over the years of neglect, pieces of the stone structure had fallen off and now lay strewn around the base, along with old wooden planks and pieces of driftwood.

A rough driveway or, better yet, a path ran from where I stood to the caretaker's place. Deep trenches, the width of a truck bed, ran its distance on both sides. Potholes larger than wheelbarrows, some deeper than the ruts, were strung out like moon craters, leading to the building. A truck, with a seahorse painted on the tailgate, sat tilted sideways in one of the potholes halfway down the driveway, its front left wheel crinkled underneath the axle and lying flat on the ground.

Hands on my knees and breathing deep, I raised my head and looked at the lighthouse, its seventy-foot-tall, white masonry cylinder standing guard over the east coast of Bonaire. *"I'll bet it has a great view,"* Tiffany had said. Emptiness grabbed me, making camp in my soul. It does have a great view, and she should be here experiencing it.

Compartmentalize.

I placed the .38 back between my belt and shorts and walked the path as far as possible, eventually needing to venture onto the lava rock toward the lighthouse.

The sharp edges of the hardened lava tried to poke through my thick-soled Nikes, continually jabbing the undersides of my feet. Careful not to fall, I worked my way across the rough ground, the randomness of my stride necessary but unsettling. A few years ago, one of my guests at the YellowRock got careless and fell on this patch of ground. He left the hospital with twenty stitches and a compound fracture of his forearm.

The shoreline along this section of the island was a sharp, ragged drop-off of thirty feet or so. The wind drove the sea against the steep shoreline, causing the water to jet skyward twenty or thirty feet in large columns of foam and spray, falling back to the ground in drops that pooled in the crevasses of the hardened lava. Water flowed between the small pools, eventually finding its way to the shoreline, where it fell back to the sea. On any other day, I might sit motionless for hours, mesmerized by the rhythm and spectacle of the show.

Not today, though. I inched forward, watching the jagged ground with every step. As I neared the lighthouse, two forms emerged from the backside of the structure and stepped out of the shadow. One was male and had a one-arm death grip around the neck of the other, a female.

I drew the .38.

To my surprise, the female wasn't Arabella.

It was Ruth.

In his other hand, pressed against Ruth's head, the guy held Wilbur. Ruth's chest heaved in and out as she stood in front of me, her ripped shirt exposing bruises below the neck on her upper chest. Duct tape sealed her mouth shut and clamped her hands together. Blood ran from her nose and lips, and streaks of mascara and dirt coated her flushed face. Her eyes, red and watery, darted from side to side and up and down. Although scared, her face swam with anger. She had fight left in her.

Spray from a wave misted over us as my eyes moved from Ruth to her captor. The man used the forearm of his gun hand to wipe the spray from his face. He placed the muzzle back against Ruth's temple.

"Hello, Conklin," he said, motioning with his head. Confidence rang in his voice, knowing he had the upper hand. He stood straight and solid, the Chicago Bears hat pulled low across his brow. A crooked smile swept across his face. "Let's start by having you drop the gun."

CHAPTER 50

"I said drop the gun."

I didn't drop the .38 but held it with the muzzle pointed down. Every police officer is trained to never surrender their weapon. Nothing good ever comes of it. Once empty-handed, the chance of survival—the officer's and the hostage's—drops to nil. Countless case studies prove the point.

"I know who you are, Mandy. Or should I call you Wayne?" I extended a hand, palm up. "It's over."

"Yeah, it's over. But not the way you think it is."

"It doesn't have to end this way."

He laughed. "What *way* do you think it'll end?"

The remnants of another wave dropped on us. I didn't answer Mandy's question, but instead, gave what I hoped was a reassuring look to Ruth. She narrowed her eyes.

Mandy pointed the weapon at me. "I could kill you right now."

Sweat dripped off my fingertips onto the ground. I worked up as much saliva as I could and swallowed, the spit stinging my dry throat. I'd had guns pointed at me before. It'd been a long time ago, and I had forgotten, until now, how it felt.

Not pleasant, I remembered.

"Why don't you?" I asked.

He shook his head. "All in good time. But first, I have a surprise for you."

Having not fired a weapon in years, I regretted not accepting Arabella's invitations to go to the range. Too risky to try and get a jump on him. The snub-nosed .38 had a short barrel and was inaccurate beyond a few feet. Anything beyond point-blank range was too risky.

My death was one thing, but Ruth shouldn't have to pay for my stupidity. Too many deaths already. Wilbur was the weapon that killed Malfena, proof that the worn firing pin wasn't an issue. The gun worked perfectly.

I took a step forward.

"Careful." He placed the weapon back against Ruth's head. "Wouldn't want Blaze here to eat a bullet, would we?"

Ruth twisted and jabbed Mandy in the kidney with her elbow. Mandy winced and tightened his grip.

"Stupid bitch," he said and smacked Ruth on the head with the barrel of the weapon.

Ruth slumped for a moment, tears running down her cheeks, her chest heaving. She let out a small moan. Steel always wins against flesh and bone, but after a moment, she straightened, angrier than ever.

"Why don't you let her go?" I said. "I'm the one you want. She means nothing to you."

"Damn it, man, do you think I'd go for that? You're not that good, Conklin. Besides, Ruthie here is a means to the end. That's all." He raised an eyebrow, as if in thought. "And call me Wayne. My dad would've wanted it that way."

"Okay, Wayne, what's the plan?"

"We're going for a ride."

"You know I—we—can't do that."

"Oh . . . I think *we* will." He laughed.

I needed to keep him talking. "The ad was clever."

"Jeez, good work, Detective. It took you long enough."

"Your alias, that was . . . cute."

"You don't miss a thing, do you? Especially when it's all laid out in front of you."

"But I don't understand leaving the gun behind at Ryberg's."

"It's the missing link."

"The missing link? What missing link?"

He raised his head as if in prayer. "God? How stupid did you make this guy?" He refocused on me, all spirituality—if any—abandoned. "It proves my dad was innocent."

"How?"

He sighed, shook his head. "That was his gun. Don't you see? He couldn't have shot that guy if he left his gun at home." He pointed Wilbur at me. "My mom knew it. That's why she used it to kill herself. That's why I used it to kill Ryberg. Because he put an innocent man in jail, destroying my mom." He wiped his eyes with his arm and gritted his teeth. "*You* put an innocent man in jail. *You* killed my mom."

The last part of his ramble may have been correct. I didn't know and would never be sure. Wayne Dow may have been innocent of murder and gone to jail for a crime he didn't commit. But the .357 Magnum had nothing to do with it one way or another.

Mandy—Wayne—was delusional, and now wasn't the time to argue.

"Wayne, you need to clear his name. I can help you."

He let out a short laugh. "Clear his name? I've done better than that. Everyone to blame is dead." His face tightened. "Or soon will be."

"What about Marybeth? Or Malfena? They had nothing to do with any of it."

"Malfena? Was that her name? That piece of trash from the snack shop?" He mocked a confused look. "Didn't you hear, Detective? Sadly, she committed suicide. Poor girl."

"I liked Marybeth," he continued. "But the look on Ryberg's face when he saw his beloved wife dead was ... priceless." He tightened his grip on Ruth's neck. She jerked and pawed at his elbow with her duct-taped hands. Even with tape across her mouth, she gnawed at his forearm, trying to bite him. Mandy jerked her sideways and tightened his grip, forcing her to let up. He returned his attention to me. "At that moment, he knew how it felt to lose a loved one for no reason. Like me when my dad died. Then my mom." He exhaled and dropped his gun arm to his side and lowered his head. "For no reason at all."

If I got the chance, I'd try to take him one-on-one. But, so far, he hadn't given me an opportunity. I took another small step forward and, ever so slightly, raised the .38. Mandy snapped his head in my direction, straightened, and pressed the weapon harder against the side of Ruth's head.

"Drop the gun. That's your last warning," Mandy said. "Next time—" he put his mouth near Ruth's ear—"Bang!" Ruth flinched, but didn't scream and tried to elbow him again, but came up short.

Mandy pointed the weapon at me again and moved the barrel up and down. A crooked smile crossed his face. "Not yet, but soon."

If he planned to kill me, he could've easily done it by now. I wasn't sure what his intentions were, but for the sake of Ruth's safety, I needed to give in and cooperate with him. At least for now. "Okay, Wayne, you win." Going against years of training, and with a sweaty, shaking hand, I slowly knelt and laid the .38 on the ground between two small crevasses. Standing, I looked him in the eyes. "And Tiffany?"

"I messed that one up. I had planned to get rid of that dweeb Lester first. I wanted to shack up with her for a few days. Man, that bitch had a nice little body. Could've fucked her for days. Would've given me a nice little workout. What do you think, Conklin?" He winked at me. "Hey, maybe she would've grown to like me. Just like my little red-headed whore, here." He buried his face in Ruth's hair for a moment, then kissed her on the cheek. She tilted her head as far from him as possible. "But when she went diving by herself, I figured it was as good a time as any. I think you pros call that a 'crime of opportunity.' Or something like that."

Mandy squinted and glanced at the sun, forcing Ruth forward as he repositioned in the shadow of the lighthouse. I took that moment to make a quick move but stumbled in one of the crevasses. Mandy leveled Wilbur in my direction and shot, the bullet striking the dirt to my right and behind me, leaving a cloud of dust in its wake.

My experience told me that people familiar with firearms always checked the ammunition load after picking up a weapon. From habit and training, I had done so with the .38 after Arabella handed it to me in my apartment. Not sure Mandy possessed those instincts. Counting the bullet that killed Malfena and the warning shot wasted at me, Mandy might not realize Wilbur only had two cartridges remaining. If true, I needed to use that to my advantage.

A familiar noise approached from beyond the horizon, and a few moments later, an airplane flew over at low altitude. I couldn't read the tail number, but a red stripe ran down the plane's side. Chuck's mission had slipped my mind.

My jaw dropped as I realized *Mandy* was Chuck's client.

That's all I needed. Or as Arabella might say, "*Ook dat nog.*"

"Looks like our ride is here," Mandy said. He motioned with the weapon in the direction of the road. "Let's go meet him. No hurry. We still have a special guest to arrive before we leave this fucking rock." He kept his position behind Ruth but stopped to pick up the .38. "Won't need this." He smiled and threw the .38 behind him, as far away from me as he could. I hoped to turn that into a mistake on his part.

Always have as much firepower as possible.

"Keep going." He motioned forward with the weapon again.

I stumbled on the uneven ground, and, in catching my balance, twisted my torso, aggravating the injured rib. I held in a moan and stopped for a moment to press my hand against my side, letting out a long breath through pursed lips.

"Oh, are you hurt?" Mandy said and smiled. "Ain't that a shame. Not much of a fighter, are you, *Detective*? You need to toughen up a bit, old man. Maybe hit the punching bag a little and learn to take some punches."

I fought back a dozen responses. With Wilbur pointed at me, Mandy stood tall and confident in his position of authority. I'd get my chance—just wasn't sure how to make it happen.

A half mile from us, Chuck banked the plane, made a ninety-degree turn, and lined up for a landing. He navigated the crosswind and planted the main gears on the dirt road, the Tundras working as designed and cushioning the plane from the rough touchdown. He taxied in our direction to a wide spot and killed the engine. We arrived at the edge of the lava surface by the time Chuck had gotten out of the plane and walked around to the front.

He saw Mandy holding the weapon against Ruth's temple. "What's going on, R?"

"Stop," Mandy said when we were ten feet from the plane.

Mandy pointed the gun at Chuck. "Turn around and put your hands behind your head."

"R?" Chuck said, eyes wide.

"Now, Flyboy," Mandy said.

Chuck did as Mandy had told him, turning his back to Mandy and putting his hands on his head. He stood at an angle to me.

"Now," Mandy said, "on your knees."

Chuck glanced over his shoulder as he lowered himself to his knees. Once kneeled, he became ridged, focusing straight ahead, staring at the horizon.

Mandy pointed Wilbur at the back of Chuck's head and gave me a sideways smirk. "This is because of you, Conklin."

Mandy is killing everyone I come in contact with.

Chuck remained taut, although his breathing increased, becoming rapid and audible.

"Wait!" I yelled. Chuck flinched and Mandy snapped his head in my direction. "You've only got two cartridges left. You sure you want to waste one on Chuck?"

I saw the confusion on Mandy's face as he glanced at the gun.

"Did you check the magazine? Ruth only had four cartridges," I said. "Count what you've used. There's two left."

Mandy frowned and moved his lips, almost imperceptibly, probably doing the math in his head. Would he now go for the .38 snub nose he threw away? If he could even find the weapon, he'd have to drag Ruth with him along the jagged, volcanic rock ground, and it was a long distance back.

As he contemplated his options, I expected Mandy to take a quick glance back, trying to remember where he had thrown the weapon. But he didn't. Amateur Hour for Mandy. He had become fixated on the outcome and no Plan B existed. To put it simply, tunnel vision. Getting to the end of this thing as fast as possible was his primary goal. Lucky for us, he'd forgotten about the .38.

After a moment, Mandy straightened and said, "Two is enough. But don't move, Flyboy, or I *will* waste one on you."

Chuck closed his eyes as his entire body slumped.

Mandy pointed the gun back at me. "Remember what I said, Conklin. Two is enough."

As I breathed a sigh of relief in keeping Chuck alive, a faint siren sounded in the distance. A police truck appeared from around a bend headed straight for us. It skidded to a stop behind the plane, and Arabella and James jumped out with their weapons drawn. They carefully made their way toward Mandy, spreading out as they approached so he couldn't aim at both simultaneously.

"That's far enough," Mandy said before they got close to him. He moved closer to the plane, turning around and placing his back against the fuselage to keep Ruth between him and the cops.

Arabella and James were on Mandy's right side, Arabella being forty-five degrees and James ninety. With me in front, we formed a makeshift semicircle around Mandy. If only I hadn't surrendered the .38.

"Drop your weapon," James said. "Put your hands behind your head and lay on your stomach. Do it now."

Arabella's chest heaved with every breath, her eyes wide, glued to Mandy. I tried to imagine her thoughts. Training had kicked in, and she was assessing the situation. The worst nightmare for any cop was arriving on the scene and realizing the victim was a family member.

"Drop it," James said, again.

Mandy didn't drop the weapon. One by one, he jabbed the pistol in each of our directions. "Three against one. That don't seem too fair." He looked at me. "Or should I say, two and a half against one."

"How about I even the odds a little?" He aimed the weapon at me and paused a few seconds. Without moving his head, he shifted his eyes toward Arabella. Before I could say or do anything, he spun to his side, a shot rang out, and Arabella stumbled two steps backward.

She raised her left hand to cover her right shoulder like a mirror-image Pledge of Allegiance. She bowed her head, blood seeping between her fingers, and staggered a step sideways before falling hard on her butt, feet straight out in front of her. She wheezed two breaths and, as if in slow motion, lowered her upper body onto the molten lava ground, coming to rest on her back.

Ruth screamed and struggled in Mandy's arms. He hit her on the side of the head with the butt of the weapon, this time hard enough to cause her scalp to split open. Blood soaked her hair and ran down the side of her neck. She went quiet.

Frozen in time, I watched the blood ooze from Arabella's chest, soaking her uniform in red. Her hand still clutched the Walther P-5. Her sunglasses lay on the ground as the wind blew her hair across her face.

I wanted to go to her; to help her. But my mind couldn't will my body forward. My feet felt riveted to the ground. All I could do was stare at her, not believing what had happened.

She raised her head, ever so slightly. Her lips moved, but there wasn't any sound. Then she closed her eyes, moaned, and lowered her head. She went silent, and the weapon fell loose in her hand.

Numbness overtook me.

Waves crashed against the rocky shoreline, and the wind blew across my face. Light pulsed from Spelonk Lighthouse. On the other side of the island, boatloads of divers were jumping into the sea, savoring their vacation and enjoying life. Vinny's had cold beer, a good view, and Ole Blue. ME N RC would be there, waving me up to the bar.

Off to my right, Arabella lay motionless, blood running down the side of her body, soaking the jagged, rocky ground.

How could I have let this happen?

"Ain't that a shame," Mandy said.

I slowly turned my head in his direction. He had one cartridge remaining. A single shot could do a lot of damage, though. I had to get word to James, but in doing so, would that prompt Mandy to shoot me? Or worse yet, Ruth?

One option was to yell at James, and rush Mandy, let him waste the last cartridge on me. He might still panic and shoot Ruth. That would be unacceptable. I couldn't let her get hurt. All I wanted to do was tear Mandy limb from limb. But I had to maintain control and figure a way to beat him.

With the weapon, Mandy motioned toward the plane. "Get in and start the engine. You, me, and Red here are going for a little plane ride."

Somehow, he knew I was a pilot. Maybe Lester told him. Or possibly Tiffany.

Mandy turned to face James. "Don't get any ideas or I'll kill them both."

James didn't know the whole story. He had seen Mandy shoot only once and, as far as he knew, Mandy's weapon still contained a near full magazine. Standing motionless, breathing heavy, alternating his gaze between Mandy and Arabella, he wanted to take a shot, but he couldn't risk it. Chances were, he had never been in a situation like this before. Most cops go their entire career and never draw their weapon in the line of duty, let alone fire it. Punching holes in targets at the range was vastly different from drawing on a moving, breathing person capable of shooting back.

"Fucking move, Conklin," Mandy said. He jabbed the weapon in Ruth's neck and kept her in front of him using her body as his protective shield.

Taking a last look at Arabella, I climbed into the pilot's seat. I fumbled with the seat belt as my shaky, sweat-soaked hands made it difficult to buckle. I had no intention of taking off, but I wasn't yet sure how to avoid it.

Mandy kept his eyes on James, who had taken a couple of steps toward Arabella. When James took another step, Mandy said, "That's close enough. I have nothing against you, so don't make me kill you."

James held his ground.

Mandy yelled into the cockpit. "Start the fucking engine."

I opted to skip the pre-start checklist and turned the ignition key while pumping the throttle control. The propeller spun, and the engine fired to life. I set the RPMs to idle.

A thought went through my mind. If I was the only pilot on the plane, which I believed to be the case, I should be able to exert a level of control over the situation. I'd give Mandy the ride of his life and maybe jar the weapon out of his hands. Unless he knew how to fly, he couldn't shoot me while we were in the air. Suicide on his part.

But he could still shoot Ruth.

Maybe suicide *was* his plan, taking Ruth and me with him.

"Okay now, Red," Mandy yelled over the sound of the engine and the force of the prop wash. "We need to get in the plane. I'll back in, and you climb up on my lap." He cupped a hand around her waist and smiled. "Feel free to enjoy yourself as I wiggle us into the plane. But don't try any funny stuff. If you allow Asshole over there a shot at me, I'll shoot you first. Do you understand?"

Ruth was having trouble keeping her head up, her eyes barely open, but managed a slight nod. For a few seconds, as they squirmed through the door of the plane, Mandy would have his back to me. I searched the plane's interior for something to use as a club. Unfortunately, unlike the condition of his apartment, Chuck kept a clean, sterile airplane cockpit. Only the essentials.

I leaned over and ran my hand under the two front seats, finding nothing, not even a dust bunny. Same result from the tiny, useless glove compartment. The back seat was empty, but I noticed a bulge in the pocket on the back of the copilot's seat. I remembered the small fire extinguisher Chuck kept there within easy reach of the pilot. When Mandy moved into the cabin, I'd grab it and smash his head. For good measure—and some payback—I'd continue pummeling him until someone pulled me away.

Mandy backed up to the passenger-side door. I reached into the pocket and gripped the fire extinguisher. He pulled Ruth in his direction, but she straightened and kicked him full force in the shin, perfectly placed directly below the kneecap. Mandy screamed in agony, bent sideways, and reached down, grabbing his knee. His grip on Ruth loosened; she twisted sideways and elbowed him in the jaw as she slipped away.

Mandy was exposed.

A shot rang out, and Mandy flinched. James hadn't moved, nor had he fired. He remained in the same spot, frozen, eyes wide, his weapon still pointed at Mandy.

Mandy staggered a couple of steps, caught himself on the wing strut, and leaned against it for a moment, gasping. Blood dripped from his mouth. He closed his eyes and wavered back and forth.

The bullet had struck and passed through Mandy, drilling into the motor compartment. Smoke began leaking from beneath the plane's cowling. The engine sputtered and the propeller, although still turning, did so in a herky-jerky fashion, shaking the plane in the process.

Mandy opened his eyes and spied the weapon still in his hand. He used his non-gun hand as leverage on the wing strut and pushed himself to a standing position. Straightening, then staggering a step forward, he wavered as he tried to maintain his balance. Blood stained the upper portion of his shirt and trickled onto his pants. His mouth opened, and he mumbled something unrecognizable, crimson-colored drool dripping from his lower lip.

He pointed the weapon at me, his brown eyes glossy, the dark spot in the white of his left eye noticeably clear. *Unique and somewhat distracting.*

My heart pounded. I pulled the fire extinguisher into my lap and repositioned it, bringing it even with my right shoulder so I could throw it at Mandy, maybe knock Wilbur loose.

"James," I yelled, "waste this sonofabitch!"

Two more shots rang out in quick succession. Mandy flinched twice.

Double tap.

James still hadn't fired.

Mandy slumped and fell forward over the wing strut, into the sputtering propeller. I grabbed the fuel control knob and pulled it back, shutting off the fuel, starving the sick engine of gas.

But it was too late.

A semicircular spray of blood whisked across the plane's windshield and cowling as the propeller sliced through Mandy's head and neck. It took five seconds for the propeller to come to a complete stop.

Mandy was dead in one.

A spinning propeller can ruin a vacation.

I jumped out and ran to the passenger side of the plane, passing in front of the blood-splattered propeller. The ground below the prop was a swamp of minced bone, brains, and human tissue. Nothing remained of Mandy's body above the shoulders.

James knelt beside Arabella and Ruth stood in the shadow of the Cessna wing. Arabella lay in a prone position, head up, arm extended and holding her Walther P-5. When our eyes met, she smiled and lowered the weapon.

I had to pry it from her grasp.

CHAPTER 51

My morning swim complete, I sat at the end of the pier across the street from the YellowRock. Several green and red parrot fish rode the mild surf, circling the pylons scavenging for food, their dorsal fins occasionally breaking the surface. It was Saturday, and a few children bounced and played in the shallows along the small beach. Several of them wore brightly colored masks and snorkels.

A Boeing 737 flew low overhead climbing for altitude, having just departed Flamingo Airport, its massive turbofan engines momentarily drowning out the sound of the ocean and the nearby kids. Full of tourists headed home after a vacation in paradise; the sun glared off its wings as it made a gentle turn to the northwest, pointed toward the good ole USA.

Exactly one week ago, I leaned on the fender of my Wrangler in the airport parking lot. I finished a beer and watched an identical jet, also full of departing tourists, roar down the runway and lift off into the Caribbean sky.

Buried somewhere in the cargo hold of that plane were two coffins.

Tiffany's parents were also on board, along with Lester Jeffrey's sister. Although none of us had known each other for more than a few days, it had been a tearful goodbye. A kinship existed between us. We all had loved ones in those coffins.

The one bright spot was when Tiffany's mom told me that Tiffany's cousin and his wife wanted to adopt Ozzie. Maybe the kid would have a chance in life after all.

I dried with a beach towel and slipped on a T-shirt while crossing the street toward the YellowRock. Erika hung up the phone as I entered the office.

"That was the hospital," she said. A tear formed in her eye, but her smile told me it was a tear of happiness. "Arabella can now take visitors."

Erika walked over and hugged me. I hugged back. "I'll be back in a little while." I kissed her on the top of the head and headed for my apartment. I needed to change before going to the hospital.

"Mr. Traverso called," Erika said before I left. "He needs to talk to you."

I shrugged, shook my head. No doubt he wanted information about Mandy Driver and the murders. The Rockford team was tying Mandy to the identity of Wayne Dow Jr., and because Mandy's head was destroyed by the airplane propeller, identifying him by dental records was impossible. Fingerprints were inconclusive because Dow Junior's prints weren't in the system. Penn said they were going to use DNA and try to prove a family connection.

It wasn't my problem anymore, and I hadn't paid attention as he rambled through an explanation a few days ago on the phone. As Schleper had said, I was retired. Besides, I didn't care about any of that right now. All I wanted was to get to the hospital.

*   *   *

I walked the hall of the hospital and thought about the last time Arabella was here. Doubtful any evidence would be recovered linking Mandy to the sabotage on my Wrangler. But it didn't matter. Not anymore.

Ballistics had confirmed Wilbur was the weapon used to kill Malfena, which implicated Mandy for the murder and, subsequently, the theft and arson of the rental car. Somehow, the only prints on the weapon were Mandy's, and the police were unable to trace Wilbur to Ruth or anyone else. A complete dead end for them.

A complete luck-out for Ruth.

Regardless, it was over.

Arabella would be fine.

Mandy was dead.

Arabella sat in her bed, resting against the back, propped at a forty-five-degree angle. Face gaunt, hair matted to her head, there were identical tubes running into her body connected to the same machines as before. As far as I could tell, the same numbers were on the screens, and I still had no idea what any of it meant.

Ruth sat in a chair near the open window. When I walked in, I caught a few brief words of Ruth's reprimand to Arabella. Ruth immediately went quiet when she noticed me.

Arabella saw me and smiled. "Conklin." Her voice scratchy, forced through dry, chapped lips. She glanced at the two brown paper bags I set on the sliding tray alongside her bed. A bag for her; one for me; none for Ruth. The grease spots gave away their origin. "Burgers!" She tore into one of the bags, spilling fries onto the sheets.

I sat sideways on the bed, careful not to cause any undue motion or agitation to Arabella, and placed my left hand on the side of her face. I leaned close and kissed her on the lips. "How was your nap?"

"I've had better," she said, not bashful about talking with her mouth full.

"I'm proud of you."

She blushed.

"You saved the day," I said. "Not to mention my life." I motioned toward Ruth. "And your sister's."

"Thanks," Ruth said.

I wasn't sure whether Ruth was thanking me for mentioning her or thanking Arabella for saving her life. Either way, I ignored her.

"I've made a decision," Arabella said, glancing at Ruth and back to me. She dipped some fries into a mound of mayonnaise. "I'm not going to take the inspector test right now."

I didn't say anything, as the predictable beep of the medical equipment paced off the seconds. A small blood spot had dried in the center of her shoulder bandage. "I wouldn't make that decision right now. Give it some time."

"No, I think it best." She reached up with her right hand and placed it on my shoulder. "It would mean leaving you, and I do not want to do that. Not now. Not ever."

I held her hand and removed a spare key to my apartment from my pocket. I slipped it into her palm, rolling her fingers into a fist. *"Hier is mijn sleutel."*

Her eyes widened. She opened her palm and held up the key. "I never . . ."

I leaned over and kissed her on the cheek. She set the burger on the table, then wrapped her one good arm around my neck and squeezed.

"Ik hou van jou," I whispered in her ear.

She squeezed harder and said, "I love you, too . . . R."

CHAPTER 52

I HAD MY feet propped on the office desk, playing my banjo, having been practicing the same song for about twenty minutes. Two of the five strings were out of tune, and, because it annoyed Erika just enough, I left them that way.

"Are you not going fishing with Jan soon?" she finally asked. "I have work to get done, and it will not get done with you here, old man."

I stopped playing and pulled my feet off the desk. "Yup. He'll be picking me up any minute." I latched the banjo into its case. "By the way, I'm not old. I'm a *classic*."

"Well," she said, turning around to look at me, "my English is not as perfect as yours, but I think *classic* is just another word for old."

"Maybe, but don't wait up. He's taking this classic out for his birthday."

She shook her head. "Lord help us." She stood with a stack of papers and walked to the filing cabinet. She muttered under her breath, "Lord help the whole island."

I chuckled, but not too loud.

A horn beeped, and I caught a glimpse of Jan's truck through the window. He had pulled into the lot and was loading my gear into his truck bed.

I poked my head out the door. The buzzing of tools and the chatter of men working came from the alley between the YellowRock and the building next door. Boards dropping, hammers hitting, an occasional laugh or command. Marko Martijn and his crew were finishing the foundation work. I had agreed to pay him half of the remaining balance if he'd get back to work, then the rest upon completion.

I yelled to Jan, "I'll get the cooler and be right out."

"I already have plenty of beer on the boat."

"Ha! No such thing as 'plenty of beer.' I'll be right back."

I took my banjo upstairs and grabbed the cooler, already loaded with beer and ice. Heading downstairs, I anticipated an afternoon of sun-filled sea fishing and an evening of island nightlife, all of which I'd regret tomorrow morning.

I set the cooler outside the door for Jan to load.

"You ready?" he asked.

"Just about." I turned to Erika. "I'm leaving."

Before I got out the door, the landline phone rang. Erika looked at the phone, then at me.

Second ring.

I looked at the phone, then at Erika.

Third ring.

"I'm going to lunch," she said and squeezed past me.

Fourth ring.

Jan stood by his truck drinking a beer, fiddling with a fishing rod.

The phone rang a fifth time as I closed and locked the door behind me.